ROSE CLARKE
AND THE
BODY IN THE CHAPEL

ROSE CLARKE
AND THE
BODY IN THE CHAPEL

Paul Ryley

First published in Great Britain in 2023

ISBN 978-1-3999-5604-8

Typeset in Goudy by Falcon Oast Graphic Art Ltd.
Printed and bound by ImprintDigital.com

1 3 5 7 9 10 8 6 4 2

CHAPTER 1

Wednesday 21ˢᵗ December 1803

MISS ROSE CLARKE SAT HERSELF down with the matrons at the Christmas Ball at Somerset House to catch her breath. She wished her wig wasn't so itchy, and wondered why her hands were trembling as she sipped her glass of lemonade. Looking out over the array of exquisite dresses and immaculate tailoring, she considered the throng. There was her brother Sir George, dancing with Lady Hawkesbury. The man at the end of the line looked vaguely familiar too, but she couldn't put her finger on why. At least she was able to enjoy this ball, most of the time. The last time she had attended a London ball, as long ago as May, she had been so very bored – though that had certainly not been the case at the ball at Trumpington barely two weeks ago, when all manner of excessively exciting things had come to pass.

Nonetheless she was not really sure just how she felt at this gathering. The party was the farewell event for the various officials of the Government departments before they returned to their estates in the country, or to the bosom of their families wherever situate for the Christmas celebrations, and as her elder brother Sir George Clarke, Bt, was something important in the Foreign Office, she had been invited, along with her twin brother Charles. Though, speaking of Charles, she hadn't seen him for a while, which usually meant he would be getting up to no good.

1

She decided on reflection that she must be nervous, for some reason, in spite of having danced with several men already, in marked contrast to that other ball hosted by Lady Swaffham, back in her interrupted Season, when she had been gravelled for partners. And, more surprisingly, she had not felt the need to be sarcastic to any of the men tonight. Her unusual activity on the floor had doubtless been because this ball was more in the way of a party for government staff than a marriage market, though she had overheard several conversations which suggested that topic was never far from the minds of mothers of young ladies. Also, there were fewer elevated personages present, and since many of the guests worked for a living, the attendees included more of the sort of person who did not require an heir for their title, and hence did not see a woman simply in terms of breeding stock. Hence, perhaps, the lack of waspish comments falling from her lips.

She had nonetheless been introduced to, and danced with, several personages who could only be described as elevated, including George's ultimate superior at the Foreign Office, Lord Hawkesbury. She had been surprised at his relative youth, considering the importance of his office, and she had become muddled about his recently-acquired title and how to address him, and surprised when the great man had suggested she simply call him Mr Jenkinson. He had a roguish twinkle in his eye as he said this, and Rose came over pink as she realised he was flirting with her, however mildly. Her embarrassment caused her to mis-step three times in the dance, and struggle to think of sensible replies to his conversation.

There was another explanation for her difficulties with his lordship though: mainly that she was quite out of practice at being a girl, after spending the last three months disguised as a boy from Nova Scotia, by name Richard Cox, in order that she might attend the university at Cambridge to study mathematics, and other fascinating subjects not usually available to a young lady. Mr Pemberton's ball at Trumpington had been the one day she had spent in her true feminine form during the last term, and she had only been back in London for two days, and in her dresses again since yesterday. She had been sad to leave her rooms at Emmanuel, and her closest friend there Edward Hever, who was staying up in college both to save money on the trip back home to Keswick, and to earn money by organising his tutor's books and papers. Nonetheless it was most pleasant to receive compliments and to mix with both sexes, rather than just men.

So what was really bothering her? She had danced without difficulties with some of George's other colleagues: Mr Warburton with his broken nose, whom she had met at Trumpington: she now knew him to be an expert on French artillery. Then there had been a rather peaky-looking Mr Terrier from the Home Office, about whom she was sure there was something she ought to remember, but she simply couldn't bring it to mind. Perhaps she was on edge because she missed having her cousin Louisa with her, both to talk to, and also as a source of less exalted partners, but Louisa was back home in her parents' Cheshire rectory. Maybe she would be able to see Louisa again if she returned for a second visit to the Season this Easter – albeit briefly, as in her guise as Richard she would be expected back at Cambridge just ten days after the paschal celebration.

Then it struck her. She didn't want to admit it, but what was really keeping her on thorns must be the absence of one Mr William Blackburn, a lieutenant in the 51ˢᵗ regiment, but attached to the military only in name, while in reality seconded to the Foreign Office to uncover hostile agitators attempting to destabilise the morale of our troops and working to discover military information useful to our enemies. To say she knew him well would be an exaggeration; to say she wished she knew him much better would be nearer the mark. And she had so hoped he might be here. She could count on one hand the number of times she had met him in the flesh, and letters had not the same intimacy. She believed he might share some of the feelings she realised she was developing for him, in spite of their enforced separations, or perhaps she only hoped that he shared them, or imagined that he did?

She brought herself back to the moment with difficulty. 'Mrs Seddon,' she enquired of the lady nearest to her, who was acting as her chaperone, 'do you recognise the man in the last place in this figure?'

The lady raised her glasses to her eyes. 'I'm afraid I do not. Why, do you wish to be introduced?'

'Not at all, thankyou. I just thought I had seen him somewhere before. Never mind. Er, another thing: may I ask when you last saw Charles?'

'I rather thought I saw him heading out through the door behind the orchestra,' she said, 'about three figures ago. He was with, er, Sir Peter Mackenzie's eldest, and two other gentlemen I didn't recognise.'

'John Smart and James Eldridge,' put in her neighbour, leaning across. 'They both have something of a reputation. Need I say more?'

Rose wished she might indeed say more, but decided instead that she would have to go and find out for herself what Charles was up to, and remind him that he was on show here, that the family name he bore also was carried by George and herself, and how he ought to think of them when he was carousing in such a place, and other such elder-twin-sister homilies. Mrs Seddon would not miss her: she had been enjoying the Madeira wine quite freely. The faintly familiar man and Mr Blackburn's absence would have to wait.

She made her way around the large ball room keeping a close watch on the faces that passed before her. No sign of Charles, and her brother Sir George had now disappeared at the ending of the dance, no doubt to discuss with some colleague matters of national importance. Nor for that matter was there sign of Mr Blackburn, though she saw numbers of red coats of officers. She slipped through the door and closed it behind her. She moved forward a few paces and listened. The sounds of the ball were muffled, but still too loud to hear if anyone was in the nearby rooms.

Moving carefully along the echoing corridor she had to wait for a while to allow her eyes to adjust to the relative dimness of the scattered candles, and then noticed a faint line of yellow light escaping from a room a short way along. She crept closer and listened. The doors here were all very well-fitting, but she could hear sounds of revelry. She put her eye to the keyhole, but could see nothing. Slowly she turned the handle and eased the door ajar. Through the crack she could see a number of inebriated-looking young men all clutching miscellaneous drinking vessels, and among them – was that a sight of pale lemon muslin?

She risked opening her viewpoint more fully. Yes, there was a girl there with the men. And, she could see Charles among them, but she didn't recognise any of the others – or did she? She wasn't sure, but that rather dishevelled one with blond hair looked awfully like Charlie from the four-oar at Cambridge. The Honourable Charles French, officially. And what was a young lady doing unchaperoned with this crew?

They seemed to be trying to arrange themselves into two parallel lines sitting on the floor, four facing one way in each group, and one facing the rest. And the girl was being half-carried and set into the position at the end of one line facing the others: Charlie headed the other group. Someone thrust a glass of what looked like wine into the girl's hand, she seemed to be having trouble sitting upright. What was going on?

With a start, Rose recognised the girl. It had not been obvious before because her hair was most disarranged, but it was surely Julia Winton, the sister of her friend Peter from college, with whom she had attended the Trumpington ball? She ought to do something. But what?

There was a brief hush, then someone shouted 'Three, two, one, Row!' The two single participants immediately started drinking their potions as fast as they could and when they had finished put the vessel upside down on their head. Then the next in line, and so on until all had drunk in sequence. Rose realised that it must some sort of

5

drinking game in the form of a boat race – bad enough that Charles was involved, of course, but surely not Julia?

Julia slumped to one side as the baton passed to the last in line and Rose acted. She drew herself up to her not-inconsiderable height of five foot seven, flung the door wide and made as dramatic an entrance as she could manage. She started to say, 'What do you think you are doing here?' but it was drowned out in the cheering as Charlie's team were victors. She marched up to her brother and clipped him over the ear instead.

'Charles, your attention please!'

Charles looked at her blearily. 'Rose! Um, what . . . ? Do you want to join in? We've just raced the tie-breaker.'

'Certainly not! I need you to help me with Miss Winton here, she appears very much under the weather and I must help her to some-where she can recover herself.'

'Shame!' came from one of the other jolly boys. 'You can't take our cox!'

Rose pulled Charles to his feet by his newly-clipped ear and led him over to Julia, who had fallen over with her limbs all asplay. 'Come on, Charles, between us we can move her to . . . ,' she considered, 'to somewhere less improper for a young lady.'

Reluctantly and rather uncoordinatedly Charles hoisted Julia to her feet and they supported her to the door. She made little effort to walk, but mumbled incoherently from time to time.

'The race was French's idea, y'know, Rose, he does rowing up at the University.'

Rose almost slipped up badly: she had to bite back a sarcastic 'You think I don't know that?' as it reached her lips. Of course she had only met Charlie in her guise of Richard, and she was doing her best to keep her back to him in case he recognised her; not to mention that Charles would wonder how she knew Charlie in the first place if she admitted the fact. It was so confusing having two identities, and keeping everything in its place. But now they were in the corridor, she was at a loss as to where to take the poor girl. She couldn't of course go into the ballroom, and she didn't know the layout of the building, but she was fairly sure it wouldn't have any bedrooms, or none nearby at any rate. She looked around in rising anxiety.

'Do you know who she came with?'

'No idea. One of the men brought her after dancing with her, I think. She was already a bit disguised then.' He belched loudly. 'Look, can't you manage on your own? I need to get back to the rout.'

'You will stay here, thank you very much. I need to think. She must have a chaperone, she wouldn't be here at the ball alone. So I must find her. And you will have to stay here with her, much against my better judgement. No, on second thoughts, we will find an empty room, lay her on a couch or whatever there is, and you can stand guard outside the door. Come on.'

This programme accomplished, she left Charles lounging against the doorpost with no strong belief he would be there when she returned, and made her way back to the ballroom door. As she entered, the noise and the heat and the brightness buffeted her so she took a moment to realise she was being addressed by a tall man in a scarlet uniform. Mr Blackburn! Now, of all times! She felt herself colouring, and trembling with more than just anxiety for Julia.

'Miss Clarke! I was so hoping you might be here. I have been searching the ballroom for you, as I arrived late.'

'Er, Mr Blackburn,' she said, curtseying jerkily. 'Yes, er, I'm, . . . I'm on something of a mission, at the moment, I'm sorry.' She made as if to carry on her progress.

'May I be of assistance?'

'No, I have to . . .' but then she remembered. Mr Blackburn was a confederate of Peter Winton, so he would probably know his sister.

'Well, actually . . . do you know Julia Winton?'

'Assuredly, she is the sister of my colleague.'

'Yes. Well. Do you know who she came with? Her chaperone, I mean? Is it her mother?'

'Indeed. I saw her sitting by the statue in the far corner.' He indicated.

Rose balanced the complexities of etiquette in her mind. None of her instruction at Miss Snape's School for Ladies had prepared her for this. 'I think, it would be best, if you wouldn't mind, if you were to ask her to come over here and meet me in the corridor just outside this door as soon as possible, without alarming her. Do not explain why. And she should come alone.' A thought struck her. 'Mr Winton is not here, is he? Peter, I mean?'

'No, he is quite engaged with some investigations, in Ely I believe. And his father is still abroad.'

'Well, please fetch Mrs Winton with all haste. I will explain later. But do accompany her, I might need you.'

Mr Blackburn looked puzzled, but gave her a small bow and set off without delay. Rose slipped into the corridor again and saw as she had expected that Charles had forsaken his post already. He was going to be in such trouble later. But for now she had other fish to fry. With one eye looking over her shoulder at the ballroom door she made her way to Julia's room and peeked in. The reprobate was snoring loudly, one arm drooping off the couch, but otherwise seemed safe to leave until she had collected her mother.

She hopped from foot to foot as she waited. Really, men!! Why did they have to behave like this? And ensnaring a young lady, too, someone whose reputation mattered so much for her future happiness.

The door from the ballroom opened again. Mr Blackburn ushered through Julia's mother, who looked most alarmed.

'What is it, my dear? Is it Julia? I have not seen her for some time.'

'Mrs Winton.' Rose curtseyed. 'I'm sorry to say that it is, Julia, I mean. But she is not seriously . . . that is to say, she is quite . . . I think you had better see for yourself.'

She led the way into the room she had selected as being convenient and unoccupied. Julia had not moved. Mr Blackburn hung back, by the door. She turned to him.

'Mr Blackburn, would you be so good as to see that nobody comes in to disturb us? I did set my brother Charles to the task but he absconded almost immediately I had gone.'

Without a word, the gentleman left the room and closed the door. Turning to their patient, she was relieved to see Mrs Winton was not indulging in hysterics, far from it. She was counting the girl's pulse, smelling her breath, and shaking her gently to see how deeply she was unconscious.

'Dead drunk,' she pronounced. 'As bosky as a wheelbarrow. Do you know on what tincture she has been dipping deep?'

'Er, the last glass looked like wine, madam, but I cannot vouch for the previous ones.'

Mrs Winton shook her gently. Then tapped her smartly on the bridge of her nose. Julia opened her eyes briefly, said 'Whaaa?' and shut them again.

'Is there a vessel in the room?' she asked. 'Anything moderately large will do.'

Rose cast about. In a cupboard she found a chamber pot. 'Will this do, Mrs Winton?'

'Capital. Now,' and she plucked a feather from her headdress. 'Can you roll her over and hold her on her side?' Rose hurried to comply. 'And pinch her nose?' Rose fumbled for that organ.

Mrs Winton thrust her fist into Julia's opening mouth and intro-duced the stiff feather firmly. Julia gagged, and then cast up her accounts copiously into the chamber pot, groaning ferociously, and trying to force her mother's hand away. But to no avail: the procedure was repeated until nothing remained to regurgitate.

'Mostly red wine,' Mrs Winton pronounced, inspecting the efflu-ent. 'And cake. Julia is very fond of cake.' She set the pot down, and looked at Rose. 'Could I trouble you or your friend to procure a large glass of water please? As soon as convenient?'

'Certainly, madam. Er, you seem very conversant with this condi-tion, if I may venture to say?'

'Three brothers, one husband and two sons, my dear. This is the first, and I fervently hope the last time, however, for my daughter.'

Rose hurried out, deciding to fetch the water herself, as Mr Blackburn would do better as guard than she would. As she passed him he contented himself with a mild 'Top-heavy, then?' which she answered with a brief nod.

Mrs Winton gave Julia a drink, repeated the feather procedure once more, then made her daughter drink the rest of the water. She left Rose with her while she went to 'see a man about a dog' and within a very few minutes had managed to arrange for the removal of the girl to their carriage by a back entrance. She by some sorcery achieved this all without alarming the party-goers, or so it seemed to Rose. Once they had left, Rose stood in the corridor alone with Mr Blackburn, twisting her skirts and feeling . . . well, unsure how she was feeling, yet again.

'Are you alright, Miss Clarke?' he enquired. 'You look a little, er, put about.'

'Indeed, sir. Several people I am acquainted with have been behaving most intemperately; shall we not add to their number by remaining here alone in this corridor?'

'Of course. Allow me to escort you to the ballroom.'

'I'd rather you escorted me to the supper room and let me sit down for a moment, with a plate of something settling and a large negus, if such is available.'

'After seeing all that unpleasantness, Miss Clarke?'

'Because of seeing all that, as you say, unpleasantness, sir.'

'Very well,' and he offered his arm and conducted her by way of the ballroom into an alcove some little distance from the supper table and was most assiduous in fulfilling her requests for sustenance.

'So,' he began, once she had consumed two slices of cold meat and some cheese, and her cup was half drained, 'what have you been doing since I last saw you?'

Rose felt a moment of panic. She had not worked out what to

say if she saw him: she had been in the guise of Richard Cox for three months but he was not privy to her subterfuge. Indeed the fewer people who knew about her disguise the better. What to say?

'Last I saw you was at the *débâcle* at the Pemberton ball, I never found out what happened, we were too busy fighting a gang of ruffians outside; but for some reason you were there and had become embroiled in the affair. Someone tried to explain but I couldn't hear what she said properly. Also, I think I may have had a blow to the head, so I was feeling a little woozy. I don't remember much of it, after the mill outside that is, very clearly. And then when I had recovered I had to rush off up North, so I didn't get the chance to speak to you.'

Rose thought quickly. The best lies were the simplest. 'Well, it was just that I was near the colonel when there was a disturbance and I got carried along with the crowd. I was staying with the Wintons at the time, Julia is a friend; and then about ten days later I returned to London and I've been living here in the hotel where you called on me in September. George hasn't told me his plans for Christmas but I expect we may go to Kilcott.'

Mr Blackburn's face fell. Or did it? Was she just hoping it would? Maybe he was just swallowing a mouthful of bread?

'I shall be staying in London for the festivities,' he said, 'though I'm not sure that it will be very festive in my lodgings.'

Rose tried to work out what her movements might be. She (or rather, Richard) was due back in Cambridge around the 13th of January, and although George had not told her his plans for after this ball, she did know he had no intention of making the long journey to Gloucestershire over the muddy December roads, as he needed to continue working, wars not respecting festivals. It was too complicated, she decided. She must just seize the moment while she could.

'Whatever may be in the future, I am most pleased we have been able to meet today. I so hoped you would be here at the ball; I was about to give up hope when I had not been able to find you.' Was that too blatant an encouragement to him to constitute good manners?

'It was my wish too, Miss Clarke. I know it is an over-used excuse but I was detained by business. Or more accurately, by the coach from Lincoln returning me from my business with the troops in Lincolnshire. It broke a wheel outside Huntingdon and we were severely delayed.'

'Oh!' exclaimed Rose. 'Were you injured?' She looked more carefully at his face, his hands, stretched out a hand as if to caress. 'I see no wounds, are you well?'

'Fortunately, I was not thrown from the carriage when it over-turned, but I have a fair set of bruises that it would not be polite to show to you.' He shifted in his seat at the memory and Rose tried unsuccessfully not to speculate as to the bruises' exact location.

'Unfortunately, one of the outside passengers was less lucky and broke a leg; and the coachman had a nasty gash to his head: he was quite knocked out.'

Rose's hand went to her mouth. 'How terrible! But you are well? I'm so glad.' She looked in concern up at his dark brown eyes and shivered slightly. She took his hand in both of hers and pressed it warmly. 'I should be so distressed if you should come to harm.'

Mr Blackburn seemed a little disconcerted by this intelligence. He averted his gaze for a moment, and coughed. 'You realise,' he managed finally, 'that my work is necessarily dangerous? You saw my appearance at Trumpington after the fracas with those ruffians?'

'Indeed I did; and I admire you for it. But I can still worry about you while believing you are doing what you must do.'

'Thankyou, Miss Clarke, for your confidence in me.'

Rose wanted to know so much more about this man, his likes and dislikes, his quirks, his past experiences. If she had been Richard, she could have asked all the intrusive questions she wanted, probably over a beer or two in a tavern, but as Rose she was constrained. On the other hand, Richard wouldn't feel towards him as she did. Oh, it was so complicated!

'So, tell me a little more about yourself, sir. If you cannot report your doings over the last months in any detail, what can you disclose?'

'Ah, where to begin. There's not much to know, I don't think.'

'The more trivial the better, I find, they tell one so much more about a person. What is your favourite kind of dog? Do you go to watch the horse racing? What irritates you the most? Have you ever walked into the ladies' necessary room in error?'

Blackburn laughed. 'Not the last, I'm glad to say. I went to Newmarket in late October but it was in the line of business, I'm afraid. It seemed very exciting all around me, but I had to concentrate on the people I was trying to sound out. That was my first time at the races too, you must think me very dull.'

'Not at all,' Rose burst out, perhaps too enthusiastically. 'Did you not watch any races? I'd so love to go.'

'Really? Well, I'd be most glad to take you some day, if you wish. Especially if we could go with someone who knows what to do and all that; I'd be a poor guide.'

'That wouldn't matter, sir. I'm sure you would be at ease in any new situation.' Good grief, she was laying it on a bit.

Mr Blackburn coughed again. 'Now what was your other question? Dogs? I must say I'm not fond of dogs. Or any house pets, actually. Pack of hounds for hunting's fine, they stay out in their kennels, but yappy lap-dogs, terriers and so on, no thanks, nor any other sort knocking into your legs and getting in the way. I'm sorry, are you a big dog-lover?'

'Not really. I quite like smaller ones, but my father kept two or three bull mastiffs at any one time, and I was scared of them. They were used to catch poachers and guard the house. Since he died we haven't kept any animals, except the horses of course.'

'My father used to hunt when he was younger, but I never took to it. I like to know what's the other side of a jump before I set my horse to it. Perhaps I'm a bit cautious, d'you think?'

'Sensible, rather, I'd say. Courage is all very well but you need planning too. I definitely like to know what is going to happen and to anticipate eventualities.'

Mr Blackburn made to stand up. 'Can I get you anything else? I'm in need of another glass of port wine, and I should like to anticipate your eventualities for you.'

Rose smiled and held out her cup. 'Another negus, if you would. And is there any cake?'

She watched his lovely back as he bent over the table to replenish her plate and fill her cup. He looked so dashing. And he didn't seem to have realised what she had been doing at the Pemberton ball: perhaps it was the knock on the head in the *melée* that he mentioned, as she was sure he'd been there when her role in exposing the bomb was explained quite clearly by the colonel to Mr Pemberton, in spite of her protestations. What else could she ask him when he returned? She really hadn't got used to being a girl again, she felt her conversation was stilted, her attention over-sensitive.

'Met a fellow over there by the tureen, most interesting chap. Says he studies rocks and fossils,' he said on his return, carrying a most indecently large slice of gooey cake for her. 'He's just coming over to pay his respects.'

Rose looked up and suddenly realised who the man she had half recognised earlier must be. Of course, she had attended some lectures of his in her role as Richard. He was the Professor of Geology at Cambridge, Mr Hailstone.

'He said he thought he knew you from somewhere. Is that right?'

Rose found her heart racing. Surely he hadn't penetrated her appearance? After all, she had sat some way away from the front in the lecture room, and had not said anything, as befitted a student who knew as yet nothing of the subject in question. But he was coming over to them!

'I thought I recognised Mr Blackburn's companion,' he said. 'We met at the Pemberton ball. I handed you over to one of our Trinity students, Noakes. I'm dashed if I can remember your name though, Miss, very rude of me.'

Rose gave a great, but internal, sigh of relief. 'Miss Clarke, Mr

Hailstone, sir. Yes, I recall very well the occasion. You danced with me, and you said you ought not to bore me with talk of rocks and fossils, but I was most interested to hear more, as it happened.'

Mr Hailstone clapped Mr Blackburn on the back. 'Best of luck with the lady, lad. A real bluestocking, I'll be bound. None the worse for that, though.'

Turning back to Rose, he asked, 'Have you had a chance to learn anything of geology in the short time since we spoke, Miss?'

Rose considered. Should she risk it? She could mention something she had learned at one of Mr Hailstone's lectures, perhaps. 'Well, sir, I have indeed. A gentleman showed me what he called an Oxfordshire pound-stone and told me that it was the petrified remains of a sea urchin from longer ago than he could credit. And that there were many other such remains of long-gone creatures scattered all over the country, and that nobody could account for them fully.'

'Capital! You are correct, Miss, and it is our work to try and fathom how these artefacts came to be so. Were they created as they are now; or have they transmuted in some way to their present form, and if so, over what period of time, and how have they come to be in sites so far from their natural dwelling?'

Rose had already regretted her lack of caution, thinking of how it would lay her open to potential recognition if she were to attend more of the professor's lectures next term. So she cast her eyes downwards modestly, and then looked up into the face of Mr Blackburn admiringly, at which Mr Hailstone took the hint and bade them farewell.

'How do you know about poundstones, Miss Clarke?' asked Mr Blackburn, looking impressed.

Rose paused, trying to keep her lies simple again. 'I was shown one when I was staying at the Wintons'. It was a curiosity.' As he didn't say anything, she added, 'I do like to acquire odd nuggets of knowledge, you know. It may not be very ladylike, but . . . Have you read Mrs Wollstonecraft?'

'I can't say I have. What is the title?'

'"A vindication of the rights of woman". I could lend you a copy if you wish?'

'That would be most kind. I know nothing of the subject. I should be glad to read something that is important to you.'

Rose discerned that he was most anxious to please her, which she took as a good sign. She wondered how she could render their relationship more intimate at such a public gathering, while retaining propriety. Perhaps a promenade outside? Or perhaps not, it was very cold and it had looked like rain when they arrived.

'Would you care to dance, Mr Blackburn? I think I have finished eating.'

'Certainly. Would you care for me to invite you to do so?' he said with a mischievous grin.

Rose grinned back and fluttered her eyelids at him as best she could, not being practised in the art.

CHAPTER 2

I

T WAS DURING THE DANCE-BUT-ONE after this that she suddenly remembered Charles. Ought she to be checking up on him again?
She probably ought, but she was having such a good time dancing that
she didn't want to leave the ballroom. Anyway, she was booked for a
second turn with Mr Blackburn in two dances' time, so that was that.

'How's my favourite sister?' came in her ear as she left the floor
with one of Mr Blackburn's colleagues from the 51st regiment. It was
Sir George; he had a look about him which said he wanted her to do
something for him.

She gave him an excessively low curtsey and said with downcast
eyes, 'I am yours to command, my liege. Only say the word.'

George looked taken aback for a moment. 'No, be serious, Rose. I
do need your help. Could you come with me out of the crowd, please,
so we can talk?'

Rose followed him into another alcove. This building seemed spe-
cifically designed for clandestine conversations. And indeed, perhaps
it had been, she mused.

'So, how are you finding the ball?'

'Fortunately, less exciting than the last one, you will be pleased
to hear.'

'But more partners than back in the Season?'

Rose inclined her head in acknowledgement. 'Get to the point,
Doddie.'

'I've told you not to call me that in public! Anyway, the point, yes: have you seen Lady John Barnes here?'

'No, really? Isn't she . . . I mean, her husband was arrested with those French sympathisers, wasn't he?'

'Indeed. It seems however that she was only a carrier of messages. We believe. We hope. However, we do not fully trust her, so she is being carefully watched. I am surprised to see her here tonight, and it is not clear why she is here. What I want you to do, if you will, is to sit down with the matrons near where she and her coterie are located, and see if you can find out with whom she is associating. Or anything else that may be of interest to us: you can do this whereas I or one of my agents could hardly pass unnoticed in such feminine company.'

'Hmmm. Now, how might I end up there without it seeming deliberate? Let me see.'

'I wondered if you could find a lady you know, and promenade a little, and then sit for a rest? How about Miss Winton? I know her to be here: I saw her earlier?'

'Er, not Julia, George. She has gone home with her mother. She was, er, unwell.'

'So then? Will you do it?'

'Of course. It sounds fun. I think I shall ask Mr Blackburn to deposit me in the correct place after the next dance. Will that serve?'

'Excellent. I shall point out where she is, so there shall be no mistake. You remember her appearance from, er, well, from before?'

Rose remembered the intimacy she had observed between Lady John and her brother that she was not supposed to have seen, and grinned. 'How could I forget, brother?'

George had the grace to colour a little, but led her back to the ballroom and indicated the location to her. Soon she was out on the floor and explaining in a low voice what she wanted to Mr Blackburn, who seemed discomfited by how close she necessarily stood to him; she noted this and smiled to herself, before moving a little closer.

Sure enough, after the dance, they had contrived to be in the right quarter of the room and she sank into a chair exclaiming how exhausted she felt and begging Mr Blackburn to fetch her some lemonade. He departed on his errand and she fell into conversation with her neighbours on such topics as the heat of the room, the splendour of the decorations, the quality of the supper, and such commonplaces. Mr Blackburn brought her glass and then withdrew as she had asked, and she quickly found herself part of a group of women who watched the dancers, and commented on anything that struck them as worthy of sniping at.

Rose commended herself for having found a seat where she could almost overhear the conversation behind her from Lady John and her friends, and moved it a little under the pretext of being better able to talk with a stout elderly lady who seemed to know all the government gossip.

'So as I said to Lord Hobart, Surely it isn't safe for us to let these foreigners into the country, you never know what they may be up to, and he said, Madam, they need to be here in the interests of trade, and we are quite capable of keeping an eye on them, but I said, Surely not those wicked Frenchies, and he said . . .' but Rose let the diatribe wash over her and focussed on picking up snippets from the ladies just behind.

'. . . my son James I am afraid is running quite wild these days.'

'Well, Mrs Eldridge, the young of today, you simply can't do a thing with them, I put it down to the . . .'

'Lady John, what do you think about . . . ?'

'How long do you think before she gets an offer from Mr Smart? Mr Philip Smart, I mean?'

'I live in hope, my dear, I live in hope, but the signs are not propitious at present.'

And so on, and so on.

It was most taxing to work out what these people were saying, especially as her back was towards them, and she could not put names to faces. However, it seemed there was a Mrs Eldridge, who might be the mother of one of the men involved with Charles in the drinking game she had interrupted, James she thought he had been called by Mrs Seddon's friend; a Mrs Smith who was very hesitant in her answers but who seemed to be most anxious to please Lady John; someone called Georgiana who was smartly rebuffed when she enquired about Lord John's health; and a Lady Elizabeth who spoke so quietly that Rose had not made out a single word she said.

The topics of conversation were mostly about the dissolute behaviour of the young, in particular their own children and other relations, the difficulty of bringing men with a fortune up to the mark to propose marriage, and the cost of luxuries now the war had started all over again. It was all depressingly like the conversation she was pretending to listen to in front of her.

'Miss Clarke, did you hear me? I asked you whether you agreed with Lady Westley?'

Rose started. 'I'm terribly sorry, I was woolgathering. I am feeling most fatigued as I slept most poorly last night.'

This seemed to satisfy the ladies next to her, and she concentrated on their conversation properly for a few minutes. Her neighbours moved onto the unreliability of certain English aristocrats in the face of the French threat, and (in a very low tone) a series of 'Did you hear?' and 'How terrible!' intimations concerning the sudden disappearance from society of a certain noble gentleman, and how strange it was that (whispered) his wife should be here tonight, and surely she must have known, and so on.

'Lord Hobart said everything was under control when I tasked him with that very point,' said the stout lady with vigour. 'He said he had every faith in his officers, and we were quite safe.'

'But wasn't there a large explosion that the gentleman set off, somewhere near Cambridge?'

'I heard it was in one of the colleges, and several people were killed.'

'Was it? I thought they said that three young ladies were mortally wounded, I do not think they would have been in a college?'

'Little you know of the behaviour of young men let free of restraint, my dear. I understand the colleges are full of women at all hours of day and night, and not just the common sort: ladies who should know better too.'

'I heard that another young lady was involved, actually in the plot. An accomplice of the gentleman we were discussing, and an English girl, too!'

The stout lady broke in. 'Exactly. I said to Lord Hobart that I didn't believe him for a moment about his so-called security precautions, and that Something ought to be Done.'

They moved off onto the manifold inadequacies of the government, the iniquity of Mr Addington reintroducing the Income-tax, the price of tea, the impossibility of buying decent brandy and so on, and Rose tried to focus her attention on the other group once more.

She succeeded in picking up a couple more names, but nothing else of import; the ladies were starting to round up their charges from the dance floor, and call for their carriages. There was just one more snippet that she thought might interest George: Lady John was planning to spend Christmas in Oxford, as a guest of the Rector of Exeter College.

The ball seemed to be drawing to a close, though it was only just past one o'clock, as she made her way around the room looking for George. He was not in evidence, and so she returned to Mrs Seddon who had fallen asleep in her chair, and simply waited. Her mind was buzzing with trying to remember names, to the point that when Mr Blackburn stopped by to bid her farewell and wish they could meet again soon, she spoke to him quite distantly. He told her his address for the Christmas period, and she wrote it on her dance card together with a couple of the names she had been trying to hold in mind, while reiterating that she expected to be in Gloucestershire, but if not she might be found at the hotel at which he had previously visited her.

George returned at length, minus Charles, for whom he had been searching without success. They set off in a hackney, due to the lateness of the hour. George returned her to the door of her hotel and then walked the short distance to his rooms, leaving her to assemble her thoughts and write down any more names that she might forget before retiring.

George presented himself early on Thursday, eager to know whether she had gathered useful intelligence. They had not liked to discuss matters before, at the ball with everyone milling about, or in the carriage, but the salon was quite empty at the hour of eleven.

'Lady John was sitting with I believe four people: Mrs Eldridge, Mrs Smith, someone called Georgiana, and Lady Elizabeth something,' she said consulting her notes. 'I did not think it discreet to look towards them so there may have been others who did not speak.'

'Excellent,' said George, 'I think Georgiana must have been . . . well never mind, do go on.'

'Mrs Smith appeared to be in a dependent position; Georgiana was not party to Lady John's affairs and made a couple of mild faux pas; and Lady Elizabeth was most reserved and spoke quietly so I could not hear what she was saying.'

'And did they speak of anything of interest? Could you discern why they were sitting with Lady John?'

'Not that I could tell. Somebody's daughter was hoping for an offer from a Mr Philip Smart: but I can tell you a little about him, I think, or at least about his brother.'

'I am all ears.'

'Well, it was much earlier in the evening,' she began. 'You're not going to like this, it concerns Charles.'

'What has he been up to now?'

Rose took a breath. 'I had not seen him in the ball room for some time, and enquired of my chaperone and the other ladies if they had noticed him. It appears that he had left the room in the company of, er, Sir Peter Mackenzie's eldest.'

'Jacob, yes, I know of the man. Sir Peter is at the War Office working for Lord Hobart.'

'Oh, that is who Lord Hobart is. One of my new friends was boasting about talking to him, and telling him his business. So this Mackenzie was with John Smart, who is the brother of Philip Smart, I found out later, and,' she refreshed her memory, 'James Eldridge. Mrs Eldridge said he was running quite wild and she despaired of him, and I heard the same from Mrs Seddon's friend, Mrs Lanscombe, who said John Smart was similarly unreliable.'

'Neither name is known to me. As yet. I shall make my own enquiries.' He made some notes, then sat back. 'But what of Charles?'

'I came upon him engaged in a drinking game, a kind of boat race.'

George grimaced. 'And were they all quite hell hocused?'

'If you mean by that uncouth expression, drunk, then yes of course they were. Now, I recognised two others in the group besides Charles, one was Charlie French whom I have only met before in my guise as Richard Cox, he is one of the men I have been rowing with, but he was too disguised to recognise me as I now am; and the other was, er, Julia Winton, whom I had to rescue before she was utterly ruined in public.'

'No? Miss Winton? So, what . . . ?'

'I summoned her mother, who was most competent and spirited her away from the revelry without fanfare.' She pulled a face. 'After ensuring she, er, shot her cat profusely.'

'Yes, to reduce the continuation of intoxication. I understand.'

'Hence I lost track of Charles. He did not return to your chambers last night?'

'No indeed. Well, he will turn up again when he is out of blunt again, I dare say.' He held out his hand for her paper. 'And is there anything else? Any snippet, any chance remark, any tiny morsel?'

'No, don't,' said Rose, withdrawing it quickly from his reach. I have certain other information recorded on this card that I wish to keep. You can make your own notes.'

'Very well.' George raised his eyebrows at her, but she ignored him. 'Anyway, anything else I should know?'

'Only that Lady John is to spend the holiday at the Rector's Lodge in Exeter College in Oxford.'

'Exeter? I wonder why? I do not know the Rector there – but I shall look into it. Well done, Rose, you have been most useful. Some of those names . . . well, I had better not say any more at present.'

'Now, George, can you tell me what are your plans over Christmas? This hotel is satisfactory for a few days, but I don't know what I shall do with myself if I have to stay here until next term begins, with you working all the time. As you know, I have few friends in London, and almost all of them will have gone to the country within a day or two.'

'Will you not be entertained sufficiently by daily visits from Mr Blackburn?'

Rose glared at him. 'I believe he may call, yes, but he has his work to do, the same as you, I imagine? Also, at any time he may be called away to investigate a regiment with difficulties.'

'Indeed. So, I have been trying to think. Do you want to go to Kilcott? It would be quite dull there for you.'

'Yes, very.'

'You could perhaps visit Louisa in Cheshire if it were not such a long journey on bad roads.'

Rose shuddered. 'Hours and hours of bumping and rolling, with lots of stops for all kinds of delays, no thank you.'

'I see why that does not appeal. Well, I shall think about it hard today and join you for dinner. It is served here at five o'clock, is it not?'

'Indeed. And I shall occupy myself until then with the Principia.' She grinned at George.

'Rose! What would the other guests think!'

'Calm yourself, brother dear. I shall read in private, in my room. I don't want to cause any more embarrassment; Charles is quite good enough at that for one family.'

But by dinner time George had not come up with any suitable plan. However, as they sat in the salon afterwards, drinking tea, a footman entered and coughed discreetly. 'Miss Clarke, there is a lady here to see you. Are you receiving at this hour?'

'Certainly. Show her in, please.'

It was Mrs Winton, looking worried. She took her seat and after acknowledging Rose's connection to Sir George, whom she already knew well through her son Peter, asked him to stay for the interview, in case he could be of help. She begged Rose to tell her the circumstances of her daughter's misbehaviour, knowing Sir George would be discreet. After hearing the sorry tale, she paused, looking embarrassed, and then addressed herself to Sir George.

'I have something to ask of you, not that I expect you would be willing, it being Christmas and probably totally inconvenient, but . . . Well, Julia has been most odd this morning.'

'Unwell, of course.'

'More than that. She has been frightened, and won't tell me why. She can't remember last night after about nine o'clock, she says, which is a mercy in some ways, but I am worried.'

George hesitated before asking, 'She hasn't been, er, . . . compromised personally in any other way, has she? Other than the drinking, I mean.'

'No, thank the Lord, I think not. And we removed her from Somerset House without being noticed by the *ton*, I believe. But I think she must have been with a group of very unpleasant men earlier, and heard or saw something, or was a party to something horrible. And I thought, but it's too much to ask . . .'

'Go on.'

'Well, would Miss Clarke be willing to come and stay with us for a few days to be a companion for Julia, to help her settle herself after this experience? Obviously, I should like it if she were also able to see if she can find out what it is that troubles her? Julia won't talk to me, because she thinks I'd be angry, I expect. And she's right, I'm fuming. But I suspect I ought to be directing my ire at some unscrupulous men rather than at my daughter.'

Rose looked at George, questioningly.

'You seemed to get on quite well the short time you were with us before, you see . . .'

George nodded. 'Would you like that, Rose?' He grinned at her, and raised an eyebrow. 'It would certainly fit in very well with *almost* all your needs.'

Rose controlled the urge to punch him, folding her hands on her lap instead. 'That would be most agreeable, Mrs Winton. And if I can be of service to you as well, I should be most glad to come.'

'Capital, I do hope it is not upsetting your Christmas arrangements?'

'No, no, we were just talking about our plans, because sadly Sir George is needed in the Foreign Office daily, so we are not able to go together to his estate for the festival.'

'We travel tomorrow at ten, if that would be suitable for you? Our carriage is quite new, and . . . but I forget, you have travelled in it before.'

They made arrangements about where Rose's luggage was to be picked up, as some of her things were stored at Sir George's apartments, and parted. As soon as she had gone Rose checked there was nobody else in sight, then took up a pugilistic pose. 'You'd better be careful, Doddie, I've learnt a lot of things in the last few months; don't you give me grief over a man I happen to like or you might find you need a few days off work.'

'You are funny when you're in a snit, Rose. But very well, I'll not mention your paramour more than, well, twice a day?'

Rose landed a hefty blow on his shoulder and snorted. 'Be careful, George. Be very careful.'

CHAPTER 3

THE JOURNEY TO MILTON PASSED more equably than Rose had feared. The turnpike still seemed in rather better repair than roads usually were in December, and it was a lot smoother in the Wintons' carriage than in the mail coach that had brought Richard to London only five days before, if not quite so rapid. She had debated as to whether she ought to bring the box containing all of Richard's clothes and possessions, in case she might stay long enough to go directly to college from Milton, and had decided against it. However, she had tucked her copy of the Principia at the bottom of her regular box, in case she might have a chance to read it without causing alarm.

The coach was crowded with the three ladies and the Wintons' maid, and all the parcels and boxes of dresses and sweetmeats and bonnets and books and ribbons that had been the main purpose of the visit to London, and which were too delicate to be tied on the roof. Julia, pale of face, remained silent for the whole journey and looked out of the window, though Rose doubted if she observed anything of the countryside through which they passed. The maid took out her mending, and Rose was grateful that Mrs Winton made conversation.

Fortunately she did not catechise her about how she had spent the time since she left Milton after the ball, which would have been awkward to answer in a believable fashion, but rather asked her about Kilcott, and showed considerable interest in Uncle Hugh's researches on the Rosetta stele, not to mention a good deal of knowledge of the problem. She was able explain to Rose what a cartouche was, and why it might be important in the decipherment, and Rose came to consider that there must be considerably more to this lady than she had imagined.

Mrs Winton was also sympathetic about her brother Charles and his erratic behaviour, but said that he would probably grow out of it, it was what they called a phase of development, which sounded like an excuse for bad manners, which it was, but at least it gave hope to suffering parents (and sisters). Rose felt she ought to reciprocate by enquiring about Julia's younger sister, whom she had not spoken to before. It seemed she was a quiet and placid child of twelve, called Elizabeth, who spent most of the time when she was not with her governess in reading, but it was clear that her mother doted on her.

In spite of the comforts of the coach the journey was long, and it was late before they arrived at the house. She was shown to the same room as she had occupied previously, which made her feel quickly at home, and after secreting her Principia in a drawer near her bed, went downstairs for a light supper leaving the maid to unpack. There was no sign of Julia, but Mrs Winton said she had agreed to take a cup of chocolate in her room.

The next morning she came down late to breakfast to find the house in a flurry of activity. Servants were carrying boxes and parcels up the stairs, and the hallway was filled with excited children. It seemed that Mr Winton's brother and his family had arrived from Ely, at such an early hour as to be in good time to go out to gather greenery and prepare Christmas decorations. Elizabeth was milling around with them, and it was with some difficulty that they were per-suaded to come to the breakfast table, as they all wanted to be outside and visiting the gardeners to start culling the shrubs.

Rose ate her bread rolls and honey cake, marvelling at the number of different preserves provided, while the children got up and down from the table and bickered and demanded as children will. Julia's aunt, Mrs Jane Winton, sat by Rose and was most friendly, explaining that her brood had not seen their cousin for upwards of four weeks (!) and were consequently having to pass on all the news and establish who was the leader all over again.

Hugh, who had just had his seventh birthday, wanted to be in charge because he was the only boy; but his sister Jane, at eleven, and Elizabeth, at twelve, had other ideas. Little Marian concentrated on getting plum jam all over her face, interspersed with complaints that the others never did what she wanted, and it wasn't fair, and that Hugh had lost a tooth and she had wanted to lose one too but hers were quite fixed in her mouth and why was that?

Mr Hugh Winton was also most cordial, pleased that there was another young person to join their party and be a companion for Julia, and interested in what she had to say about Gloucestershire, and the new kinds of carrot that their gardener Jenks had been trying out (though Rose carefully omitted to mention that she had been the one to dig over the test beds while building up her muscles for her role as Richard). He was in business buying and selling farmland and other property, and had interests in canals and in Fen drainage, and in renovation of buildings.

The other person present, seated at the end of the table, was Miss Charlotte Churchill, Mrs Elizabeth Winton's much older, unmarried, sister from Huntingdon. It seemed she had been in residence for ten days already, and was somewhat sniffy about her sister and Julia having gone off to London and leaving her, though she had not wanted to accompany them on their shopping expedition as she saw no need for purchasing frivolities. Besides, the roads were so dangerous at this time of year, and she had seen it as her duty to be at the house on St Thomas' Day, to supervise the giving of gifts to the poor of the parish (carried out by the butler and housekeeper) even though Elizabeth had chosen to cavort at a ball instead.

Miss Churchill ate sparingly of dry toast and very weak tea, and sat upright in her chair. The children kept a wary distance, and Rose thought she might follow their example. Julia had not appeared, so

Rose thought she would be left hanging between the very young and the older generation, until Marian came up to her and held out a (still slightly sticky) hand and asked her to come with them to cut branches. 'You can lift me up to reach,' she said, 'the others always get the best bits else.'

She rose, therefore, and followed her small host into the hall where they donned coats and headed for the garden. Marian confided to her that she was five now, and a big girl, so she wanted to pick the Missles toes this year herself, and they hadn't let her before but she did want to and could Miss Clarke make sure she did?

It was a beautiful sunny morning, though cold, and the gardener greeted the children like old colleagues. 'Morning Miss Jane, Miss Elizabeth, Master Hugh; come to help me have you? And Miss Marian too? Who is your assistant, Miss Marian? Won't you introduce me?'

'This is Miss Clarke, and she's going to help me pick the Missles toes, John.'

The gardener touched his cap to Rose and said that he hoped she was good at climbing as the mistletoe was quite high up on the apple trees this year. He armed the girls with strong scissors and gave Hugh, to his delight, a large knife with many reminders to be sure to cut away from himself. They marched in procession first towards the shrubbery where stood a wheeled barrow. The children gathered armfuls of yew and holly, bay and laurel, until John had to tell them to stop or the barrow would be too full for the other plants. Next came the scented herbs, rosemary in particular, which John had them put in a large trug he produced like a kind of rustic conjuror. Lastly, for the *pièce de résistance*, they entered the orchard, and looked for the bunches of green sitting high on the bare branches of the fruit trees.

'Lift me up, lift me up,' begged Marian, 'I want to reach.'

Rose did as she was asked, and set her on a branch at head height. 'Hold on to that bough by your right hand,' she instructed. 'Can you reach the bunch from there?'

It seemed not. Marian leaned as far as she could and almost let go of her hold on the bough. 'Hold there, Marian,' Rose cautioned, 'I'll need to come up myself to help you.'

John produced a set of folding steps and with their aid Rose ascended to the point where she could catch Marian around her waist and lift her far enough to snip with her small scissors at the 'Missles toes'. Pieces of leaf and little sprigs fluttered to the ground but cutting the whole spray was beyond her. Presently Rose's arms tired and she lowered the child first to her branch and then to the ground. Marion knelt and collected all the little pieces into her lap, and counted the berries.

'I've got fourteen-three Missles toes, Miss Clarke, look!'

Meanwhile Hugh had climbed up high into a large tree (after being disarmed of his knife by John until he had ascended) and, on being passed the blade, had cut a beautiful bunch of foliage. The girls had not been outdone, and had ascended rather more cautiously in their skirts, but had both been successful. All the trophies were places with the herbs in the trug and then it was placed on top of the greenery in the barrow, John wheeling it with them in procession to the French doors of the drawing room, Marian clutching at her skirts which held her treasure.

Hugh knocked on the doors and, with what Rose imagined he thought was a stentorian voice, ordered, 'Open for the entry of the Christmas wreaths!' The door was opened at once by his mother, who presumably had been observing the action, and they all trooped inside.

Rose stood back to watch while the family dressed the room with their trophies. Marian sat at table where there was a framework for a mistletoe ball, and with Aunt Jane's help began wiring it with greenery and herbs. Her shards of mistletoe were carefully shepherded to one side to be added later.

In the midst of all this activity Julia entered the room with her mother, looking sullen. She was in a loose morning gown and pinafore, and her hair was dressed extremely simply.

'See dear, you have missed the gathering of the evergreens already,' said Mrs Winton brightly. 'Why don't you go over and catch up with Rose, now, and watch what the others are doing, if you don't feel like taking part?'

Julia drifted across to Rose and sat down a little distance away. Rose smiled at her, and getting no response turned her attention to Elizabeth and Jane who were manufacturing a complicated arrangement out of scraps of shiny paper, offcuts of fabric, and sequins. From what Rose could see the main component however was glue, liberally applied.

'Can you tell me what you are making, girls?' she enquired, 'or is it a secret?'

'It's not working very well,' said Jane, 'but it's supposed to be an angel.'

'You've put that bit of muslin over his face,' said Elizabeth. 'Look, it's better lower down.'

'Julia, are you any good at this sort of thing,' asked Rose, 'I'm all fingers and thumbs.'

'Yes, come on, Julia,' said Elizabeth, 'help us, you know you made that lovely set of stars last year.'

Julia reluctantly moved across and inspected the confection. 'What you need,' she said quietly, 'is a stiffer base. You can't just glue the bits together, you need to stick them to something. What have you got?'

Elizabeth riffled through their pile of materials. 'There's some paperboard somewhere here, I think.'

'So, girls, one of you needs to draw the angel and then cut him out, and then you can stick the materials to him.'

'I'm the best at drawing,' said Jane, 'I'll do it.'

'Alright, I'll cut him out then.'

'Give me the pencil.'

Julia went to sit back down. Rose moved across next to her. 'You did some stars last year, Elizabeth said. What were they like?'

'Oh, it was nothing.'

'I'd like to know.'

'Well, I made several strings of them, we hung them over the door-ways, they were silver and gold. They looked lovely.'

'Lovely,' Rose echoed. 'Do you plan to do anything this year?'

'No, I'm not feeling in the mood.' There was a long pause. She raised her head and looked Rose in the eye. 'Rose, tell me something. Why did mother invite you here? Is there something going on, or . . .' she trailed off.

'Something going on?'

'Yes, like last time, when Peter brought you to take you to the ball, and asked me to pretend we'd known each other for ages. I'm not stupid, you know. And I don't think you've set your cap at him, you don't look at him in the right way, although I wouldn't blame you if you did, he is a wonderful brother, when he's here I mean. But at the ball, there was a commotion at the supper table, I couldn't see what happened, and people were running around and shouting, and then they came to fetch mother and nobody would tell me what it was about really, but the gossip said you'd destroyed the special cake, the one they brought in as a present for the militia.'

'Ah, yes, the cake. Um, do you know what Peter does for a job?'

'Not really. He's very secretive about it.'

'Well, let me just say all that was to do with what Peter does, so it's secret too. I'm sorry, but I can't tell you, much as I'd like to. But that's not why I'm here now, and I don't know where your brother is at the moment.'

'Do you, um, like him?'

'Well, of course I do. As you say, he's a fine man.'

'No, I mean, do you want to . . . to marry him or anything?'

'Not at all.' Rose thought she'd spoken a bit too definitely, as if she thought ill of Peter. Now she was going to have to admit who she did like. Bother. 'I, er, well, there's someone else I am becoming quite fond of, to be honest. Except, we rarely seem to be able to be in the same place at the same time, unfortunately.'

'Was it one of the people you danced with at Somerset House?'

'Er, well . . .'

'I saw you with Lord Hawkesbury: it can't be him, he's married.'

Rose gasped. 'No, no! He must be nearly forty, too.'

'Nor Mr Terrier, not unless you haven't heard the gossip.'

Rose felt puzzled, and then she remembered. Mr Terrier had looked peaky, and Sir George had intimated in May that he'd contracted an unfortunate infection . . .

'I have heard the gossip, thankyou,' she said, blushing. 'No, not Mr Terrier either.'

'Perhaps it's rude of me to ask, though? Do you think it is?'

'Well, maybe a little bit. But I don't have to tell you, do I?'

'I didn't see who you danced with after that,' she continued. 'I was, well, I wasn't dancing.' She suddenly hunched her shoulders and fell silent. Rose let her be, and watched Hugh trying to get some yew branches to stay put on a display of swords and armour on the wall. She heard Julia sniff.

There was another rapping on the doors, and two roughly dressed men came in dragging a large log. Mr Hugh Winton went over to help them after summoning the footman, and between the four of them they carried the log over to the fireplace where it sat somewhat awkwardly half in, half out of the hearth.

'Happen that'll do, Madam,' one of the men said to Mrs Winton, mopping his face. 'If you light the end that's by the chimney, then you can push it in as it gets consumed. Might be a bit smoky at first, but it'll burn a fair time. Maybe not till Twelfth Night, mind. But it's good oak, that is. Fell back in February, in that big wind we had.'

Young Hugh left his yew branches and ran up to Mrs Winton. 'Can I light it, can I light it?' he carolled.

'Very well. You must fetch the piece of last year's log that we kept over for the purpose, though.'

'Where is it, where is it?'

'You'll have to look, you'll have to look,' she replied. 'But it's in this room.'

Hugh ran here and there looking in all the likely and the unlikely places. The older girls climbed down and joined him, and eventually Hugh ran the charred remnant to earth in the coal basket. His father lent him his penknife and showed him how to shave bits off the wood to make a bed for the spark, then produced his tinderbox and between then they got the flame going.

Carefully Hugh took the burning brand, laid it in the kindling in the fireplace, and watched as the flames slowly took hold.

'Julia, do you always have a Yule log?' asked Rose, 'I've never seen one before.'

'It's not very fashionable, I know,' she said, 'but we've always done it since I can remember. We do all the old traditions. Father likes them, and he says they're coming back into fashion. Shame he won't see them this year, he's still in Barbados.'

She coughed, then moved a bit closer to Rose. 'Look, if you aren't here on secret business for Peter, then mother must have asked you to trick me into telling you about . . . about what happened at the ball. So you're spying for her. Like I said, I'm not stupid.'

Rose was taken aback by the girl's forthrightness. 'Well,' she temporised, then realising that honesty was the only way forward, said, 'You're right, Julia, she did ask me to do that. Not trick you, quite, but be company for you, and find out what is upsetting you, try and help. And I don't think you're stupid, far from it. I've not known you for long, but I know Peter is highly intelligent, and your mother seems to know everything about everything.'

'She does. But, I don't know, I can't, I mean . . .'

'Your mother is quite angry about, er, what happened, but she suspects it wasn't your fault exactly.'

'I can't tell you.'

Rose considered. It might be better if they went for a turn around the room, or better, away from the room, where nobody could hear them. She leaned in closer. 'That's alright. But I have something I ought to tell you first, though, and you don't have to say anything in return, unless you want to. Shall we go and walk in the gallery if you have one, or somewhere a little more private?'

'Julia,' called Elizabeth, 'Can you come and help us, please?'

'I'd better go,' she said, and the moment was lost.

The activity continued all day. Rose was tasked with taking Marian up into the attics with a big basket, to where the apples from the autumn sat neatly in rows, not touching so they would keep, and bringing enough down for the apple bobbing later. Marian was very careful to select only the reddest ones, and placed each one tenderly into the scrunched-up cloth in the bottom of her basket.

'Hugh won't be any good at this this year,' she confided, 'because he hasn't got all his teeth.'

Rose found herself sat at lunch between Mr and Mrs Hugh Winton. After having, perhaps incautiously, expressed herself interested in agriculture in their earlier conversation, she learnt a lot that she hadn't expected about experiments with growing beet from Silesia to produce sugar; drainage, sluices and management of water generally; and advances in crop rotation. Mrs Winton intervened at one point to suggest her husband may be boring Rose, but her interest had been piqued and she implored him to continue.

Once lunch was over she found herself leading an expedition on foot to Baits Bite lock, to work off some of the children's excess energy, and to take advantage of the wintry sunshine. Marian held her hand the whole way, Hugh spent most of his time swiping with sticks at anything swipable, and the older girls planned further decorative extravaganzas. Julia had excused herself and gone to her room, leaving the older generation to tidy up the debris of the children's decoration and add their own touches.

On their return, she delivered Hugh to his mother for a change of clothes following his falling into a ditch while reaching for his latest stick which he had inadvertently thrown into a tall bush, then ascended to Julia's room and knocked. There was a vague sound which she decided to take as assent, and entered.

Julia was lying on her bed staring at the ceiling. Hoping she was doing the right thing, she planked herself down on the nearest chair and began to talk, in the manner of a witness in court, addressing the air.

'So, I was at the Somerset House ball, and after dancing with a number of men, I thought I ought to look for Charles my brother who I had not seen for some time. I imagined he would be involved in some escapade that we, that is my older brother Sir George and I, would find embarrassing. My chaperones told me that he had left the room in the company of three men they thought to be undesirable: to whit Jacob Mackenzie, John Smart and James Eldridge. I am not acquainted with any of these; my own brother I would describe as easily led but not malicious. Leaving the ballroom I saw light showing in a chamber off the main corridor and looked inside. I saw Charles engaged in a drinking game involving the imitation of a rowing race, and with surprise saw there was a young lady present who appeared to be in her altitudes.'

'Er, that would be you, Julia,' she said, more directly to her friend. 'Do you remember that bit?'

There was no reply, but Julia's breathing had changed, it was more jerky somehow. Rose ploughed on.

'I enlisted the assistance of my brother, Charles I mean, to remove you from the scene, and lay you on a couch in a nearby room. You appeared unaware of this manoeuvre, I may say. Next I summoned your mother with the aid of a gentleman who I know to be completely discreet, and she, er, caused you to cast up your accounts so as to limit the amount of alcohol you would absorb subsequently. She then effected your removal from the building without anyone, as far as she knew, becoming aware of it.'

'I imagine you felt terrible the next day, did you not? You had not previously experienced this, er, degree of intoxication?'

Julia groaned, and turned away from her.

'I thought I would explain this so that you knew I am in possession of at least some of the facts. I will leave you now to think about whether you wish to confide in me at all, since I know a fair amount already?'

She stood up and made to leave the room, alert to any suggestion that Julia wished to talk, but there was none. She returned to the drawing room hoping she had not made things worse, and was immediately engulfed in a game of Hoodman blind, in which all but Aunt Charlotte were participating.

After everyone had had enough of this – or at least the adults had, and insisted they were quite exhausted, and had to sit down, and that the small people must bring them refreshment immediately or they would faint – Mrs Winton drew Rose aside and asked her if she had made any progress with her undertaking. Rose paused while she considered carefully what to say, and eventually begged to be allowed to keep her counsel until she had ascertained the facts fully, if she was indeed able to do so. She explained that she was doing her best, and that Julia was aware of the commission her mother had laid upon her, but she thought it better . . . and so on.

Mrs Winton was quite understanding and most grateful to her for her efforts. She hoped she was not too fatigued with the activity of her nephews and nieces, and was finding everything quite comfortable, and was there anything lacking? The idea flashed through her mind that what was lacking was the presence of Mr Blackburn, but dismissed the thought as ridiculous even to think, and far more so to mention.

Mrs Winton took the head of the table at dinner, and afterwards there was cards; and music, because Julia was prevailed upon to play the pianoforte, though she refused to sing, and Jane showed her beginner's abilities on the instrument after much persuasion. Then in the middle of her slightly halting rendition of a Scotch air, there came a rather more robust sound of singing from outside the French doors.

Mr Hugh Winton advanced and threw the doors open to reveal a crowd of about ten labouring men rendering 'God Rest Ye Merry,

Gentlemen' with gusto. Mrs Winton advanced with a large bowl full of spiced wine, and once they had finished singing they all dipped their cups in it and wished the family good health for the year. Rose had to whisper to Mrs Jane Winton to ask about this custom, as it was another ritual she had not previously seen. She was told it was called wassailing, and was a very ancient practice. Hugh tried to slip underneath the men's legs and sneak a drink of the wine but he was discovered and extracted by his father before he had done more than dip his fingers and suck them.

Next figgy pudding was produced and passed out, the whole family having a share too; the men departed only after a performance of 'While Shepherds Watched' and after a clinking purse was passed to them.

Rose found she was having the best time she could remember for, well, since she could remember. Since before her mother had died, probably. It was so good being with a big and comfortable family, with little children, and friendliness all around.

It was so much fun that Marian was most reluctant to go to bed, having been allowed to sit at the dinner table and stay up late, until after the wassailers had been; Hugh was also dispatched to his nurse, and Jane and Elizabeth given notice of their following the smaller children in about a half hour. On hearing this Jane whispered to her cousin, and they went up to Jane's mother and, holding hands in front of her, curtsied and begged her to sing 'Robin Adair' for them. She said that her voice was croaky, that she was most clumsy on the keys, and she was too shy to perform. Nonetheless she was prevailed upon, and roundly applauded when she had finished the song, pre-dictably without any evidence of her purported weaknesses.

The evening carried on in this vein until late; Rose judged it not a time to make further attempts to gain Julia's confidence, and anyway she was enjoying herself so much she had almost forgotten why she was there. Mr Hugh told some riddles; Mrs Winton regaled them with an account of the London shops they had recently visited, and

Rose described the new attractions in Bath, as none of the Wintons had visited for some years. Julia, after her playing was finished, sat quietly with her embroidery and said almost nothing.

Christmas morning was bright, though breezy. They walked to church in a group, except for Aunt Charlotte who was taken by carriage due to her rheumatism. Rose thought privately that she did not seem to have any trouble walking up the church path, or in standing while telling the vicar at length what she thought of his sermon. The church was completely full, with people standing all around the walls and sitting in the aisles. It was a most joyful occasion. Julia remained withdrawn, sang in the quietest of voices, and after the service left the building promptly, to stand outside the churchyard alone, to avoid interrogation by those who knew her.

Rose decided she ought to leave any questioning about the ball until after the festival, but she went to Julia so as to be friendly, and contented herself with asking her about any young ladies that emerged from the porch, in case they were known to her. Three small groups of neighbours came over to pass pleasantries, and one young gentleman also, whom Rose surmised from his manner to have a *tendresse* for her friend, but he received little or no encouragement for his addresses. In fact, Julia seemed almost rude to the boy, who was handsome, well-spoken and courteous.

As they walked home with the others, Rose contrived for them to fall a little behind, and enquired in a low voice about the lad, saying how she could see he had great admiration for Julia. Julia replied that he was called James, she had known him for years, he was the son of a most respectable gentleman farmer, but that she could not be doing with young men at the moment, especially ones like him who she knew were interested in her. She then fell silent and did not respond to any of Rose's further attempts at conversation.

CHAPTER 4

As THEY ARRIVED AT THE front of the house a horseman overtook them on the drive. Mrs Winton rushed up to him as he pulled up his mount, and almost dragged him from the saddle with her hug. It was Peter, grinning all over his face. He jumped down, lifted his mother off her feet, then bowed low to Elizabeth and Jane, doffing his hat in the finest style and kissing their hands to much giggling from the girls.

'We weren't expecting you until much later in the week, Peter,' accused his mother. 'Not that you aren't welcome, of course.'

'I was surprised myself at being allowed to leave so soon, mother,' he said. 'And how is Mr Hugh?' to the boy. 'Somebody told me you were seven now. Surely you can't be, I thought you were only three!'

'I am seven, and I'm very big,' he retorted. 'I stopped being three ages ago, that's a baby's age.'

'I'm not a baby either,' said Marian, 'and I'm five.'

'And a very beautiful lady you are too.'

Peter saluted his aunt and uncle and then turned to Julia. He started to greet her then almost jumped. 'Oh! Er, Ro. . ., I mean Miss Clarke, what are you doing here?'

Julia looked at the ground and fidgeted with her handkerchief.

'Er, Mr Winton.' Rose curtseyed to give herself time to think. 'Your mother was good enough to invite me.' Peter seemed to be still waiting. 'To be company for Julia,' she added, weakly. 'We met at the Somerset House Ball.'

'Ah,' Peter said, as if that explained everything. 'Well, welcome.' He turned back to his family. 'I'm the prodigal son today, so I hope there's a fatted calf waiting for me.'

'No, Uncle Peter, it's venison and goose, silly, it's Christmas, didn't you know?' This from Marian.

'Oh, yes, I'd forgotten,' he replied, clapping his hand to his forehead theatrically. 'You'll have to remind me what I have to do then.'

'Come with me, I'll show you everything,' she said, holding out her hand. 'We've done lots of decorations and I cut the Missles toes this year all by myself.'

A groom began to lead the horse to the stable and Peter crunched along the gravel with Marian chattering away. His small guide bounded up the steps to the front door, as he asked her with a low bow to tell him what exactly happened at Christmas. Rose, grinning to herself at the seriousness with which Marian took his questions, was just about to say something to Julia when there was a loud bang and she looked up to see little Marian lying on the top step, with Peter at first bending over her, then looking round scanning the distance in all directions. In a moment he left the child, raced to retrieve his horse from the groom, flung himself onto it and hared off in the direction of a covert some hundred or more yards away, riding low over the horse's neck.

The rest of the family stood for a moment in shock before hurrying forward to the little girl while at the same time trying to keep the other children from seeing too much. Marian was unmoving, and it was clear she was bleeding copiously from her head. Her mother cradled her, unminding of how soiled her dress was getting, and wailed. Nobody seemed to know what to do, Mr Hugh Winton was fully occupied with his other two children who were respectively weeping and screaming, and Julia had her hands clutched to her face in horror. Rose stepped forward hesitantly, unsure whether it was her place to try and help. Peter's mother however joined her and together they examined the child. She was breathing, that was certain, though she was unconscious. Mrs Winton stepped back to comfort her sister while Rose tried to see where the blood was coming from. Marian's hair was matted with it, and she had to feel rather than see what damage there might be.

It appeared from her gentle probing that there was a shallow groove in her head almost at the crown, it was hard to tell, but all the blood appeared to be coming from there. Rose called out to a footman who had appeared at the door for some linen to press on the wound, something, anything would do, and meanwhile fumbled in her pocket for a kerchief. Though it was far too dainty for the job she pressed it to the bleeding, and once a towel appeared in the hands of the butler, added its bulk and held it in place as firmly as she could.

Mrs Winton instructed the butler to carry the child inside, allowing Rose to keep pressure on her head all the time, while she tended to her sister. And so in due course Marian was laid on cushions on a couch in the hallway, and the other children were taken off to the nursery.

Rose knelt by Marian, not understanding at all what had happened, but sticking to her task of applying pressure to the child's wound. Mrs Winton, delivering her sister into the care of her husband, took charge.

'Rose, has the bleeding lessened at all yet? Is it possible to release the compress?'

'I don't think so, Madam. I don't like to look and see. There was such a lot of blood.'

'Very well, we shall leave it be for another few minutes. Let me look at the child. Does she stir at all?'

'Not at all, I fear. But her breathing seems adequate.'

Mrs Winton called for the servants to bring hot water, and more linen, and brandy, and bowls, and then sat by Marian with Rose and simply waited.

Rose, finding her eyes were wet with tears, asked Mrs Winton in a low voice if she knew what had happened.

'She has been shot, my dear. Shot, I should say, from some distance. Peter has galloped off to try and apprehend the assailant; I do hope he is careful. Not that he will be, I constantly worry about him.'

'Shot? But why?'

'Yes dear, shot. Yet I hope only a glancing wound, or else she would not still be with us, now would she? And why? Well, I scarcely think she would have been the target, now would she? She is no danger to anyone.'

Rose, trembling now, concentrated her mind on her task of stemming the bleeding, and tried not to think about who, or why, or a multitude of other questions. But it must have been Peter who had been the intended target, her mind kept telling her. Her friend Peter.

After a few more minutes the child began to stir, her eyelids flickered open for a moment, and she started to cry.

'There there, Marian, lie still, you've bumped your head, dear,' said Mrs Winton. 'It's all right now, we're looking after you.'

Marian's cries became a wail, mixed with calls for her mother, and struggles to stop Rose pressing on her wound. Mrs Winton whispered to Rose she could release the pad and they looked together at what they could see of her wound while trying to comfort the child. Her mother, looking terrified and trying to avoid seeing the blood, nonetheless edged close and held Marian's hand, stroking it with her other hand and repeating, 'Mother's here, darling, Mother's here.'

Mrs Winton called for scissors and cut away the hair for several inches around the bloody area, revealing a long track of still-oozing wound across the crown of the girl's head. She took a razor, and carefully scraped away the remaining short hairs until it was clear there was a cleanly incised three-inch line of injury passing from front to back of the scalp.

'Rose, can you hold this bowl under her head, please?' And then to the child, 'This is going to sting a bit, Marian, you must be brave.' Pouring first hot water and then brandy down the length of the wound, she dabbed at it with a clean cloth. The bleeding restarted, but not before it was clear that the wound was clean, and the skull underneath not broken.

She put a new, freshly-laundered wad of linen over the cleaned area, and indicated to Rose to resume her pressing. Standing up, she went over to the housekeeper who was standing with a worried-looking knot of servants, and spoke quietly to her, before going off with the woman.

Rose tried to collect her thoughts. Somebody had shot at Peter, but hit Marian instead. Why? Well, of course, it was obvious, it would be his enemies, the people involved with the French spies, the people whose bomb she had frustrated so recently. And, well, would they be after her too? Or maybe not after Rose, but after Richard Cox, perhaps, because after all they had ransacked his room in Emmanuel? What should she do?

It seemed clear to her that at the moment she should do nothing but tend to Marian, and wait for Peter to return, but she trembled with the urge to do something, anything, to get back at the man who had hurt poor Marian.

Mrs Winton reappeared holding a spoonful of something golden. 'Marian, dear, please would you take this honey medicine, it'll stop your head hurting, really it will.' She placed the tip of the spoon on Marian's lips and the child stopped her crying for long enough to swallow the sweet liquid. Gradually her distress lessened, and soon she relaxed and seemed to be sleeping.

'What did you give her?' asked Mrs Jane, 'will she be alright?'

'Just honey with two drops of laudanum, sister dear. Just enough to soothe. She is going to be fine. Once the bleeding stops again, we will bandage her head with a butterfly dressing, and then all she has to do is rest. And, of course, not tug at the bandages, that will be your task to prevent once she has woken.'

At this point Peter entered, looking disconsolate. 'Lost him,' he told the company, 'his horse was far fresher than mine. He was headed towards Newmarket, but he could have turned off anywhere once he was out of sight.'

Going to Marian's side he asked how she was, and what they had done, and embraced his mother, telling her what a fine woman she was, and how sorry he was to have caused Marian's injury. And turning to Rose, congratulated her too for keeping a clear head, and doing what was needed.

'I could see the ball could only have grazed her head, so I knew I could rely on you and Mother to care for the child while I chased off trying to catch the varmint,' he said. 'Are you alright yourself though? It must have been horrible for you.'

Rose mumbled something about being quite fine, then focussed on pressing on the pad so he wouldn't see her tears. Tears both of pity for Marian, and of relief that Peter was safe. Richard wouldn't cry, she told herself, so why would Rose?

Gradually normality was restored. Marian was removed to her nursery, where her wound was dressed, and she was put to bed. Her mother stayed by her side, sniffing tears back occasionally as she looked at her poor mite. Miss Churchill made her entrance, having arrived by carriage, and was most put out to find such disarray among the servants, whereupon she withdrew herself to her chamber. The blood-stained couch was removed to the kitchens to see what might be done to rescue it, and the hall floor and steps swabbed clean. Rose and Mrs Winton retired to change their soiled costumes, and rejoined the family in the decorated drawing room. Peter was absent again, and nobody seemed to know where he had gone.

It hardly seemed proper to continue with the Christmas festivities, but they decided to carry on as well as they could, if only for the sake of the other children. Lunch was served, a little delayed by the disruption, and consisting only of cold dishes, and then Mrs Winton announced they would have a game of snapdragon, as a special treat, to whoops of delight from Jane, Elizabeth and especially Hugh, who loved all things to do with fire.

Julia tugged at Rose's sleeve and murmured that she really needed to talk to her privately. Rose, emotions still in turmoil, followed her to the library, where there was a cushioned window-seat with curtains that gave a little more privacy.

'Rose, did someone really shoot at Marian? Why would they do that?'

'Not at Marian, my pet, at Peter.'

'Peter? Why Peter?'

'Because,' Rose hesitated, but then decided this could no longer be a secret from his sister, 'he is doing work for the Army, and the Foreign Office, defending us from traitors. As he was doing at the Pemberton Ball, you recall.'

'Oh! Yes, of course. How silly of me. I . . . I felt so unwell when I saw her bleeding I had to run and hide . . . I cast up my accounts, it was horrible.'

'That's quite understandable, my dear. You've been through a lot recently.'

'Well, um, yes. That's why I had to talk to you, you see, um, well, I don't want to, but it might help, I mean, I don't want not to say if . . . I mean, someone else might get hurt, mightn't they?'

Rose put her arm round the girl's shoulders. 'I'm sure it'd be better to get it off your chest, whatever it is. I won't tell anyone who doesn't need to know. And, if it would stop people getting hurt, yes you certainly ought to tell.'

Julia clasped her hands together and braced her shoulders. 'Well, it was at the ball, the Somerset House ball I mean, um, when I . . .'

'Yes, my love, go on.'

'I, well, I had danced with Mr Eldridge, James Eldridge, he was very charming, and he took me to the drinks table and gave me a glass of wine, and then I started to feel most elevated. Most unconscionably happy, I remember, much more than I would normally feel after just one glass; and I agreed to a second dance with him, and I know it was most improper so soon after the first one, but he was so very handsome, and charming. And then after, . . . after that dance he gave me a second glass, which I drank, and he said we ought to explore the building because it was brand new and he wanted to see the latest fashions in architecture. And so I followed him, which I know I shouldn't, but I felt so excited, and all, well, churning inside, in a most delightful way, um . . .'

'So we went into a room and there were some men there, they were talking about someone called Barnes and how things had all gone wrong, and how the next move was to target - well, somebody or something I didn't properly hear. I think they said something about a bakery, and about trifles, but it didn't make sense that they should be discussing cookery. And then when they saw me with James - Mr Eldridge I mean - they went quiet and then started to threaten me, they said I was never to mention that I had seen them, or it'd be the worse for me.' She coughed, and shivered, and put her head in her hands. 'They said they'd find me and drag me away into a dark alley and . . . I can't say what they said, it was too awful.'

Rose just squeezed her shoulder again and waited.

'And then they made me drink some more wine, and I started feeling quite dizzy, but some other men came in and they made me do this Boat Race kind of game, I had to drink some more, and I didn't want to but I was so frightened, and then . . . I don't remember any more until the next day when I woke up with such a horrible head, and kept wanting to be sick, and didn't know what to do, so I just said nothing, and Mother got worried, and I still didn't dare . . . so here we are.'

'You did the right thing telling me. Really. You understand, I need to tell Peter, he'll know what to do. About the things you heard, you know. And I don't need to tell your mother any details, except that Peter will be dealing with it. Though I think you might want to tell her yourself, in time. She's a remarkable woman, you know.'

Julia sniffed, but didn't say anything.

'Did you know who any of the men were? Did they say any names?'

'I'd never seen them before, never. But one called another one

Jake, I think. He was the most horrible. He put his hands on my . . .'
she gestured, vaguely, 'and it was so horrible.' She shuddered, and
clenched her fists.

'That's fine. You've done really well. So, would you like to stay here
a bit longer? Or can I get you anything? A bowl of tea, maybe? I saw
you hardly ate anything at lunchtime.'

'Nothing, thankyou. But please stay with me, if you will.'

'Of course.'

Julia drew up her knees and hugged them, rocking gently. Rose just
sat, and thought. Julia hadn't known much about those who threatened her, but she thought they might well have been Jacob Mackenzie
and John Smart, from the intelligence she had received from Mrs
Lanscombe. Though she had said to Julia that Peter would be dealing
with the matter, she (or rather, Richard) would be doing her bit too.
In fact, there was something she wanted to do now. Why hadn't she
thought of it earlier?

'Julia, if you're feeling a little better, would you like to do something to help Peter, something we could do together, right now?'

'What could we do? We are only girls,' she said with a sniff.

'Well, girls can do things too, you know. I mean, we ought to
find the ball that struck Marian, it might help find the musket-man?
Would you like to come with me and search?'

Julia looked up. 'Would it help? Really? I'd like to help.'

Together they made their way to the front steps. Julia looked
warily around in case there might still be someone with a gun in the
vicinity, but then set to with Rose to search for the ball. Rose stood
at the foot of the steps and considered where Peter and Marian had
been when the shot had been fired. Marian had been on the top step
and Peter at the bottom, bowing low to her. She had been facing . . .
that way, and the ball had grazed her head on a direct line front to
back, so it ought to be . . . at such and such a height, and in such and
such a direction.

'We need to look near the bottom of the left hand pilaster, Julia,' she instructed. 'I think the shot came from over near that covert.' She waved her hand in the direction that Peter had galloped.

Before long, Julia spotted the ball, embedded in the wood of the pilaster, and Rose prised it out with her pen-knife. It was about half an inch in diameter, and had scratch marks on its surface.

'We need to keep this carefully, it might tell us something about the man who fired it,' Rose said. 'I'll wrap it in my kerchief, and put it in my pocket.'

She did as she said, tucking her pocket carefully away inside her costume, and then suggested that they should both take a short walk and look for where the man had hidden to take his shot. Nervously, Julia agreed, and after finding their boots they set off to the covert, which stood just beyond a stout wooden field boundary.

Casting along this fence in each direction, sticking together because, for all the peace of the countryside and the nearness of the mansion, they were both quite frightened of a further attack, they eventually found a place where the undergrowth was trampled down beyond the fence, and branches had been woven behind the bars of the barrier to provide cover. There was sadly nothing of note to be seen in the hiding-place, not a half-smoked cigar, or a discarded piece of paper, or a dropped pin or brooch that could lead them to the perpetrator of the outrage. Still, they had found his hidey-hole, and that was something.

Julia tied one of her hair ribbons to the fence so they might more easily find the place again, and they retraced their steps to the house, looking for Peter.

The butler said that he believed he had changed his horse and ridden off soon after it was clear that Marian was recovering. He could not undertake to say where he was headed, but he could enquire of the stable master if Miss Julia liked? She did like, but no further intelligence was forthcoming.

It was not until dinner-time that Peter reappeared, looking tired and hot in spite of the December weather. He explained that he had ridden into Cambridge to 'see a man about a dog' and that what he really needed was a plate of roast venison, and one of goose, and several large glasses of wine, if they didn't mind. So Rose and Julia had to wait to question him, as at table he refused all enquiry from his family, saying he needed to gather his thoughts before any explanations could be given, but that he was almost certain none of them was in danger at present.

And then after dinner there were games for the children, and singing, and everyone seemed determined to forget the events of the day, except that Mrs Jane Winton left every half hour to check on Marian, even though the nursemaid was in attendance, and Rose had to hold herself sternly in check to stem bursting out with the news of their discoveries, and interrogating Peter about the nature of his 'man' and 'dog'.

At last the children had been sent to bed and Rose thought she would be able to have Peter to herself. He however was deep in conversation with his mother, and then abruptly took himself off to his chamber, where she could not follow. So it was a frustrated Rose who sat for the rest of the evening with the others, and attempted unsuccessfully to amuse herself with a novel, before the cards were brought out and a game of loo was at least a little more absorbing.

At breakfast Peter was no more communicative than before, and said he hoped 'you young ladies were able to amuse yourselves' as he had several things he needed to do. As soon as he had drunk his chocolate he was off. Julia and Rose followed him at a short distance, as he opened the front door and busied himself on the steps.

After a little while, Rose stepped forward and, ignoring Peter's glare, enquired in a sunny tone, 'So, for what might you be looking, sir?'

'Never you mind, Miss,' he said, 'let me alone, won't you?'

Rose fished around in her pocket and turned to Julia. 'I don't think your brother will be capable of finding what he seeks, will he, Julia?'

'I am as one with you, dear,' she replied, quickly picking up the game. 'He is completely out of sorts.'

'Might you consider he was in a snit, Julia?'

'Quite, my dear Rose. Almost unconscionably so. Most unbrotherly behaviour.'

Peter looked at them suspiciously. 'Out with it, girls. What are you up to?'

'Why, nothing, Mr Winton,' said Rose. 'After all, we are only girls. What would we know of important matters?'

Peter stood up, conflicting expressions chasing across his face. 'Come on, you've done something or found something or heard something, haven't you?'

'We might have,' said Julia. 'And we *might* tell you about it if you ask prettily.'

Peter put his head on one side. 'I forgot, you both have brains, haven't you? I am an idiot. You have found the ball that struck little Marian. I am an oaf, am I not? May I see?'

Rose held it out towards him, but not too far. 'You may, and you may congratulate us on our success, Mr Winton.'

Peter bowed, took it, and examined the ball carefully. 'I'll need to measure this, and consult an expert, but I think, see, see these scratch marks, here and here, these are marks of rifling, from the barrel of the gun. Which might explain his being able to fire from . . . well, wherever he fired from. It might help us to narrow down our suspects also, knowing the type of gun he used. So, I'd better go back inside and get my dividers and rule.'

'Before you do that,' Rose put in, 'I don't imagine you have any interest in seeing the rifleman's hidey-hole? Anything else we have found, being mere girls, could be of no interest to you?'

Peter gave her a Look. 'Really? I am impressed.'

'We discovered it yesterday also. Julia has marked the place.'

Peter apologised for his attitude, and they all three walked across and inspected the marks. Rose was gratified that Peter did not discover anything they had missed, though he did cast around the covert and find the place where the horse had been tethered: nothing but droppings and cropped grass to give a clue was evident.

While returning to the house Peter measured the distance by pacing, and once he had finished counting off, explained that he had thought someone had been following him over the past day or two, but he had not been certain. Once or twice he had caught sight of a rider who was on the same road but did not get closer, nor further away. He graciously allowed them to accompany him to his instrument box, and measured the ball at just over six-tenths of an inch, which he said would with the scratch marks and the distance of 156 paces be most useful to his colleague.

Rose then turned to Julia and asked her if she would like to inform Peter of what she had heard at the Somerset House ball, but she hung her head and said, Could Rose explain. Rose relayed the few words that Julia had heard, and gave him the names of the likely speakers, Jacob Mackenzie and John Smart, together with James Eldridge, and, displaying a remarkable forbearance, he did not interrogate his sister further, but made a note of the intelligence, and then suggested they ought to rejoin the family for more traditional St Stephen's Day activities.

The news of Marian was good, in that she was free of fever, sitting up in bed and complaining bitterly of how her head hurt and how she wanted to play snapdragon. Mrs Winton therefore, together with Mr Hugh and Mrs Jane, were able to take the other children on the rounds of their tenants to dispense gifts and cheer of the season, and reward the inside servants in turn. Miss Jane and Miss Elizabeth took charge of handing out sweetmeats, and Master Hugh was deputed to be the bearer of the purses of money.

The very next day Peter announced his departure, much to the regret of his mother, and noisy disapproval of the children, and mixed feelings from Rose. She felt conflicted as to how she ought to treat him, and how he treated her, being as she was disguised as her real self. With Peter she was so used to being Richard, and seen as a near-equal, but as Rose, it was different: he was different, but so was she.

She wanted to be back at college, back as Richard, able to come and go freely, to ride with Peter, and be involved in his work against the French. But she did like being Rose too, and being with Julia, and talking of girlish things, and admiring her new dresses, and being with the children. It was perplexing.

Later, after dinner, Julia confided that she had talked with her mother and felt a lot better for it; that she wasn't in trouble, and no longer felt as threatened by the men she had met. Well, only a little intimidated by the memory, and she wouldn't be going to anywhere that she might come across them any time soon, that was for sure, and nowhere without a chaperone. In fact, the family were going to accompany their cousins to Ely, where none of the men would be able to find her, before the end of the week. As soon as Marian was fit to travel, that is, because she would be more at home, at her home, if Rose understood her meaning, and Marian's parents wanted to return, for their daughter's sake.

So her mother, Elizabeth and herself would be leaving. And they would celebrate New Year there, but what ought they to do about their guest? She felt bad about it, seeing as Rose had come to help her, but how could they impose upon their cousins, whose house was far smaller than theirs? And they would have to inform Miss Churchill, who was sure to be most put out, and would undoubtedly refuse to leave during the current season, and although Rose was welcome to stay here, well, it would be no fun for her with only the older woman for company.

Rose for her own part didn't know what was best. She needed a haircut – or rather, Richard did; and she didn't think she knew how to arrange that except with the man her brother had engaged previously. She could not consider returning to college at present, even though her friend Edward Hever was in residence, because, well, it would be too complicated to change her person either here or in Cambridge, and she didn't have her box with her, Richard's box that is, and well, no, she couldn't possibly. So she ought to go back to London, that is, if Sir George was actually going to be there. But the roads . . . and travelling on her own . . . then where would she stay, and how would she occupy herself? She ought to write a letter to her brother, but she didn't exactly know what to say.

The problem resolved itself, however. The day after Peter had left, Sir George appeared unannounced soon after breakfast, with a carriage and a number of large boxes. He paid his respects to Mrs Winton, before enquiring after his sister. It seemed he had had official business in Cambridge, came across Peter there, and resolved to make the short detour to visit Rose before returning to London. He quite understood their situation, expressed himself exceeding sorry about poor little Marian, and proposed to disentangle their Gordian knot by following the example of Alexander the Great. He would remove his sister to London forthwith. Without the use of swordplay, however. No, it was no trouble, he only regretted depriving Julia of her companion.

Shortly after – well, as soon as Rose could gather her belongings, and say goodbye to all the children, which took some considerable time, and visit Marian, who though looking pale, seemed to be well on the mend, and then say goodbye to the children all over again – they were on the London road and able to talk.

'Winton was at . . . well, never mind where he was, he was consulting with Warburton, who though principally concerned with artillery, is well versed in all things involving gunpowder. He said that the ball which you found in the door pilaster had been shot using the new Baker rifle, as its rifling marks and calibre are characteristic, which means our assailant somehow had access to the latest equipment issued to our troops. This rifle is most accurate at distances up to three hundred yards, so he was indeed fortunate to have bowed to Miss Marian at just the crucial moment. Though of course, she was less fortunate, to be sure.'

'And what does this tell us?'

'That we have a continuing presence of French spies in our midst, and perhaps ones more professional and well-equipped than the gang that devised the cake bomb plot that you foiled.'

'I see. So, when I return to college, I may have more scope for investigations, may I not?'

'I don't think you ought to go back, Rose. It will be too dangerous.'

'Pshaw! Not to say, ballocks, sir! You try and stop me. I am going to be a spy, and I am going to be an educated spy. I am about to start the Principia, and have the prospect of all sorts of other subjects to discover. Chemistry, I believe, might be most fascinating. And geology. And the company of likeminded fellows.'

George held his counsel. He set his jaw, and stared out of the window at the outskirts of Cambridge as they passed beyond Chesterton. They would see. Indeed, they would see.

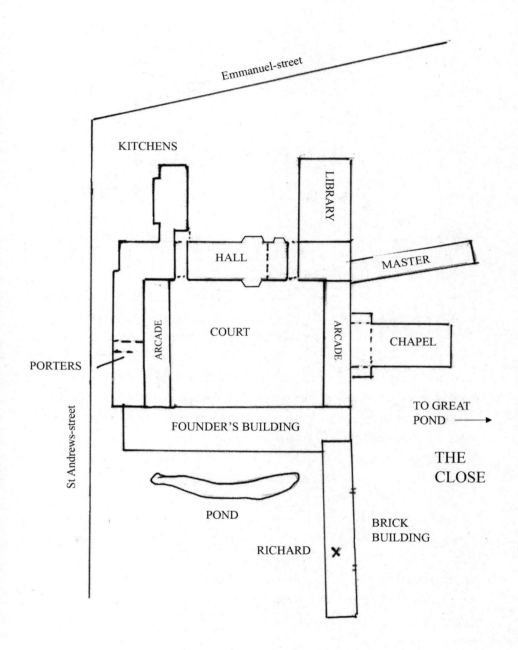

Emmanuel College buildings

CHAPTER 5

RICHARD COX SAT IN HIS room at the top of the Brick building, looking out over the Close at the pond with its swans mere ghosts in the dusk, and considered. It felt good to be back, good to be free of Rose's wig (though he passed his hand over the short hairs at the back of his neck which still felt odd), and good to be in a position to study properly, and discuss matters that, well, that mattered, with friends.

It was fearsomely cold, as the fire had not been set that morning, he having arrived well after dinner was over; and his room looked bare without the lovely painting that had been destroyed last term, his Meer. No matter, he had his scarf and gloves; and would venture out into town tomorrow, and find something to replace the picture. Not something the same, of course, but something. And he needed rugs to prevent the east wind whistling up between his floorboards. Perhaps he might go without Edward, glad though he was of his company most of the time? Not a restful companion while choosing personal items, though. On the other hand, he might well feel upset if he ignored him. Oh dear.

It seemed an age since he had left Milton with George to return to London, though it was barely two weeks. London had been almost empty, there were few social events to speak of, though Rose had attended a concert with Sir George at the Hanover Square Rooms given by the Duke of York's military band. More notably, there had been fireworks at Vauxhall Gardens, opened especially to celebrate Twelfth

Night, and she had been escorted there by Mr Blackburn, no less! Properly chaperoned, of course, by the mother of one of George's colleagues, and in the company of two other couples, but even so.

A whole evening with Mr Blackburn! He had been most correct, naturally, and had not attempted to lead her away into the wilderness where lights were few, or test her chaperone's patience in other such ways. Indeed, his attitude to her had been almost like that of a friend. Richard considered this thought, and decided it sounded most odd. Could not a woman be friends with a man? It seemed, but rarely. But was it the case that he treated her as he would if he knew her as Richard? Not at all: he was most condescending and kind, he had treated her as a lady, while yet respecting her mind.

Richard recalled the discussion they had had when she had recounted the episode where poor Marian had been shot, and how she and Julia had discovered the lead ball, and the place the assassin had hidden. He had explained to her details of the Baker rifle that she had been told was the weapon used: that following the American Revolutionary Wars the Army had decided they needed to modernise, replacing their muskets with more accurate weaponry. It had taken a while, but in 1800 the chosen rifle, made by Mr Ezekiel Baker, had been issued. He had added that he only knew all this intelligence because a consignment of such rifles had been stolen from a barracks in Woolwich, and one of his many tasks was to investigate the theft. Was it possible that the weapon used in Milton was one of those purloined? This was surely not the sort of conversation a gentleman would normally have with a lady?

But it had not only been intellectual discussion that had so enlivened the evening. He had been most complimentary about her person, and without transgressing any social rules had made it clear that he was becoming enamoured of her. And she him, and she him . . . Which was most confusing now, thinking back from his persona of Richard Cox, pensioner of Emmanuel College; but at the time it had felt, oh, so . . . so squiggly inside, is the only way she could describe it.

That evening had passed only too quickly, and Mr Blackburn had then to depart on another mission which he was not permitted to discuss with her, but when he returned her to her hotel she was able to lend him her copy of Mrs Wollstonecraft's book, and he had promised faithfully to read it forthwith. She had had to divert herself by study of Mr Newton's Principia, privately in her room, and make notes of all the questions that she needed to ask of her fellow-students and her tutor, things that were a little unclear and things that she could not comprehend at all. And then the matter of her haircut, and changing into male clothes once more, and staying again at George's rooms for a couple of nights, while she reminded *herself* of how to be *himself* – matters of how to stand and move, and how to look at people, and speak, and all sorts of tiny things she had learnt before her first foray into academe.

And now he was here, and chaperones and gentleman admirers and fashions in dresses and curtseying were past. He had travelled up on his own on the stage coach. He was a young lad from Nova Scotia, and one eager to win prizes and scholarships. And, of course, to learn how to be a spy. He lit a small cigar from the candle, and wandered about his keeping-room with a sense of pride, remembering how he had returned to the shop he had first visited so long ago, and ordered a pound of the same cigars as he had purchased before. This time, though, he had felt confident in his right to be in the emporium, and that was quite something.

He inspected the new Bramah Challenge lock that Peter had had fitted to his oak at the end of last term, following his room being ransacked, and took out his set of picklocks, turning them over in his fingers and wishing that Peter would return to college soon, so he could have a further lesson with them. In the meantime, he could practise on the simple lock on his trunk. And then some more of the Principia, and then perhaps see if Edward was in and wanting to go to supper, and then to bed as to be sure he was very tired.

The morning dawned wet and miserable. Scurrying across the

Close to the privy and thence returning very damp to breakfast with Edward, Richard was treated to a display of more of his recently acquired cant expressions. He described the weather as being shockingly low in the haft; and his employer (the tutor Mr Watkinson, whose rooms he was supposed to be tidying, organising and cataloguing) as being sick as a cushion. Richard was unsure of the correctness of these usages, but could not cavil at their accuracy: they sounded good at any rate, and Edward was extraordinarily pleased with them.

'So, how has the Christmas period gone for you?' he enquired when they had greeted Mrs Fenn and were sitting with their tea and rolls.

'Dull as . . . well, as a dunghill, my old clinker. And I haven't even got my roommate any longer, since Smith got himself in clink.'

'I see you have been studying hard in the streets and the taverns? Have you applied yourself to any books: mathematics, or maybe Greek? Just asking?'

'Not exactly, old whippersnapper. Had too much of bally books in Watkinson's rooms, don't you know. Fellow has hundreds of the things, wants them all putting in alphabetical order and a catalogue made. And paper, you wouldn't believe now many papers he has, and it's deuced hard to work out what they're about because half of them are in Latin, and some in Greek, and others in some incomprehensible scribble.'

'Russian, perhaps?'

'Don't know, don't care. Put all of 'em in a separate pile for later.'

'Good old Edward, you know your priorities, don't you?'

Edward looked slightly offended. 'Sure I do. Pass the exams, get a degree, but no need to work all that hard, don't y'know?'

Richard, remembering how keen Edward had been when he first arrived to win college prizes and perhaps a scholarship, just grinned at him, raised his eyebrows a few times, got a punch on the shoulder for his pains. It was good to be back.

He saw a printed sheet on the table, reached for it, had a squint. It seemed to be a list of, well, dubious phrases. He turned it over. It was headed 'Cant for those that can' and it was attributed to one E Hever. No, on second thoughts, it probably read G Heyer. It was roughly printed though, and it might have been Edward's name at the bottom of the sheet.

'What's this? Crib for your favourite field of learning? Or did you write it and get it printed yourself?'

'Hey! Give that here!' He snatched it away, tucked it in his coat. 'Never you mind what it is.'

Richard grinned again. 'I'll wager that this Mr Heyer, whoever he is, made up at least half of those phrases. "Sick as a cushion", indeed? And what did you call the weather? "Low in the haft"? I think you'd better check those out before you look more of an idiot than you usually do.'

Edward looked mutinous. 'Well, it was only two pence from a street hawker, I thought it a bargain. And what would you know about it, anyway?'

'Just bamming, lad. Just taking a rise. It's good to see you again, really.'

Gradually undergraduates drifted back into residence. It was frustrating though: there were no lectures until the division of term, it seemed a waste. He walked to Grantchester on a Tuesday with Edward to see Rev Laughton, though it seemed he had far outstripped his friend in mathematics and they might soon have to alter the arrangements. He spent time with Abel Johnson on Greek, and managed to persuade Mr Griffith to begin tutorials for them again, early in term, by dint of flattery and enthusiasm for the tutor's special interests, as before. The chaplain was willing to give further instruction in divinity, though he learned much more from the sermons of Mr Simeon at Holy Trinity.

He attended the fencing club, and found his muscles had lost some of their capability over the Christmas break, but that he was able to master one or two new moves, and felt quite proud of himself. Having defeated a taller opponent one day, he wondered how brother Charles was doing, and whether he would defeat him now, if they were to have a match. That would be most satisfying, though he could not imagine when he might be able to challenge him in either of his personas. All in all his week had filled again with all kinds of fascinating pursuits.

Of Peter Winton there was no sign, but he was invited out in the four-oar again, with another Jesuit filling in at number 2. Because it was so cold, he was less nervous of showing his figure with his coat off, since he wore extra layers under his shirt, though these were still not quite enough when the wind whistled through the gaps in his window-frames of an evening. He tried to row as tidily as he could, and pull as hard as the others, for fear of drawing attention to himself: he was concerned that Charlie at cox might have recognised him after seeing him as Rose at the Somerset House ball, but he discerned no flicker of puzzlement crossing his face, and after the outing, when they all repaired to an alehouse, he felt a little more secure, and risked a few questions, hoping to find out about more of what had gone on at that event.

'So, Charlie, what did you do over the Christmas break?' He sipped his whisky, and examined his hands, which had begun a couple of blisters, having softened after the weeks away from the water.

'Oh, this and that. Went and saw the folks, did the usual round of being polite to deaf old aunts. What about you?'

'Mostly in London with my cousin. It was a bit dull actually, did quite a bit of reading in fact. I did go to the fireworks at Vauxhall though, that was quite something.'

'I saw those, but only from the river. I was out on a boat some chaps had hired for a party. Two of them fell in: good job the Thames isn't quite as filthy as the Cam or we might have had a repeat of poor old Tom on our hands.'

'Yes, poor man, though I never met him, of course.' He paused, out of respect. 'So, being in the right circles, didn't you get to any balls or things like that? See any likely young ladies? Make any conquests?'

Charlie grinned at him. 'Looking for tips, are you? Good for you. Well, no fish that bit on my bait anyway. I did go to one ball, got dreadfully drunk, don't remember much about it, except that there was one gel there who was nearly as cut as I was. Poor thing. Can't have done her reputation any good.'

'You say, tips maybe, but what I need is leads, there aren't many girls in Cambridge are there? Well, not ones that I might, er, well, feel comfortable with. Plenty of,' he paused, trying to find the words, and tightening up inside as he said them, 'doxies and serving wenches and so on but that's not my, er, style. I'd like to find an educated girl that I can have a conversation with.'

'Not a lot of hope for you then. Girls don't want education, they just want to snare a fine fortune. Or their mamas do, which amounts to the same thing. Anyway, what's the point in a girl having an education, what's she going to use it for?'

Richard bit back his immediate retort, settling instead for, 'What about those Society Ladies who founded the Society, um, the Bluestockings group? They were learned.'

'Fine if they can afford it. But weren't they all married women, comfortable on their husbands' incomes?'

'I don't know. But I'd like to meet a girl about my age who is interested in mathematics and history and science and so on. The Blue Stocking Society is sadly no more, I understand.'

'Well, best of luck, lad. Don't know as I could help you though. I didn't meet any intelligent girls at that Somerset House ball, as far as I remember before I got shot in the neck. I was with old Jake Mackenzie, he's too much an Exquisite to be bothered with matrimony, and he has enough, er, lady friends, to fill a Venetian Breakfast. He was more interested in trying to keep up with me in the matter of ale. Smart, though . . . I don't know. He was trying it on with that gel when she was only slightly disguised, had a bit of a row with Eldridge about it. Thought she might have a few stockings of the wrong hue, I seem to recall, before the lights went out in her peepers. Though I did hear

John was supposed to be engaged to some Friday-faced wench or other. He's up at Caius, you know. Trying to make it to the blessed apostles, I heard.'

By which, Richard understood after some consideration and much thought, that Mr John Smart, alumnus of Gonville and Caius college, who had been at the ball with James Eldridge, was not a reading man, hoping merely to pass the ordinary degree by the skin of his teeth. Since it was almost impossible to fail, this was quite a target. Also, and of some interest, he had had a girl marked out for him as a future wife but he didn't sound as enamoured of her as he might be. If only he had his notes from the ball about what he'd overheard from Lady John Barnes and her friends, but they had been left behind with George in London. He was sure there was something he ought to remember.

'So, are your other two friends up in Cambridge too?'

'No fear. Jake's too flush to need to come here, and too lazy. I believe Eldridge has sunk himself to be at that other low-class place in the Thames marshes. Exeter college, I heard. And they're not really friends of mine, y'know. More, occasional drinking buddies.'

It was on a Tuesday evening towards the end of January that he found the body. He'd been to Grantchester to see Mr Laughton (now without Edward, who had decided they were moving far too fast through Euclid for his wishes), and then he'd met Edward as he returned to college, and eaten a slightly late dinner with him. They were heading to their rooms, after which Richard intended to spend a couple of hours at his job in the library. Passing the open chapel door he noticed something odd.

'Edward! Hang on a minute. Come here, see in chapel, what's that do you think?'

There was what looked like a heap of clothes on the step up to the communion rail. He'd only noticed it because he'd been wondering if he'd left his Ovid in his seat at that morning's service, and half thinking he ought to go in and check. The two lads turned aside and investigated. The light wasn't good, because it was now nearly quarter after four on a dull January day, but there were a few candles still alight in their sconces.

'It's not a heap of clothes, it's a drunk,' opined Edward. 'A Bingo boy, if ever I saw one.'

'In chapel?' Richard bent over and tried to roll the man over. He moved freely, and flopped onto his back. On his bared throat, easily visible even in the flickering dimness, was a livid mark circling his whole neck. His lips were bloated, his eyes stared open, his whole face was dark with blood.

Edward started back jerkily. 'It's a corpse, pon rep! A dead body, by Jingo!'

Richard took a closer look at the man. 'Edward, if you want to help, go and fetch some of those candles over here so I can see what's happened.'

Edward, surprisingly, obeyed mutely, carrying the altar candles to near the man's head. When he set them down, it was to hear Richard reporting that every pocket of the dead man's clothes was empty.

'I wanted to see who he might be, you see. Someone's picked him clean.' He fumbled in the man's waistcoat. 'All but, look here, I missed this cross on his watch chain before you brought the lights. No watch, though. See, the chain's been broken off, where they yanked it away.'

Edward stood a little distance off, looking down at his feet, breathing noisily. Richard continued to examine the man. The mark on his neck extended all around, and the skin had been broken at the back, where his cravat had been stained with blood. He wore an ordinary set of clothes, several years behind the fashion, with breeches rather than pantaloons, and well-worn boots. His hair was rather unkempt as if he did not regularly have it cut, and his chin rough with patchy stubble. He looked about twenty years old. Richard stood up, turned to Edward.

'You alright? You look a bit, er, well, if I could see properly, you might be greenish?'

'He stinks. How can you get so close?'

'Of course he stinks. He's dead, and his, er, muscles have relaxed, so he has relieved himself into his clothing. Haven't you seen animals that have been slaughtered?'

'No, never. We sell dry groceries, not meat and such.'

'Well, tell me then, from the safety of your detachment, what you notice that is odd about him?'

Edward maintained an averted gaze. 'Odd? Well, he's dead, that's fairly odd, don't you think? Very odd, I'd say, for a chap in chapel.'

'And?'

'What d'ye mean, "And"? Isn't that odd enough for you?'

'Well, what else ought he to be wearing here? You don't recognise him, do you?'

'Huh? No, of course not. Well, er, I didn't get a good look at him, did I?'

'He looks about twenty, I don't think he's from this college, it's after dark, so he ought to have his . . . ?' He grasped his own lapel, and nodded meaningfully.

'Huh? Oh, I see, his gown. How does that help, though?'

'Well, look, your gown is different from mine, isn't it?'

'Of course, you're a pensioner and I'm only a sizar. Don't rub it in, cully.'

'So, this chap isn't an Emmanuel man, I don't think, is he?'

'Nobody that I know.'

'So what gown would he be wearing?'

'His own college's . . . Oh, I see. We could tell which college he's from, and maybe what sort of cove he is, by the type of gown.'

'Exactly. Of course, he might not be an undergraduate, but I think he probably is. Ink on the fingers, a vaguely unkempt appearance but gentlemanly clothes, and so on.'

'So what do we do now? I mean, what are you going to do?'

Richard sat back on his heels and thought. He wished Peter Winton was here, but he was still not up, though most of the other college members were. To whom should he report it? Who was the proper authority? In London, he might have tried to find a Bow Street Runner, but not here. Anyway it had happened in college, which as far as he knew, operated as its own kingdom. That was it, he ought to tell the Master. If he could find him, that is.

While he thought, he unfastened the remains of the chain and its cross, and slipped it in his waistcoat. He had an idea about it, how it might lead him to the identity of the victim. Then, deciding, he took Edward by the sleeve and told him, 'Come on, you, let's get you out of here. I have a job for you.'

He closed the main chapel doors behind them and stood Edward with his back to them.

'Stay here, don't move, don't let anyone in. You're in the fresh air, so you will be fine. Chapel service isn't for ages, so there probably won't be anyone to stop, but stop them you must. I'm going to find the Master.' He looked back as he left, but Edward had stayed put, at least for now. It reminded him of leaving Charles to guard poor Julia, but he hoped Edward might be a bit more reliable.

First he looked into Hall, but noone remained from dinner. Then, ascending the dais, he peered round the door of the Fellows' parlour, which contained five or six men drinking wine, but not the Master. So, before approaching the Master's Lodge, he went over to interrogate the porters.

'Mr Chapman, I have an important message for the Master. Do you know where I might find him?'

'Sir, he's in the Lodge. He dined there quiet-like, with two guests. That's where you'll find him for sure.'

Nervously, Richard knocked on the Master's door. A servant answered, and he, almost forgetting himself and curtseying, but some-how turning it into a small bow, asked if he might speak to the Master privately on a matter of urgency. He was shown into a small drawing room and soon was with his college head.

'Dr Cory, sir, um, I have something unpleasant to report, and I thought you were the best person to tell, er, first.'

'What is it, lad? I'm sorry, I don't recall your name, you're one of the new pensioners, aren't you?'

'Yes, sir, Richard Cox, sir, I'm a cousin of Sir George Clarke. Um, when I first met you I brought you greetings from Dr Thomas Young, if you recall.'

'That's right, I remember now. Well, what is it?'

'Er, well, we've just found a, um, a body in the chapel, sir. A dead body.'

'A dead body! What, did someone have an apoplexy or some such calamity in God's house?'

'No sir. I don't think that's what happened, sir. I think you ought to come and see for yourself, um, if it's convenient, sir.'

'Well, it's deuced inconvenient: my guests, you know, but . . .' He seemed to think for a while. 'But I must, mustn't I? A death in college, eh?' He seemed to make a connection: he nodded, slowly. 'I see, you're saying the man did not just, er, die, but he was . . . killed?'

'Er, yes, sir.'

The Master rang for his servant, and gave him some instructions in a low voice. Then the two of them headed for the chapel, where Edward was surprisingly still on guard. Richard explained his presence, and they left him outside while they went to see the corpse.

After demonstrating the mark on the man's neck, Richard told Dr Cory about the complete absence of contents of the pockets, though he kept to himself the finding of the little cross. Struck by an idea, he felt again the man's exposed neck, his forehead, his hands. He was still very warm, even though the black-and-white tiles of the chapel floor were icy.

'The poor fellow's been garotted,' opined Dr Cory. 'I've seen this once before, a long long time ago . . . must have been when I was at

69

Bath and Wells, that's right. There'd been a lynching in the town. Terrible business. Never forgotten it.'

'Sir, I hoped you'd know the proper thing to do, I'm so new in the college. And in this country, to be sure.'

'Right. Yes. The correct thing. Not had this happen here since I've been Master. Hmm. I must consider.'

After a moment, he decided. 'Would you be so good as to run and ask the Head Porter to join us? He is a man of great resource in practical matters. Yes, that is undoubtedly correct.'

Richard hurried away and soon returned with Mr Chapman.

'Master, good day to you. How can I be of service?'

'Where is Dean, then?'

'He's not in college, sir. I'm in charge today.'

'Very well. If he is not available, then. You see here, we have a man, he appears to have been murdered on the very steps of our altar. Disgraceful, terrible desecration. But the question is, what is the proper procedure?'

'Well, sir, I should say, we need to move the poor man's body before evening service, that's for sure. And house him decently. I can arrange for him to be taken to the town mortuary, straight up.'

'Excellent. And you can do it without fuss?'

'Surely, Master. All quiet-like.'

'And who is the proper person to inform of this calamity?'

'Murder, you say? Well, the magistrate is the gentleman I should say, yes, the magistrate, sir.'

'Excellent. Would you see to that too? Request him to wait on me in the Lodge at his convenience.'

'Yes sir. Right away, sir.'

'And . . . do your best to keep this whole business quiet, won't you? It reflects negatively on the college's reputation, don't you know?'

'Sir.'

Privately, Richard thought there would be no way the matter would remain quiet, the whole college would be buzzing with rumour and surmise before supper. Nonetheless, he followed the Master and porter out of the chapel, retrieved Edward who was still at his post, and took him back to his keeping-room for a stiff peg of his whisky.

'What d'ye think of all that, then?' he enquired once Edward had spluttered over his first, incautious, sip of his spirit.

'Don't want to think. Don't want to know. Not our problem, is it? Silly cove gets himself done in, we leave it to our elders and betters, that's what I say.'

'Where's your spirit of enquiry? Curiosity?'

'Left me when my stomach heaved. Hever by name, heaver by nature, cully.'

Richard smiled to himself. He must be feeling a bit better if he could jest about it. 'Very well, that's fine. Now, look, I have to do my stint in the library, so if you are finished with my fine Scottish liquor, I need to eject you from my chambers.'

'Rot-gut you mean. I think I might go and seek out some fellows in the Eagle an' Child, there ought to be some Trouts there, and decent liquor.'

In the library, which was quiet, as usual, Richard set to thinking. Thinking, and writing a list. A list of what he knew, and what he needed to find out. With much crossing-out and rewriting, to be sure, but it helped his thinking. After half an hour he sat back and studied what he had:

Things Known
1: Man about 20 years, gentleman but not well-off (clothes out of the fashion, down-at-heel boots), in need of barbering.
2: Not of Emmanuel. (?)
3: Probably an undergraduate? Ink on left fingers, and on outside of right palm.
4: No gown or possessions except cross.
5: Must have died in the hour or so before I found him as still most warm.

<u>Things to find out now</u>
1 & 2:   Check with porters in case bedders report anyone
missing.
3: Find out about his cross – is it like one the Simeonites wear?
4: Look for his gown around college; bulky thing to take out
unobserved.
5: Ask porters about those outsiders entering college between,
say, two and four o'clock.

<u>Things to do later</u>
1: Once we know who he is, investigate his friends.
2: Is there a connection to the French sympathisers?

He crossed out the last line, feeling it was going too far, but then reinscribed it, because . . . well, because of poor Marian, really. And Peter being absent: perhaps he was on the King's business? And, of course, last term's outrage. And, also, it seemed to him to be quite likely. Possible. Anyway.

He issued a couple of books to a Fellow, which was quite unusual; not many were in residence, he had thought. He tidied away some returned books, and found the broom which as usual had been left in one of the bays and not put away, and swept the floor, which was part of his duties. He wrote out reminders to three borrowers whose volumes were over-due, and then returned to his list.

So. Once he had finished his time in the library, he would go and have another look around the chapel in case there was anything else to find. And he could look for his Ovid: it would be a fine excuse in case anyone wondered why he was searching. And then, perhaps, Mr Chapman might have returned from the magistrate, and he could question him. Good.

CHAPTER 6

ONCE RICHARD HAD BEEN RELEASED from his library duty, and walked the few steps through the arcade, he found the chapel door to be locked. A notice affixed to it announced that evening chapel was cancelled due to the indisposition of Reverend Burton. Which seemed to Richard unlikely to be a true statement, as he had been quite well when he had seen him drinking wine in the Fellows' Parlour only two hours previous to the usual service time of six o'clock.

Repairing to the porters' lodge he found Mr Chapman returned from his errands and, using as an initial pretext his search for his Ovid, sat with him by the good fire he had blazing there, and made his enquiries.

'You see, Chapman, I was the person to find the body, so naturally I'm interested. And you don't need to worry about spreading rumours, 'cos I already know about it, don't you know.'

'Well, yes, sir, but the Master was most insistent.'

'I know, I heard him. It is a great cause of embarrassment to him, I could see. But what did the magistrate say?'

'Not much, sir. He just said he'd call and see the Master in the morning. And that's what I told Dr Cory.'

'Is there any sort of constable or anyone who would look into the murder?'

'I don't rightly think so, sir, not in a place this size. They have constables, but they usually deal with fighting and drunkenness.

73

And what with it happening in college 'n'all, they might say it's not their business. Proctor might, maybe, but he's more used to dealing with young gentlemen milling and being out of college without their gowns, to be sure. And he doesn't have any authority inside college, either, now I think of it.'

'I thought so. Now, did you or any of your colleagues recognise him when you, ah, transported him to his rest?'

'Not a one, sir. He wasn't from this college, anyway.'

'And, were you on duty in the Lodge all afternoon?'

'Surely. I came in after my lunch about twelve, I was here all the time.'

'So did you notice who came in and out?'

'Not to speak of, sir. We don't check on the gentlemen, as you might say. And the tradesmen ring our bell, of course. I did notice a big party arriving about, what, a while before dinner, maybe a little after three o'clock or so. All in their gowns, seeing as they'd be here after dark, naturally, and anyway, they were going to Hall, I reckon.'

'Did you notice anything that would tell you where they were from?'

'No sir, I was dealing with the college post that had just arrived.'

'No unusual gowns? Dons', or fellow-commoners'? You might notice the velvet or the braid, and so on?'

'Well, not's I'd've noticed, sir. Could've been, could've not been. Mind, though, there was a couple of blue gowns, now I come to think of it.'

'Caius men?'

'Or Trinity, of course; that's right, sir, I noticed what with all the others being black, of course, you see. I thought, mind, that'll be the gentlemen going to Mr Davies' rooms for their drinks before dinner. Party of hunting fellows.'

'Did anyone come in after that?'

'Not so's you'd notice, sir. Well, there was you, and Mr Hever, of course. That was just a while after the big group.'

'And before that?'

'Very quiet it was, sir. There was a few came and went, but I can't mind myself as to who they might have been.'

'Well, thankyou anyway.' He slipped a couple of coins into the man's hand. 'For your trouble, Chapman.'

Richard made his way towards Queens' College, clutching the cross he had found. He sought out one Mr Benson, with whom he had exchanged a few words on Sundays in Holy Trinity: he knew he was a keen Simeonite, and might well know others of like persuasion. He explained he had found the cross, but carefully omitted to mention the circumstance, merely implying he wished to return it. On being shown the remembrance, Mr Benson recognised it at once: he said it was one kept by many of his co-evangelicals. He pointed out the chasing along the edges of the simple design, which was the only ornament.

'So, you can only think the owner was one of your friends?'

'Indeed. Well, not all of them are friends, I do not know all of like persuasion, but I do know many.'

'Are any of them sinister-handed?'

'Really? Why do you ask?'

'I just wondered.'

'Well, there's, let me think . . . the only one I can call to mind is Stephens, of Caius. Most men have had it beaten out of them at school, y'know. Don't know the fellow at all, really, just had him pointed out as a curiosity.'

'None other?'

'No, I don't think so. Now, what's this all about?'

'I'm most sorry, I'm not at liberty to explain just at the moment. It's a bit of a . . . well, a private matter, not mine to share. When I can, I'll tell you though, it shouldn't take long to unravel.'

'Most mysterious, lad. Well, glad to be of use to you. Hope to see you on Sunday, Cox.'

'Surely.'

Leaving Queens' he made his way up King's-lane and Trumpington-street to Caius and enquired of the porter where Mr Stephens' rooms might be found. He was not surprised to find no answer to his knocking, and applied himself to the list of residents at the foot of the stair. He saw that one neighbour was a Mr Sterne, and recalled the wine party he had attended at his rooms the previous term. Perhaps he would try him first?

'Go away!' was the initial response to his knock, but he persisted, and eventually opened the door a crack and eased his head into the room. Ah yes, he recalled the windowsill from which Mr Burgess had let fall his glass, and the prints on the walls.

'I'm truly sorry to bother you, sir, but I am enquiring about your neighbour Mr Stephens.'

'Can't you see I'm in the middle of a confounded mathematical maze, bottle-head? Shove off!'

Richard considered. 'I think he might be dead,' he ventured.

Mr Sterne looked up from his papers. 'Dead? Not dead drunk? Actually cold meat?'

'I fear so, sir.' Richard insinuated the rest of himself into the room. 'Mr Sterne, sir, I had the honour to be a guest at a wine-party in these rooms last term, hence my presumption. You know the gentleman?'

'He's a right old chum, he is.'

'Would he be of height about mine, with dark hair that needs a barber, and a pair of boots that have seen better days? And left-handed to boot? A Simeonite, and a man who studies?'

'Indeed. This boots ill, I sense.'

'And when did you last see him?'

'Lunchtime, we ate together. So where is he now?'

'I fear, in the town mortuary.'

Mr Sterne roused himself to a flurry of action. He knocked up every one of his neighbours, none of whom had seen Mr Stephens since lunchtime; he enquired of the porter, who had seen him leave college a little before two o'clock; he called upon the Master to appraise him of the situation, and he led Richard off to the mortuary to see if he could positively identify the body. It was indeed the late Mr Stephens who lay there, he pronounced, God be with his soul, and he returned to Caius to relay the news to the Master and hence to the lad's parents, while Richard trudged back to Emmanuel to likewise report his success, though a success that had somewhat hollow feeling to it.

The following day, Richard felt decidedly under the weather, which itself was lowering and dull. He ought to go and interrogate Mr Davies of the large group of visitors, but somehow he couldn't face it. It was feeble of him, but there it was. He kept thinking of the bulging eyes and lips of poor Mr Stephens, and the great welt around his neck, and was full of questions as to why? and when? and how? but with no answers. He cut morning chapel for the first time, and couldn't even keep a veneer of politeness to fend off the questions of Edward, who came round as he was eating his breakfast; well, not eating, just taking a little tea, and pushing away the rolls. Edward left in a snit, and Richard just sat in his best chair and tried to empty his mind.

Eventually he roused himself to go for a walk by the river. He headed across Christ's Pieces and Barnwell Causeway, and then meandered along the towing-path, occasionally turning up his collar against a flurry of drizzle, and at times stopping to watch some swans or a passing barge.

Which reminded him, there was an outing in the four-oar before dinner. Perhaps that would snap him out of his mood? He couldn't miss; it would let down four other fellows. But he didn't feel like it at all. Not anyhow.

After a sketchy sort of lunch he made his way to Jesus Green, and climbed into the boat as usual. The Jesuits were all talking about the murder, but the story seemed to have been elaborated considerably since it had begun to spread. Supposedly the victim had been stabbed through the heart with a crucifix, or according to another source, there had been rivers of blood running down the altar steps which had necessitated cancelling chapel as there had been so much cleaning to be done. Richard kept quiet, concentrated on his rowing, and wished he were somewhere else.

As they turned the boat up at the Pike and Eel, Rob commented on his silence, but he excused it by saying he was tired, and might be coming down with a fever, though he hoped not. However, by the time they were mooring and clambering out before removing the oars and thanking the boatman, Charlie cornered him.

'Something's up, Richard. Out with it. What's happened?'

Richard looked at him and couldn't be bothered to try and deceive him. 'It's that chap who was murdered, the one you were talking about. It was me who found him, and it wasn't like you've been saying at all. He was strangled – garotted – and it was horrible. I felt so responsible, I don't know why, and after I'd told our Master, I had to try and find out who he was, because someone had taken away his gown and everything from his pockets. So his parents could be told, I think, and to make it better, somehow. And I did, find out, I mean. I felt better having something to do, but now I feel awful, I don't know why.'

'You found out who he was?'

'Yes. Well, he had this cross on his watch-chain, you see, the watch had been taken, and I could tell he was left-handed from how there were inkstains on the wrong hands, and so, um, I asked someone who knew the Simeonites, because I thought I'd seen the cross before in church that is, and tracked him down to Caius, and now I . . .'

'Really? Young lad like you? That's pretty smart work, you know.' He thought for a moment. 'Not surprising you feel bad, it's like a comedown after a battle, I guess. You just keep going and going, when you have to, and then you feel totally flat after, and scared witless, thinking about the things you've seen.'

'Have you been in battle?'

'Yes, only once though, the peace came soon after I joined up and then I thought it would be better to come here and study a bit before I maybe went back to war; I mean, anyone could see old Boney was going to start it all up again.'

'But what about your bad back?'

'Oh, that. Happened after I came back to old England, that. Rotten luck.'

'So I'm not . . . a coward, then?'

'Not at all, Richard. Sounds like you did a grand job. So who was he?'

'A man from Caius called Stephens. Second year, that's all I know. Due to take the Little-go any day now, I should think. Well, not any more, though.'

Charlie gave him a slap on the back. 'Don't you bother yourself too much. Anyone would feel like that, even old soldiers, every time there's carnage. You'll get over it soon, everyone does.'

The following day, though the weather was worse, Richard felt a little better in his mind, and managed to brave the rain to call on Mr Davies, a lordly fellow-commoner, who roomed in the Founder's range like Peter Winton, but on a different stair. His rooms were furnished sumptuously, as was his person, but he was surprisingly helpful to Richard's enquiries.

'You see, sir, I found the body, in chapel, um, on Tuesday, so I'm concerned to discover what happened.'

'Friend of yours?'

'No, sir, I didn't know him. But, I feel responsible somehow. Having discovered him, you see.'

'Fair enough. So how do I come into it? You're not accusing me of doing the dastardly deed, are you?'

'No sir, of course not. But, um, I know you had a large party come to dinner with you on Tuesday; I wondered if . . . well, I am trying to rule out people who came into college before dinner, and if they were with you they couldn't have been murdering the gentleman in chapel, you see.'

'I follow you. Dashed cunning of you.'

'So, I know it's an imposition, but might you be able to make a list of people, I mean all those you remember being in your rooms and then at dinner in Hall with you? It's a bit of a cheek, I know.'

'Should be fairly easy, they're all my hunting buddies. Good eggs, all of them. D'ye want me to do it now?'

'If you could, sir, please. And could you write their colleges with their names? It'll be most useful to me if you would.'

Mr Davies set to promptly and soon had a list of thirteen names including his own. 'Unlucky for some,' he observed, as he sanded it and handed it over. 'I can vouch for all these fellows, and they were all with me from just after three until, well, when did the cove get his cool-crape?'

'Before four, certainly, sir.'

'We were all in Hall or in this room past six, for certain, lad. So, is that all I can help you with?'

'Thankyou sir. Yes, that is most kind.'

Back in his rooms Richard studied the list. There were men from several colleges, but what interested him was that there was only one name from Trinity, and none from Caius. But Mr Chapman had definitely said there were 'a couple' of blue gowns, and only those two colleges affected blue robes, all the rest wore black like Emmanuel. He recalled the suspicions he and Peter Winton had had concerning one Mr Noakes of Trinity, and his own discomfort around Mr Burgess of the same college, but neither was the name inscribed. He ought to visit Mr Chapman and ask him some more questions.

Mr Chapman was fairly certain there had been more than one blue gown in the crowd that came in for Mr Davies, two or possibly three Trinity or Caius men. And no, none of the gentlemen was exceptionally tall, as far as he noticed. No, he didn't know Mr Burgess of Trinity, but he thought he would have observed someone of six foot five passing his gates. And he suggested Richard might ask the Hall servants if there had been any more guests from either college that day. Richard did so: there was only the one blue gown that anyone could remember, with Mr Davies' party.

Of course anyone might have been coming to college to visit anyone else, but less likely just before the dinner hour? Not all colleges still ate so early, but Emmanuel men would mostly want to dine if they were in. He consulted his list of questions to answer, and considered whether he ought to look for the missing gown. It hardly seemed worthwhile, since he had identified the victim as a Caius-man, but still. He wasn't going to be able to concentrate on his books, and it would be something to do. He didn't relish the alternative, of visiting Caius and talking to Stephens' friends. Not just yet, he still felt trembly about the whole business.

Remembering his Ovid, he first visited the chapel. It was now unlocked, and empty both of the living and the dead, though a shiver went through him as he stepped from lobby to chancel, not just because of the chill in the air and the damp on his coat. Amigoni's painting over the altar seemed to want to tell him what it had seen, but (fortunately for his nervousness) stayed silent. All the benches were empty of helpful traces: just prayer books and a couple of pieces of stale rolls. He thought he'd found his Ovid under a kneeler, but it was only an old copy of 'The Castle of Otranto' that some bored undergraduate had been reading instead of listening to the service. It seemed an appropriate book for how he felt about the scene: death, a religious house, and terrible weather. Checking in case it had any useful inscription inside (which it did not) he replaced it and paused in the lobby before leaving the building.

Why commit a murder in the chapel, he wondered? Surely it was too public, too likely to lead to discovery? But then, if the time chosen was between half after three and four of the clock, everyone would be dining, and the murderer would be safe. But then, why would a man from Caius be there: would he not be at his own meal? And similarly, the other, possibly Trinity man. He felt baffled by the whole circumstance.

Where would he hide a gown if he had committed the murder himself? He turned back and looked again at the altar and its painting. Could it be under the altar hangings? He hadn't looked there, it had not occurred to him to violate sanctity in that way. But this was murder, was it not? He retraced his steps, and pulled aside the cloth, holding his breath. Nothing. Well, a considerable amount of dust, and some breadcrumbs, but that was all.

Outside, he thought of the time when he and Edward had made their expedition to Chesterton to spy on the bargees delivering gunpowder. Perhaps the gown was in a bush somewhere? Feeling slightly silly, he made a systematic but miserably damp search of the college's greenery throughout the Close, which took some time, and was fruitless. At least he had only had to search the coniferous plants, others having lost their leaves.

As he passed his stair on his way to search the rest of the gardens, a head poked out of an upper window.

'What're you about, bottle-brain? Lost a nest? Taking up gardening? It's nice and warm and dry in here.'

Richard looked up at Edward's grinning face on the second floor, thought about throwing a clod of earth at him, but decided his arm wasn't up to the task.

'I'm looking for suitable wood for your coffin, cully,' he called up. But, thinking it might be good to have another mind on his task, he turned into the staircase and ascended.

'Here's the problem, Nocky boy. You're in the chapel, you've just killed someone, you want to hide his gown. Where do you put it?' He edged close to Edward's fire, his clothes started to steam.

'I'd wear it under my own,' Edward suggested. 'Easy.'

'Oh, yes. I hadn't thought of that. But if you didn't? Then where? I've searched the chapel, and the bushes out there,' he indicated, 'and I was going to look round the back when I saw you.'

'Ponds? The one in the Close is deeper.'

'Maybe, but they're both pretty shallow, and a gown would probably float up.'

'Stones in the sleeves?'

'Could be.'

'In the privy?'

'I'm not going to look there, thankyou kindly.'

'He might just leave it on a stair, people are always leaving their gowns around, to pick up later.'

'Yes, but it's not an Emmanuel one, I think it's a blue job: it would be noticed.'

'Blue?'

'Do you not pay any attention to anything? What colour is your gown?'

'Black, of course. Well, a bit grey, really, it's got all dusty from being used to clean my window.'

'And what colour do they wear at Caius?'

'Same.'

'Think, man, you have Trouts from Caius, don't you?'

'Yes, but they don't wear their gowns in the tavern, it'd start a mill.'

'Well theirs are blue with black edging, remember? And so are Trinity's. But noone else's.'

'Oh yuh, Bulldogs wear blue.' A few moments then, 'Have you done your Latin poem for the Griffith? If you have, could you have a look at mine that Watkinson has set? I've got totally stuck, my iambs are all trochaic and my pentameter is spondylated. Come on, here's my text book.'

Richard stared at him. Then burst into laughter. 'So it was you who stole my Ovid! Come on, bottle-brain yourself, I'll try and help the helpless in their need. Can't leave a Trusty Trout floundering out of water, can I?'

At dinner, Richard decided to risk asking the others about his problem. Abel suggested it'd been chucked over a wall; Will thought he'd have rolled it up and taken it with him; John Wilks, always short of money, wondered if he might have tried to sell it back to the tailor's. Then there was idea of burning it somehow, perhaps in the kitchens (impractical), burying it (but digging equipment?) and then cutting it up small and eating it (which earned a cuff on the head for Edward, served him right).

'Anyway,' said Abel, 'if you've just done a murder you're going to want to get away as sharp as maybe. Your man's going to be a foxy fellow, isn't he?'

'So he has to go past the porter, and he might be seen, is that what you're saying?' said Richard.

'Yes, of course.'

'I'd not thought about him leaving, only about him getting in here.' Richard felt quite stupid for the omission. Thinking hard, he said, 'You see, I think he might be a Trinity man, so he'd be noticed in his blue gown, wouldn't he?'

'Not if he wore the other one over it.' Edward again. 'Like I told you.'

'Yes, but the victim was from Caius, theirs is blue too. You wouldn't tell them apart in the twilight.'

And there it rested. Richard did go and check again with Mr Chapman as to whether he had seen any blue gowns leave the college between three and four o'clock, and he said he thought not, and that he would have noticed, being finished with the post by about five and twenty past the hour. There had been a handful of men both come and go, but he didn't recall anyone in particular: that was a quiet time of day, because of everyone being at their dinner in Hall. He had a quick search of the rest of the sopping-wet bushes but the light was too dim to look in the ponds. Another day, he told himself, another day.

In the morning however, he woke early to stomach cramps. His courses had started, but they weren't usually painful. Perhaps it was the upset of the murder, he wondered, while trying to decide how to get some sort of warming bottle to have in bed to ease the pains.

Fenn came to wake him, but left his tea and disappeared promptly at his groans, and soon Mrs Fenn bustled into his keeping-room, and began lighting the fire.

'Not getting up, love?' she called. 'You'll be late for chapel.'

'I'm not going, Mrs Fenn. I don't feel well.'

The bedder put her head around the door. 'What is it? Too much of that whisky of yours?'

'No, not that sort of unwell,' Richard groaned. 'Stomach ache.'

Mrs Fenn looked him up and down as he lay there, clutching the lower part of his belly, and nodded sagely. 'What you need for that is a hot bottle, my lad. I'll fetch one right as soon as I've lit this here fire and boiled you some water.'

And in not many minutes she was as good as her word. Richard snuggled close to the stoneware in its towel, and felt the warmth ease through his tummy.

'If you've any . . . soiled items you want Elsa to dispose of, Mr Cox, private-like, just say. I knows how to keep my mouth shut. I'm forever grateful to your cousin for what he did for me and Fenn, you know.' She gave a conspiratorial wink and disappeared.

So she did know about my secret, thought Richard. I imagined she would, but she's never said. Anyway, this explains why I've felt rotten the last few days. Quite apart from poor Mr Stephens, that is. And he lay back and tried to go back to sleep.

Mrs Fenn came in again later and refilled his bottle. She locked his oak after her, telling him just to rest for the day, and that she'd left him extra rolls and cheese and butter and a quart of small beer, so's he wouldn't need to go to dinner. Richard relaxed back into his blankets. What Edward would think of his sported oak he couldn't say, but at the moment he didn't care. No more than he cared about the mystery at the moment, actually. Not one whit.

The following day, Saturday, he felt fine. Better than fine, actually, full of energy. While he was lying feeling sorry for himself, he had thought about Mrs Fenn, and how protective she was of him, and how glad he was of that. He also remembered Sir George's conversation with her at the beginning of last term. She had said that George had proved she and Fenn couldn't have done whatever they were supposed to have done because they had been elsewhere at the time, they would have had to have ridden a horse faster than the great Eclipse to have gone from the scene of the crime to where he saw them early that day. George had called it an alibi, it was Latin for 'he was elsewhere'.

So, the murderer, if he was truly a fox as Abel had called him, would have wanted to get away as fast as possible and show himself to have been somewhere else as soon as he could. Without, of course, equine assistance, which would have looked odd inside the Founder's Court of Emmanuel and galloping through town.

Which meant, surely, that he wouldn't have wanted to go far to dispose of the gown: time was important to him. He was still somehow sure he wouldn't have taken it with him: he didn't know why, it was just a hunch. So, after chapel he lingered behind, standing on the altar steps and considering, trying to put himself in the mind of the assailant. Reverend Burton's exit had been followed at top speed by all the congregation, and the place was still. It was quite dark of course but for the sparse candlelight, the sun having barely risen, and quite like he imagined it would have been around, say, three thirty in the afternoon of the murder. Where to go?

He walked slowly forward. He'd searched all around the chancel; what about the antechapel? There was nothing in there, was there? To be fair, there were a few assorted Emmanuel gowns hanging on pegs on the wall in front of him, but he had checked them before: black ones only. And the room itself: just bare black and white tiles, and the small room, almost a cupboard, containing vestments used by the Chaplain. But what about those? He hadn't liked to look in there, it was private. But a murderer wouldn't consider that a barrier, would he?

In the little room, there was a closet with robes hanging in all the liturgical hues; a dresser with many drawers containing various smaller items and with the robes Rev Burton had just removed lying on its top. Under the window was an iron-bound chest, but when he lifted the lid it was just full of old moth-eaten vestments. No luck. Just to be on the careful side, though, he lifted them up and checked underneath. And there it was, a blue and black gown. He took it out, and looked at it. A Caius gown, to be sure. Success! He jigged in excitement.

What next, then? He had Stephens' gown, and knew how it had been hidden. He felt a shiver of exultation, of cracking the problem, pass through his body. What should he do with the thing? He supposed he ought to return it to its late owner, or his family at any rate. So, feeling it was far too early for expeditions across town, he retired to his room for a rapid breakfast and then with the gown slung over his arm, he made his way to Caius. In company with Edward, that is, who had heard him come in and had badgered him so much, about what he had been doing with his oak sported the previous day, that to put him off interrogating him further he had explained about his discovery, and asked him join the expedition. And been entertained in consequence by his flowery and often critical comments on several personages whom they had passed on the way. He was alright, old Edward, really, but liable to get himself in trouble if anyone ever overheard him.

The Caius porter was their first port of call. Richard showed him the gown.

'I'd like to return this. I believe it belonged to the late Mr Stephens, I found it in our chapel at Emmanuel.'

'Thankye sir,' said the porter, holding out his hand to take it. 'Hold hard, lad, this isn't a Caius gown, it's a Trinity one. Look see, there's not any black facing on the yoke.'

Richard looked, and saw, and felt even more confused. 'But I was sure this must have been Mr Stephens'. How else would it have got into our chapel?'

'Can't help you there, sir, but this ain't one of ours, for sure. Look here, sir, they're both blue, but they're quite a different pattern. Like you can see, different on the shoulder? Trinity like to think they're better than all the other colleges, see?' He handed it back. 'I suggest you apply at the lodge next door, they might be able to help you. Mind, they're awful busy at the moment, getting ready for a visitor.'

Feeling stupid, he went out into the street, and thought. Edward helpfully suggested that he was becoming a bit noddy, and to keep up his end Richard had to cuff him, and call him *sceleste*, though sadly he dodged, and didn't ask what the Latin meant. Once this matter of honour was settled he examined the gown again, in case he had missed some sort of marking, but there was none. Edward then suggested one of them could try to impersonate a Trinity man and get a better class of dinner in their hall, and received a glare for his pains. With no other obvious course open to them, they took the porter's advice and, proceeding up the street a few yards, entered the Lodge.

As they had been told at Caius, the place was a hive of activity. Gardeners were tidying the beds, and cleaning weeds from the cobbles; someone was repairing a part of the brickwork, and the entrance flags were being scrubbed. Nonetheless, enquiry soon provided them with the intelligence that this was indeed the gown of a Trinity sizar, that it seemed quite old, as if it belonged to a senior man, or maybe one who had acquired it second-hand.

'A sizar, you say?' Richard queried. 'I know a man here, slightly that is, called Noakes. Would he be a sizar? I might ask him if it's his.'

'Yes sir, it could be, he's in his second year. He keeps over the other side of the court.' He pointed.

'And there's John Burgess, I've met him.'

'Yes sir, everyone knows our Mr Burgess. But this ain't his gown, it's far too short for his height, and he's a scholar: theirs is different, you see. Now if you don't mind, we have a lot to be doing.'

After thanking the man, they took the opportunity to wander around Great Court and admire the buildings as they had on their first day in Cambridge. In the far corner was Noakes' staircase, he remembered. He looked at the names painted there. Noakes, Price and Hope were the names he had suspected last term: there they were.

Edward elbowed him in the ribs. 'Why don't we go up and see if it's this cove's gown, eh?'

Richard didn't want to risk Noakes recognising him, or rather, Rose, from the Pemberton Ball, having danced with him and, to be fair, cast admiring glances at him in the figure, but of course he couldn't say so. 'I don't want to bother him,' he temporised.

'Don't be a yellow-belly, cully. Or do you think he'd garotte you on sight?'

'Of course not.'

'Well I'll go and do the deed, if you won't,' and he grabbed the gown and hared up the stairs before Richard could stop him.

Richard, worried that Noakes might look out of his window, pressed himself against the wall and waited. Hardly a minute had passed, when Edward reappeared, still with the parentless gown.

'Not his,' he said, 'his was on his chaise-longue. All shiny, like a new one. What sort of lollpoopy fellow has a chaise-longue in his rooms anyway? But I learned a couple of useful swear-words from him. Good call.'

Richard relaxed a little. 'Let's go home,' he said.

But on the way past Caius again he havered. Ought he to go into the college and try and find out about Stephens' habits from his friends? Or could it wait? He didn't really want to do that job with Edward in tow, it would be too . . . too clumsy, maybe?

As he stood there in thought, some men came out of Caius lodge and crossed the road to the coffee house. He recognised Burgess immediately by his height, but there with him was . . . surely that was Charles? Brother Charles! In Cambridge again, and this time clearly with a group of undergraduates, not his hunting set. Quickly, he ducked behind Edward who had fortunately also stopped, though not presumably to think: his attention was focussed towards the windows of the coffee house, not the procession of men.

Richard knew his disguise wouldn't fool Charles for a second, and so he turned away and prayed. Prayed possibly irreverently, but successfully, as the six or seven fellows disappeared inside the shop and the door closed.

'Could you see that comely wench we met last term?' asked Edward. 'I couldn't, the windows were too steamed up. Maybe we ought to go in and have a nose?'

'No, no! Not now. I've had enough of all this, I'm, er, I'm quite knocked up, I didn't sleep well last night, and I want to get on with some work. You can come, or you can stay, but I'm off.'

So, back to college they went, to lock the gown away in his trunk, and to commune with Newton and Ovid and more restful kinds of fellows.

CHAPTER 7

THE FOLLOWING DAY, BEING SUNDAY however, he took the opportunity of catching Mr Benson in Holy Trinity church and letting him know what had transpired concerning his friend. Benson was most concerned about the occurrence, though he reiterated that he had only known him slightly. He was most ready to assist with all he knew about Stephens' friends. He introduced Richard to several Simeonites who had known Stephens through the church, but again, none were his intimates. Except one, that is, a Mr Danns, who was also a Caius man though not a great friend. He suggested that he ought to apply to Mr Sterne, who he said was a sound fellow, though sadly somewhat Popish in tenor, who he rather thought was Stephens' closest friend. Which is where Richard had thought to start anyway, but as he said to himself while walking the short distance to Caius, nothing had been lost by the diversion.

Mr Sterne was at leisure, and indeed welcoming, his foray into the Little-go having passed off satisfactorily. He offered Richard a glass of his wine, and expounded on the virtues of a new vintage he had recently had delivered, an up-country Spanish wine from the Ebro valley. Dashed decent, he had called it, but he was concerned that Boney was going to mess up his supply lines, maybe not this year, but soon, because of his plans to take over all of Europe.

'So what can I do for you,' he said at length. 'It's about this terrible business with Stephens, isn't it?'

'Quite,' said Richard, nursing his glass. It certainly was good wine, if a little early in the day for it. 'What I thought, you see, is that Stephens must have gone to Emmanuel, to the chapel, for some reason on Tuesday. He wouldn't have just been there by chance. And I imagine he might have gone with his murderer, because, well, otherwise how would the man know he would be there?'

'I get your drift, surely. So, if we find this so-called friend who went with him, we find the killer? I'm all for helping out. Philip was a fine chap, didn't deserve his wooden surcoat just yet.'

'Can you tell me what he was like? Who he spent his time with, what he studied, was he a reading man? Um, did he mostly stay in college, or was he out and about a lot, did he visit other colleges much, that sort of thing. I know he was a Simeonite, that's about all I do know.'

'Right, lad. Well look, it's time for a little lunch, would you like to join me? Bring your glass, you've hardly drunk any, and you can probably meet some of Philip's friends.'

They repaired to the Hall, which Richard was most interested to compare to Emmanuel's, while Sterne continued: 'So, to start with, I think I might have been one of the closest of his friends, don't you know? We used to have good old to-and-fros about theology, to be sure, but we mostly got on famously. And yes, he was a reading man, but not a quiz, he liked to have fun too. Liked his wine well enough, but never overdid it, I'm sorry to say. He did a fair bit of hunting; that was something he'd have done more of if he hadn't felt the need to study. Keen on quite a few academic things outside the usual Euclid and classics and divinity, I believe too. Not that I would follow him there, I'm too wedded to the elixir of Bacchus for that. But he liked this Chemistry stuff that's being the next big thing, as he used to say. And architecture, and painting, and that kind of thing. Went on trips to see old buildings, y'know. Ely's cathedral, and its old timber houses, those old ruins, as if we haven't got enough wood and masonry here in Cambridge.'

'Who was his tutor, do you know?'

'Same as mine, Hardwick; but he spent more time learning mathematics with Oliver James, he's just been made a Fellow this year, now he's a bang-up quiz if ever there was one.'

'And other friends?'

'Lots.' He considered. 'There's Paine, an' Longton, Baddeley, Dobson, . . . well, hang on a mo, I'd better do you a list. If you're serious about this, that is?'

'Never more so, Mr Sterne.'

'Call me Hugh, won't you? Can't investigate a murder on formal terms, can one?'

'Thankyou, Hugh.'

Hugh introduced him to such of the friends as were in Hall, and Richard tried to gather such information as he could think of asking about. Hugh and he then went back to his own rooms by way of Stephens'. Stephens' family had removed his books and personal possessions, but his furniture was still in place, and his pictures. Most were of either architectural sights, including (Richard recognised from Mr Griffith's collection) the Parthenon, or engravings of famous works of Art.

After making the list, Hugh most cooperatively then accompanied Richard around several of the other men's abodes, introducing him again and explaining the idea. Most were friendly, but one or two expressed themselves unwilling to get mixed up in 'that sort of thing'. No matter, Richard noted their opinion, and carried on.

David Paine was the most informative of the friends. He said that Philip (Mr Stephens, that is) had been most keen on Chemistry and as well as the University lectures, had attended a discussion group in the college concerning the subject, which Richard supposed might be similar to the one Peter Winton had organised in Emmanuel. Also, and most tellingly, that he was part of a group of mostly Trinity men who sallied forth on the expeditions to absorb culture that Hugh had alluded to. They visited grand mansions to see the paintings, and interesting buildings, and even rode out to look at quaint villages, especially those built by large landowners for their tenants.

By this time Richard's head was spinning and his notes becoming most confused, and he decided to stop for the time being. He thanked his host and guide, and begged forgiveness for retiring, but said that he would return: he felt he needed to organise all this intelligence before he could decide what to do next. And it was now time for dinner; he was dashed hungry, to boot, even after having eaten quite freely at lunchtime.

'Oh, no, sorry, just one more thing. Who does he hunt with?'

'Trinity boys again, schoolfellows of his. Don't know them, there's a big crowd of them. But I could find out for you.'

'Thanks,' and then he really did take his leave.

After Hall, he decided to sit in the library where he thought he might be less likely to be disturbed by men wanting to waste time. He laid out all his papers and lists on the table and stared at them. Taking a fresh sheet, he inscribed 'Philip Stephens' in the centre, and then wondered what to put next. His thoughts weren't organised enough to make one of his lists.

In the end he just wrote things down haphazardly around the man's name. Hunting with Trinity men; Architecture and painting, Trinity link again, but also schoolfellows; Chemistry, Caius discussion group; evangelical religion; Tutorials with Mr James; College tutor Mr Hardwick; The Gown conundrum; The time of the murder; Why in Emmanuel chapel?; Murderer's escape plan; and then in larger letters, the word 'Motive?'.

One thing was missing, he didn't know anything about Stephens as a person. What he spoke like, his attitudes, his morals, his views. Was he serious or light-hearted? Was he loyal or come-and-go? Forward or reserved? He felt these things might be telling, he needed to discover them.

Now as for the Chemistry, the Emmanuel group wouldn't probably start unless Winton came back into residence, though he could ask one of the other senior men about it. Lectures didn't start until mid-February of course, but in Caius they may have begun their discussion group already, nonetheless?

Hunting: not his field at all. He would be happier looking into the cultural expedition group, though he didn't have a way in to the Trinity set. He could talk to the tutors, maybe? Or was there someone who had known if he had seemed worried before the day of his murder?

He wished again Peter Winton was here. It was so hard to know how to proceed, he had never had to unravel such a puzzle before. And all alone, because he couldn't properly rely on Edward, not with something so important. For example, puzzles like, why Emmanuel chapel? Why at dinner time? And, of course, simply, Why?

After staring at his paper for several minutes, until his forehead began to sting, he sat back, took a deep breath and decided. He couldn't solve the mystery yet, he needed to gather more intelligence first. So, how to proceed? He could certainly make a list of things to be done, couldn't he?

Things to be done
1: Speak again to Hugh Sterne about Mr Stephens' character. Also possibly to other friends about the same. Also about his prospects, money etc.
2: Find someone from the cultural visits group to speak to.
3: Ditto, Trinity hunting group.
4: Ditto, Caius Chemistry discussion group.
5: Possibly sound out the Simeonites about any unusual signs they had noticed about him recently.

Things to be thought about
1: Why do people commit murder?
2: Why would anyone go from Caius to Emmanuel chapel on a January afternoon?

3: Why was there a Trinity sizar's gown in the Emmanuel
   chaplain's trunk? (and where is the missing Caius gown?)

He then scratched his head and added,

Also
1: What is Charles doing in Cambridge with those Caius and
   Trinity men?
2: How do I avoid him seeing me by chance?

That felt better. Much better. He folded up both papers and stowed them safely in the inside pocket of his coat. The thing to do now, quite honestly, was to forget about the whole business and get on with his studies. Mathematics, now. That was relaxing. You knew where you were with mathematics, it was all totally logical once you saw what they were driving at. Though to be fair, like his conundrum, it was often just as confusing until you got on the right lines.

Over the next few days he found time in between stretches of study, and social demands, and fencing club, and the four-oar, and indeed all the demands of his life in college, to go back to Caius and other colleges and speak with various of Stephens' friends. He discovered that he was a serious type of man, much prone to examining his conscience; that he was scrupulously honest, and had such difficulty in telling a lie that he could not be trusted to take part in any practical jokes or bamming. He was a pensioner, but reasonably comfortable with money, in that he could afford to hunt and hire horses, but he had no financial expectations from his family, and indeed hoped to take orders and go into the church. He had been about to take the Little-go when he met his demise, but had been confidently expected to graduate among the Senior Optimes in due course.

Richard went so far as to visit Mr Oliver James to enquire further about Stephens' academic abilities, feeling that this gentleman's poor eyesight and unworldly manner would surely protect him from recognition. The Swaffham ball had been nearly a year ago, and although he (or rather Rose) had met Mr James again at the Pemberton Ball the previous month he was sure he would be safe.

'Well, Mr Cox, poor Mr Stephens was a very good man indeed. I cannot think why anyone would wish to harm him. He would have been eminently suitable for a parish, or even rise to higher things. He had a scrupulous mind, and eschewed frivolity of thought. I had had great hopes for him.'

'Was he well liked by others?'

'Indeed. By all, yes, by all.' Mr James paused, his forehead furrowed. 'Pardon me, have we previously met? Richard Cox, you say?'

Richard gulped. 'Yes sir. Arrived from Nova Scotia to study at this great University only five months ago.'

'Indeed? I just thought . . . no matter. You are quite young, are you not?'

'Sixteen, nearly seventeen, sir.'

'Your voice is very light, sir. It reminds me, I cannot quite place it, but . . . no, it would have been longer ago than five months. I must be mistaken.'

'Sir. Well, thankyou for your time. I feel impelled to try and unravel the puzzle of Mr Stephens' death because of being the one to find him, you see. I bid you farewell.'

Outside the Fellow's rooms he felt a cold shiver run up his spine. That was so close. Of course, Mr James, though his sight was poor, had excellent hearing. He remembered how when he had first met him Mr James had described hearing music in terms of seeing a colour. He must keep on his guard for that sort of mistake in his impersonation. Perhaps he ought to drink a little more whisky and smoke more cigars to try and deepen or hoarsen his voice more?

He had been directed to a Mr Symes of Trinity who seemed to be the leader of the set of men who were interested in all forms of Art. Symes confirmed that Philip Stephens had indeed accompanied them on their architectural visits but he thought his main preference was

97

for paintings. Of course they would often visit mansions where they were allowed to access many works, but if he remembered correctly, Stephens was less keen on portraiture which understandably domi-nated such collections, than on other forms of depiction. He could not easily make a list of names, but made a start while Richard was there, and said he would try and complete it in the next few days.

It was in a way surprising, and in a way not so, that everyone he spoke to was quite willing to talk to him once he had explained how he came to be involved in the matter. Well, not all: he had a rude rebuff from the fellow-commoner who arranged the hunting-parties, in rooms he was told had once been occupied by Mr Newton. 'Owes us for the last meet,' he said, 'and little chance of getting his dues out of his pater, don't you think? Shove off, you. Unless you're able to cough up the blunt?'

However, a friendly porter on whose mercy he threw himself at the lodge, told him of a lesser mortal whom he could try, and who, being less high in the instep, might be more cooperative. This Mr Venn however could tell him little beyond the fact that Mr Stephens only attended about one hunt in ten days, whereas the society might arrange three a week. He looked rather askance at Richard's request for names, but eventually was persuaded to give him a list of all those who at times attended these hunts. It seemed he initially took the task as implying that he himself had personally dispatched Mr Stephens to meet his Maker, and he had to be considerably mollified with flat-tery. Fortunately Richard, when in his form as Rose, had had ample practice with gentlemen in this art, and used it with suitable modifica-tions until Mr Venn was quite affable.

Lastly, though he had thought he might have approached it first, he obtained a list of sometime attendees at the Chemistry meetings from David Paine. This one was more eclectic, containing several names from nearby colleges that did not have their own groups, such as Clare Hall, King's and Trinity Hall. Sitting down with all the lists one evening at his desk, he tried to make sense of them.

There was just too much paper to cope with. What he needed was to sieve through the information and reduce the lists to a manageable level. How to do it? Well, he could start by seeing if any men were named on all three lists: Chemistry, Art, and Hunting? It would be a beginning, though he shouldn't exclude people on only two. Or even if they only appeared on one, maybe?

After much labour he had a short list of seven names who had participated in Stephens' three main areas of interest beyond the regular academic topics. His new list read:

Stephens' associates in all three groups:

Caius   Hugh Sterne
           Joshua Little
           John Dobson

Trinity John Burgess (he turns up everywhere)
           Louis Price (French name, suspicious. Also, neighbour of Noakes)
           Hans Telmann (another neighbour of Noakes, another foreign name)

Jesus   Hon. Charles French (Charlie, it seems he didn't actually ride with the hunt much due to his bad back)

Finding Charlie on the list was a major surprise. And then he had to append the names of Oscar Seligman, Fellow of Caius, because although he did not appear with the huntsmen, he was in both other lists and was also foreign. And also Noakes of Trinity of course, though he was only on the hunting and Art lists, because he was a known associate from last term's events. He thought he'd better stop there as there were another fifteen who were on two lists, and that would make the whole thing unworkable. His brain simply wasn't big enough. Trinity was so much bigger than Emmanuel, and its societies correspondingly wide in their ambit.

After this flurry of activity the whole business stagnated for a while. Richard simply couldn't think of any more ideas, so he decided to set it aside, locking all his papers in his trunk with the gown so he might look at them afresh in a few days. Besides, he had other business to occupy him. The four-oar had been challenged by a crew from John's to a race, and therefore they were having an outing three times a week. It was going reasonably well, but the day of the race was fast approaching and Richard had some juicy blisters which didn't seem to want to heal, as well as an aching back after outings. There was the fencing club too, a different form of exercise, but one at which he had found himself quite capable.

He had been invited to attend the sermon classes that Mr Simeon gave in the Gibbs building at King's, which was a great honour as he had not expressed a desire to become ordained, but he declined, citing too many irons in the fire. Also, he had to get well ahead with his Greek, which he was still studying along with Abel Johnson, as he wanted to fit in as many Chemistry lectures as possible when they started, both because of his interest, and because of the possible connection to Stephens' death. Also, he had become more friendly with Abel, since they had now been studying together for some weeks, and had found out more about his interests, which meant he had been taken to see the bowls lawns at several colleges, on which Abel hoped to play once summer came.

And then there was Geology, which he also wanted to learn more about after his conversations with Mr Hailstone. And, because after all he was a young man in the company of many other young men, he had constant encouragement to neglect his studies in coffee houses and public houses and fellows' rooms; and in shooting and fishing expeditions and the like. Well, only one fishing expedition: it turned out to be a cold, wet and unproductive affair, much as brother Charles had described his time by the banks of Loch Ness last winter. So it was not until mid-February that anything further transpired in relation to the murder.

It was while watching a man changing his gown for another before Hall that it struck him. This man had simply picked up the wrong gown from a pile at the end of a wine-party in someone's rooms, and had to retrieve his own. It gave Richard to think. What if, maybe, the murderer had not only hidden Stephens' blue gown in the trunk, but also switched his own gown for an Emmanuel one? There were plenty of old gowns hanging up in the antechapel. Why would he think to do that? Only, he supposed, if the man was wearing a blue one himself. Then, he would be able to walk out of college without being noted as a Trinity or Caius man. But what would he do with his own, blue, gown?

Richard thought about this as he ate his dinner and hurried off as soon as he might to the chapel. Standing in the chancel he looked back and imagined himself standing over the body of his newly-deceased victim on the altar step, the victim's possessions in his pockets, the blue gown in his hands and the guilt upon his soul. Even now it gave him to shiver. Walking towards the robing cupboard he made as if to put the gown in the trunk, and then thought 'Why not conceal my own gown there too?' followed by taking the Emmanuel one and departing.

Which was all very well, but then he would be at his own college, with the wrong gown. And there ought to be two gowns in the trunk, not one. Two blue gowns. He would not want to incriminate himself by returning to the chapel at a later time to effect the exchange, now would he? And if he had done, why was it not Stephens' gown that remained? It made no sense. He should have taken his own gown and left Stephens'. And he still had no idea why the two of them had been in the chapel in the first place. It was infuriating.

That same evening Peter Winton arrived into residence, with a fair deal of baggage and several porters to carry it. Richard saw the commotion, and realised he ought to tell him about his discoveries, but baulked at the prospect as he so wanted to have solved the mystery himself. It would be galling to have to ask a man for help. Except, he pulled himself up sharply, he was a man himself, wasn't he? So it wasn't quite the same. Except, it was, it really was: it made him feel like a silly little girl having to ask for assistance.

Which is why he avoided Peter all the rest of that day, and the following morning, and then he had two lectures the other side of town, and then in Hall he tried to look invisible, keeping quiet even when Abel accused him of copying his Greek prose without asking (which he hadn't) and Edward of failing to turn up at the Pickerel the evening before (which he had. Failed to, that is). To no avail, of course, as Peter clapped him heavily on the back and enquired why the four-oar had allowed the Hogs to defeat them on the river, and said that it was surely because he was not in the number two seat, and that he'd got more muscled than last term, and why hadn't he come to raid his new bottle of whisky yet, one he'd bought on recommendation of a real Scottish laird?

All of which was so . . . well, normal, thought Richard, what was I worrying about? Well, I must have felt he thought of me as just a girl, now he knew I was a girl, but I'm not. Well, I am, but I'm not. And he was so, distant, most of the time at Milton. And with that confusing thought he followed Peter up to his rooms, trying to get his thoughts in order about the whole Stephens business, and failing signally.

'Has the Chemistry group got going yet?' was Peter's opener, and at Richard's negative he complained that nobody organised anything, did they, they left it all to him. And then he told a tale all about his trip up to the Scottish Borders, which is why he had been so late back to college, and how he'd been initiated into the mysteries of not just whisky but golf, which was a God-benighted game, and Richard was never to attempt it: he ought to play cricket if he wanted a sensible game with a bat and a ball. At least the ball was big enough to see and the bat large enough to hit it with, and you could throw it and bowl it not just attempt to get it off the ground with stupid weapons which were peculiarly ill-designed for the purpose. From this diatribe Richard deduced that Peter saw himself as a bit of a sportsman and had been embarrassed at his lack of ability at this new game. This made him feel encouraged: perhaps Peter was not good at absolutely everything, as he had seemed.

On the other hand, the whisky, he said, pouring a generous amount into a heavy glass, was a fine invention, perhaps the only good thing to come out of the country. He explained how the Scots diluted it with water, just a touch – they said it brings out the flavours better – and praised Richard for having discovered it before him. But after this encomium, he went on to criticise the weather in the country, the roads, the people, and the food, and again gave Richard dire warnings about a number of dishes to especially avoid.

Eventually, he ran out of tales, and settling back in his chair asked, 'So, how have you done with your studies without my noble influence? Are you yet sated with chasing skirt and dipping deep in the evening?'

Richard looked worried. Peter added, 'Come on, I'm only bamming you, you look shocked. How have you been getting on? I imagine it's been a bit quiet after last term's shenanigans?'

'Er, well, not exactly. Not at all, really. Um, have you not heard of our murder?'

'No? Really? A murder? I've been out of touch with civilisation for so long, I haven't heard the news at all.'

'Well, um, I found this body in the chapel,' he began, and haltingly explained how he had worked out who the victim must be, and why it had not been at all obvious.'

'Good work, lad. Couldn't have done better myself.'

'I've got totally stuck after that, though.' He recounted finding and then trying to return the gown, and how it had led only to more obscurity; about investigating Stephens' friends and interests and how the intelligence had been overwhelming in volume; and about his recent idea about the murderer changing his gown for an Emmanuel one, except that that hadn't worked out because of there being only one gown in the chest.

'I am truly impressed, young Richard.'

Richard inspected his expression carefully, but he seemed to be genuine. 'I think I've been very stupid somewhere,' he said, 'I must be missing something obvious. And I can't think of any reason he might be murdered, or why it would have happened in our chapel, or anything. It seems far-fetched to think it's French spies again. I can't see how it could be.'

'Has anyone else been looking into this? The Master, the magistrate, the proctors?'

Richard confessed he didn't know. 'I wanted to do this myself, I felt responsible, seeing as I found the body.'

'And have you checked all the obvious places around college for the other gown?'

'I tried, I searched as well as I could. The bushes in all the gardens; Edward and I poked around in both the ponds with sticks; I asked people if they'd seen a Caius gown lying anywhere on their stair; I checked with the porters.'

'Curious. Most curious.'

'I expect you can see the answer straight away.' He sighed.

'Not at all. No ideas at all. Well, one: I think we ought to go and visit the Caius Chemistry discussion group, if it has started up again this term, you didn't say you'd done that.'

'No, I didn't like to, and I didn't know what I would be looking for.'

'Well nor do I, really. But given what we know about these French blighters, I think if it's to do with them, which it might well be, in spite of your reservations, your very reasonable reservations, I think we're more likely to find mischief in the Chemistry department than in the hunting field or the picture galleries. Well, as a start anyway. But before that, I'd like to have a look at the gown. Have you still got it?'

'Yes. And I've got all my papers, with all the names on. I bet you'll recognise somebody, someone well-known to your Foreign Office friends,' he added disconsolately.

'Maybe, maybe not. Let's look first.'

CHAPTER 8

T HE GOWN TOLD PETER NOTHING new, other than that it was well-worn and dirty. The lists of names he spread out on Richard's table, and whistled as he saw how much work had gone into them.

'This is a monumental achievement, lad. Surely you didn't do it all yourself?'

Richard confessed to assistance, such as it was, from Edward, and from the concerned Mr Sterne who had rallied all Stephens' friends to provide information. 'But do you know any of the names?'

'Well, some, of course. Why exactly did you make this list of men who are in all three groups?'

'I didn't know how to sort out who might be more likely as a murderer, it seemed one place to start, it's probably a silly idea.'

'No, excellent idea. Um, I think we can rule out Charlie, don't you know?'

'Why? I know he's a friend of yours, but it's a bit odd that he's in these groups seeing as he's a Jesuit.'

'Ah. Yes, I see. Well, um, yes.' He seemed to be thinking hard. 'I didn't ought to tell you this, really, but Charlie is, er, one of us. He is, um, a bit like me here at Emmanuel. Foreign Office. Studying, but also looking out for useful information. I haven't heard from him for ages, but then I wouldn't have, being up North.'

'Oh. So he isn't who he says he is? And his bad back? Is that just make-believe, so he can get out of, I don't know, certain things?'

'No, his back's real enough, just he didn't get it hunting but in a rout with some Frenchies, a year or so ago. And he really is an Honourable, and so on.'

'Oh.'

'I didn't want to tell you, the fewer people who know things the better, but, well, you need to know now.'

'I see.'

He turned again to the list. 'On the other hand, we are always interested in Mr Burgess, he has fingers in so many pies. And in any associate of Mr Noakes, I see you have Price and Telmann on your list, his neighbours. Very good. Mr Sterne . . . well, I don't know. And the other names are unknown to me. Little, Dobson, Seligman . . . not a flicker.'

'Mr Seligman is a don, I wasn't sure about putting him down.'

'Seniority no guard against treason. In fact, the higher up you are the more damage you can do. So, can I borrow these papers for a few days, I'll keep them safe in my trunk? You can hang on to the gown; we might need to identify its owner at some point. Good thing we had your lock changed last year; these notes are highly dangerous.'

'Dangerous?'

'Yes, dangerous to the man who I'm sure is on one of them, and doesn't want to be.'

'Oh.'

'My money would be on Mr Louis Price, as a starter. French name, right associates. But it could be anyone. Right, well, the first thing I'll do is go and see Charlie, see if he knows anything about anything. And I'll tell him about you, so he can feel able to pass on intelligence if any reaches his ears.'

'No, don't do that! Nobody but you knows. Well, and George, I suppose.'

'Whyever not? Oh! No, not about your, er, other identity, don't worry, I'm as silent as the grave on that. Just, that you have been very helpful to me and can be trusted. Is that alright?'

Richard let out his breath. 'Yes, that's fine, I just thought . . .'

'You're far better placed with your secret intact, you know.' He got up to go.

'Can I ask one other thing?'

'Yes, what?'

'Can I book you in for another lock-picking lesson, please?'

Charlie had had nothing to report, and strangely hadn't realised Richard had been investigating Stephens' associates, though of course he knew about Richard finding the body and identifying it, and told Peter how impressed he'd been with the lad. Peter returned Richard's notes the following day, saying that he had copied what he needed, and that Richard should have them as he had made them: if he had a further look at them it might spark another of his brilliant ideas. He also said he'd been to see the magistrate, and discovered that his constables had been able to make no progress with the murder, as they had nobody like the Bow Street Runners to call on in town, and the division into college, University and town jurisdictions made it doubly hard. Dr Cory similarly had been baulked from any discoveries.

He had also organised the first college Chemistry discussion group of the term, and persuaded someone to present about the new elements that had recently been discovered. There was Columbium and Tantalum and Palladium and Cerium and Osmium . . . Richard wished he'd brought a paper to take notes, but is seemed that all you had to do was take a Greek or Roman god and add -ium to the name and you had something new. He still wasn't quite sure what an element was, though, and didn't like to show his ignorance.

However he was equally interested in the men who had made the discoveries of these new elements. It seemed that Palladium had been found in platinum ore that was being processed by one William Hyde Wollaston, the brother of the Jacksonian Professor of Natural Philosophy whose Chemistry lecture he had attended last term. And that this William had made a fortune from the platinum extraction, which seemed a whole new area of industry, certainly for someone like Richard, used only to hearing of coal and iron ore mining, and farming and the like.

'Has anyone else anything new they have heard of?' asked Peter when the topic had for the time being become exhausted. 'Any new developments in the country?' But noone had. Lectures and demonstrations were only due to start the next day, and the meeting broke up with plans for the next one on the same day the following week.

Peter went back to his rooms, but Richard wandered over to the chapel again. Surely he could work out why Stephens and his assailant had been in the chapel? He entered, walked most slowly towards the altar. The huge painting of the Prodigal Son's return dominated the scene. He didn't like it much, it was brown and dull, and everyone looked as if they were in an Italian palace rather than in whatever a Jewish house might have looked like eighteen hundred years ago. Why couldn't it tell him what it had seen?

His hand went up and felt his neck, his head tilted up as it was to look at the artwork. It was ideally exposed for a ligature, ripe for one, you might say. He shivered, felt as vulnerable as a girl in a Whitechapel rookery, couldn't stop himself looking over his shoulder in case anyone had come in with evil intent, tried to relax his shoulders. Still, no ideas came to him.

He walked back to the chancel entrance and turned back. The body had been found on those steps. So, unless it had been dragged there, the murder must have been committed there. And it had lain there so naturally, just as if it had dropped down all of a piece. So at the time of his death, Philip Stephens had been admiring the Amigoni, unless he had been trying to steal the plate on the altar. So, why was he there?

He thought back over what he knew of the man, from his endless conversations with his friends. He liked hunting, of course, and Chemistry, and architecture . . . and yes, of course, paintings. He went on trips out of town to look at them. He could have been brought here . . . to inspect this masterpiece. Couldn't he?

Which meant . . . that whoever came with him must share his interest in Art. So, he needed to go back to the lists, and have a rethink. Progress at last! Although, as he said to himself as he walked through the cloister to Peter's room, he still didn't know either why the murderer had bothered to come all the way over to Emmanuel, nor what had happened to the gowns.

Peter listened to his idea with fascination, and clapped him on the back. 'You have it!' he cried. 'Brilliant!'

Richard tried to mutter that it was nothing really, but inside he felt a warm, glowing sense of achievement.

'What about the gowns, though? And why here?' he said, expecting Peter to deflate.

'Never mind about them, lad. Real progress. You have a brain in that noggin of yours, you really do.'

They looked again at the lists. Surely the murderer must be on the Art and Architecture list? And, maybe, also from Trinity, or else why had there been a Trinity gown in the chest? That still left a whole plethora of options. There were thirty-one names of men who had at least on one occasion come on the expeditions, and nineteen were from Trinity. And as Richard rather disconsolately said, the man who had made the list had told him there might have been more, but he didn't keep any records, these were just the men he could remember.

So, Burgess, Telmann, Price and Noakes went to the top of the pile. Still, it was a big task to unravel. Little by little, as Peter said. And we have our next move clear. We shall attend the Caius Chemistry group in two days' time and see what we shall see.

The next day's Chemistry lecture and demonstration was held in a lecture-room in Wollaston's old college, Trinity Hall. Richard had never been in there before, so that was interesting in itself. It was a small college, overshadowed by Trinity, Clare Hall and Caius. And it fronted onto the river which meant that it smelt unwholesomely.

However, that was nothing compared to the odours that emanated from the apparatus as Professor Wollaston demonstrated the production of sulphur, and its reactions. One man seated too near the front collapsed and had to be removed to fresher air, upon which all the windows were thrown wide open before the demonstration recommenced.

This proved to be a useful illustration of the hazards of chemical compounds, and Professor Wollaston waxed lyrical over the tiny amounts of sulphur oxide, which Mr Priestley had called 'vitriolic acid air', or hydrogen sulphide, first described by Ramazzini as 'sewer gas', that might kill a man. This was not much comfort to the poor victim of his experiment, however, who had been left with sore eyes and a painful-sounding cough. The other uses of sulphur were described, and Richard felt the most important of these surely must be in the manufacture of black powder, or gun-powder, especially with the war having restarted, even though it had not ignited into any actual battles as yet.

Given their location in a panelled college lecture-room, however, most of the listeners were disappointed that no actual explosions were demonstrated. The Professor did show how spirits were tested for strength, the 'proof' of which was that gunpowder would still burn if soaked in a spirit of adequate concentration of alcohol.

Understandably, the Caius discussion group the following day was centred on black powder, including the production of a small explosion with a sample, which was most satisfactory. One man had spent time in the Army and explained how bothersome it was to tear open the cartridge, sprinkle some powder into the pan by the flint, pour the rest into the barrel and follow it up by ramming the ball into place with the paper wrapping serving as wadding. 'There surely must be a better way of doing things,' he said, 'even our best men can only manage four shots a minute, and with the new rifles only two.'

It seemed that the accuracy of the rifles outweighed the slower rate of firing, but that there must be some improvements that men of ingenuity could devise. 'And then we would put Boney to flight in one fell swoop,' he opined.

'When was black powder invented?' asked someone else.

'Centuries ago,' said someone. 'In China, or India, or some such exotic place.'

'So why has nobody made anything better?'

'Ask Wollaston, not me.'

'The man before him, before Wollaston, I don't remember his name, he did some work on gunpowder, I heard.'

'You mean Richard Watson? He was ages ago, just after the King came to the throne. But he didn't change the formula, it was just improvements in manufacture, I believe.'

'Oh, I see.'

After the meeting broke up, Peter and Richard spoke with the convenor, one John Eames, Richard recalled from his lists. He professed himself delighted to receive visitors, and hoped he might be welcomed at the Emmanuel group if he could find the time. He seemed to have a fair knowledge of Professor Wollaston's activities, although he said the University had not provided him with adequate rooms or equipment.

'What is he working on for his own researches?' asked Peter.

'He will not say. He brushes one off, like a spider, if one asks. I suspect it is because he hopes to make his fortune with some new discovery: you know his brother has become most wealthy from South American ores? But he is quite open about anything else. He says that he was able to learn all his chemistry in one year, and so we ought to be able to comprehend it in similar fashion. But I must say much of it is obscure to me.'

Richard thought it would be less embarrassing to show his ignorance here than at Emmanuel. 'May I ask, please, could you explain exactly what is an element?'

'Well yes, er, I can. I think. It is something that is not divisible into anything else. Yes.'

'Like, water?'

112

'No, not like water. That can be made to become oxygen and hydrogen. By electrical means. I believe. But sulphur, that is an element. And carbon. And many others.'

At least this man did not seem certain of his knowledge, thought Richard. That makes me feel better. Although I would like to know more, but perhaps I can read about it.

'Professor Wollaston does have some intriguing substances in his laboratory, I must say. I visited it once last year; it is in the Botanic Gardens, off Slaughterhouse-lane. He has a store of black viscid liquids, whose nature I cannot guess at. And flasks with solutions of all kinds of colours, most beautiful. I should like to keep some such on my windowsill to catch the sunlight. And great numbers of vessels containing powders with labels some of which carry arcane symbols, which I suspect are from the days of alchemy.'

'And black powder?'

'Assuredly so. Bags and bags of it, and sulphur, and saltpetre, and charcoal for the manufacture of the powder. I wonder he does not suffer an explosion when he is experimenting.'

On the walk back to college Peter and he discussed the men whom they had met. Neither had detected anything suspicious, and none of their Trinity quartet had been present, which was disappointing. However, as Peter said, most of his work involved negative results, it was important to persist, and eventually, with luck, something would become clearer. Which meant, he said, that one of them, by which he meant Richard, should join the next expedition to view paintings, which he had been told by Charlie was to take place that Saturday, a visit to Wimpole Hall, a ride of some ten miles.

'You can ride, I suppose, Richard?'

'Indeed, I practised when I was supervising my brother Charles at Kilcott last year. I can canter very well, and gallop if there are no obstacles.'

'Excellent. I forgot when I was planning that you might not have used a . . . no, I should not say when we can be overheard.'

113

'Indeed you should not!' Richard punched him on the shoulder. 'Shame on you, call yourself an intel . . . Oh, now I'm doing it!'

They walked a little further. 'But why is it to be me to investigate the Art-lovers? Surely you would be better placed to notice whatever it is that needs noticing?'

Peter had the grace to look slightly embarrassed. 'Ah, yes, well, actually, I might be more, er, experienced, as you say, but it is a matter of my studies. What with chasing around Scotland, I am severely behind with my Greek and my mathematics, and my tutor was most uncomplimentary when I first met him. I have to do a good deal of reading to catch up. Much as I would like to visit Earl Hardwicke's collection, other matters take priority.'

'Oh. I see. All the better for me, then.' He saw a group of rowdy men passing and remembered: 'Now, another thing. I should have said earlier but I forgot. I have seen my brother Charles in Cambridge, a most unfortunate occurrence.'

'Your brother?'

'Yes, my twin.'

'Is he an identical twin?'

Richard gave him his best Look, and simply waited.

Peter stopped too, and looked puzzled. 'Well, is he?'

Richard raised one eyebrow in the best of fashions. 'I thought you were a man of learning, Peter. Think, man!'

Peter's face went through puzzlement, dawning realisation and self-castigation. 'Oh. Yes, of course. I see. Bacon-brain,' and they recommenced their progress.

'The thing is,' Richard continued, 'Charles was consorting with University types, including our friend Mr Burgess, which means I am far more likely to come across him again, and he see me before I can avoid him, and he is bound to recognise me, and then I am undone.' They passed under the entrance to Emmanuel and nodded to the porter.

'Why is he here?'

'I don't know. Last I saw of him he was getting drunk with those lads at that ball I went to.'

'What ball?'

'Tuh! I've already told you about it. Might I remind you in private once we reach your rooms?' They ascended into the Founder's building accordingly.

Richard furrowed his brow. 'I haven't seen you for weeks, Peter, and you were very uncommunicative at your mother's. You gave Julia and me the cut most of the time you were there. Only when you realised we had discovered the lead ball and the hiding place of the rifleman did you acknowledge us.'

'I'm sorry, I have been very preoccupied since before Christmas.'

'That is no excuse, but I will let it pass.' Richard realised he had started relating to Peter as if he were Rose, and shook his head to clear it of the error. He went over to Peter's cabinet and poured himself some whisky without asking, to help him get back into his proper frame of mind as a man and his equal.

'That's better. Now look, this is how it was.'

He reminded Peter how he had mentioned the men when he told him about the business with Julia being made drunk, and that he must have forgotten all about who was with her, which wasn't like him. Peter denied a lapse of memory, or said it was just that the names had slipped his mind for the moment. Richard then explained about the discoveries he had made, that while Jacob Mackenzie lived as he pleased, John Smart was up at Caius though doing little work; and James Eldridge had a place at Exeter College in Oxford, where, Peter might wish to know, he had discovered that Lady John Barnes had intended to spend Christmas staying with the Rector.

'It was Charlie who told me the rest of this, you know. He was there too, in the drinking race.' Light dawned. 'And he is one of the intelligencers, is he not? So he was there keeping an eye on the likely lads, was he not? And does he not know Julia?'

Peter looked a little crestfallen. 'He does not. Or, he did not. And

115

he is most contrite, both that he did not protect her, and that he became much too disguised to carry out his task effectively. Whatever mischief they were up to did not become apparent to him. Indeed he spent two days indisposed after the event.' He paused to think. 'Why is Lady John staying with a clergyman? It is not her style one whit.'

'Rector is the title of the Master of Exeter College, I am informed: it is not a sign of ordination. Though I suppose he might be ordained too, so many academics are. Also, it would seem to me likely that if the traitors have been operating in the university in Cambridge they have a similar aim in view in the Other Place? Hmm?'

'They do. Though I am not party to the details. And, so I am told, it is possible that both groups or gangs are connected. Yes.'

'Are conditions at Oxford similar to those here? Are the same subjects studied?'

'They are far less inclined to Mr Newton there; there is more emphasis on Divinity and Humanities. But there is quite as little studying done, and as much hunting and drinking and, as I have intimated to you before, fighting and whoring.'

'Hmm. And what about other activities you know about? I think you ought to tell me, in case there might be other links.'

Peter pursed his lips, and seemed to be in two minds.

'Come on, it's not as if I'm going to blab any secrets, man.'

'Very well. I am not in possession of the full picture, mind, but then, nobody is. So, I was up in Scotland investigating the activities of people whom I might describe as "Neo-Jacobites" since the word they use for themselves is in Gaelic and unpronounceable. They have links to the "Society of United Irishmen" who were involved in the uprising there five years ago.'

'Sorry, I hadn't heard of that. I was in Nova Scotia at the time, you see.'

'Very droll. Anyway, I could not find out very much, other than a few names of their supporters, people who donate money to the cause, you know; and that they had connections in Lancashire with

Catholic families. And also with the French, who of course sent troops to Ireland for the recent rebellion, though of course it was fortunately unsuccessful.'

'So these Jacobite coves might well want the French to succeed in defeating us in Europe so they could have another go at getting King George replaced with a king of their choice; and the Irish want an independent Ireland, of course, which they believe would be hastened by our weakness.'

'You are quick on the uptake, as usual.'

'Any links to Cambridge?'

'Not directly. Other than that one of the Lancashire families my colleagues are interested in is closely related to one Mr John Burgess, scholar of Trinity College. And generally suspicious person.'

'Now that *is* interesting. Is there anything else you could tell me?'

'I don't think so.'

'Then I have a different question for you. Why do people commit murder?'

'Motives? Many reasons. There is drunken brawling, and political assassination, and, well, they say the commonest is love, or lust perhaps, or sexual jealousy, I believe. And for gain, money that is, and revenge, and to keep someone from talking, say if someone is being blackmailed. And some people just like killing, I think. Mostly those fellows join the Army, though, where their penchant is sanctioned.' He thought for a moment. 'There must be other reasons, I suppose.'

'Let me write these ones down, hold on for a moment, do you have paper and ink?'

Richard scratched away busily. 'Thanks. I'll have a think about these things. And I'll keep a look out for them, though how you see a motive, I don't know. You can't just recognise one in the street, can you?'

On Saturday morning a letter was waiting for Richard, having arrived by the college post. It was from Hugh Sterne, asking him to call at Caius at his convenience, as something odd had occurred. Richard left early after breakfast, since he could combine the trip with the rendezvous at the stables nearby, that had been arranged for those setting off to Wimpole Hall to view the paintings and other marvels.

Mr Sterne held out a gown to him when he arrived. 'See this? David Paine found it lying on a staircase yesterday, though it might have been there some little while I suppose.'

Richard inspected it. 'This is a Caius gown, I imagine? So why did he give it to you?'

'Indeed, one of our own. But look inside the collar.'

Richard inspected it. There, clearly written, were the initials PS. 'Not Stephens' gown, surely?' he exclaimed.

'The very same. I would know it anywhere. You recall, he was a most punctilious man, all his possessions were marked in this way.'

'So how did it get there, and why now?'

'I have no idea, none at all.'

'Was it on this stair, where he lived?'

'No, in a different building entirely.'

'So, when do you think it might have got there?'

'I should say within the last day, surely? Otherwise the bedder would have taken it up.'

'Curious. Since Stephens is in no condition to abandon his gown, it must have been put there by . . . well, his murderer? Seems a very odd thing to do. And why the delay?'

'Indeed.'

Richard asked Mr Sterne to hold on to the gown until he returned from Wimpole; he thought he ought to show it to Peter. Meanwhile he had to get himself horsed and off with his new companions.

CHAPTER 9

PETER WINTON HAD ARRANGED FOR Richard to join the group by invitation of Charlie French, who was a regular on these trips, so he made sure to greet him as soon as he arrived at the stable in St John's-lane, and ask him a few questions about the four-oar to establish his *bona fides* with the others on the expedition. He was given a rather spirited mare to ride, but managed to mount and wheel out of the stable without catastrophe, and hold up the horse in order to wait for the others. He hoped his relative inexperience with riding astride would not show him up, not so much fear that his disguise would be penetrated as concern he would lose face before fellow-undergraduates.

Fortunately there were enough men of limited horsemanship for him to fall in with, leaving the hunting types to forge ahead. He was able to talk with several as they made steady progress, first negotiating the Small Bridges and then striking out past Newnham village towards Grantchester, and by fields and small muddy roads to the Roman road that led to their goal. They found a few places to canter for a short way, but he was quite glad nobody seemed to want to break into a gallop, as his thigh muscles felt under strain as it was.

Louis Price was one of these conversation partners: Richard felt a frisson of excitement as he made his acquaintance and wondered just what he might have been doing on the day of the murder. He was a small man, shorter than himself, Richard thought, although it was hard to judge on horseback; and he had a short and irregular dark beard. Though a keen huntsman, he was with the slower group because he was friendly with another Frenchman at Trinity called Christian Martin, who rode somewhat nervously, and they talked for most of the time about the famous collections of the Hardwickes. Richard unsurprisingly learnt more about the first Earl's paintings, the second Earl's books and manuscripts, and the present Earl's architectural projects, than he did about Price and Martin's political or religious views. He did risk a question about how long they had been in the country, and it seemed that both families had been resident for some thirty or more years, and so the men had been born here.

He noticed Charlie was riding with John Burgess, and thought it best to leave them alone, in case Charlie was sounding out one of their suspects, but more because he felt most uncomfortable around Burgess. Instead he moved on a little and fell into conversation with a man by the name of Ebenezer Harmour, who was only too pleased to talk at length about the people in the society, which Richard hoped would be profitable. He had a certain aloofness of manner, quite dismissive even when saying the most ordinary things, and pale blue eyes that seemed to look right through you. Richard felt rather out of his depth in his presence, but felt he ought to get to know him.

After Richard asked if most of the men in the party were from Trinity, Harmour explained that he wasn't a member of the University himself, but lived in Cambridge and was welcomed into certain groups because he had 'connections'. He wouldn't elaborate further, but went on to talk about all those within the group with whom he was acquainted. After checking that Richard knew John Burgess – 'but then, everyone knows the Burge' – he mentioned Matthew Noakes in a most disparaging way, saying he was prone to toady to those whom he thought could advance him, and then drop them if he thought he would no longer benefit. Mr Burgess, he said, was quite antagonistic to Noakes at present: it was most entertaining when they were together, though this would not be one of these days as Mr Noakes had sensibly stayed in college.

He also knew Louis Price and Christian Martin, and said it was outrageous that Frenchmen were allowed to study at the University, and that they all ought to be interned for the duration of hostilities, and Richard cringed internally at this, while hoping Mr Price and Mr Martin were out of hearing.

Harmour expressed himself more interested to see the famous Yellow Drawing Room and Bath House than the paintings, though he had heard there were some very good landscapes as well as the usual family portraits. Also, the landscaping by Capability Brown, and the lake with its Chinese Bridge. Richard, thinking he ought to contribute to the conversation, asked if he had heard of the murder in Emmanuel, judging that this topic ought not to be too inflammatory with a man who was not an undergraduate.

Mr Harmour had not only heard of it, he had great interest in hearing all the details, asking about the appearance of the corpse, and the method of murder, and how those who found it had reacted. Richard, surprised by his enthusiasm, omitted the information that it had been he who had discovered the body, and limited himself to a superficial description of the injuries, and the embarrassment caused to the college, and the difficulty in getting anyone to investigate the crime, falling as it did between University, College and Town. He also mentioned nothing concerning the matter of the gowns, feeling this was his own special preserve.

When Richard asked about the rest of the members of the group, he looked around and said that the other three in their party were unknown to him, but that he had seen John Smart and Jake Mackenzie with the faster party, together with several names Richard did not recognise and could not of course note down while on horseback. The thrill of recognition was tempered with anxiety about how to ask about these two without revealing his particular interest.

'Are all those men undergraduates too, or are any, like you, interested Cambridge residents?' he eventually managed.

'Only Mackenzie is a visitor, he's a good old clinker. Fearless, always up for a jape, tops with the barking-irons, a real buck.'

'I'm sorry, I'm from Nova Scotia, I don't follow?'

'Only that he's the sort of man you'd want by you when you're setting out for a mill with the bargees, or shooting the hats off swells as they strut around. Crack shot at long range too, terrific on a snipe shoot.'

'I see, a bit of a daredevil and a sportsman?'

'Indeed. We were at a cockfight only last week, and he leapt into the ring and bit the head off the gamebird that was beating his fancy. Had to pay off all sorts of bets for the deed, but it was great sport.'

Richard shuddered inside, but kept quiet. 'Jake Mackenzie? I think I've heard that name somewhere. Yes, from Charlie French,' he pointed, 'I row in a four-oar with him, I think he said he saw him at a ball in London, getting a girl foxed?'

'I heard about that too, typical Jake. Seems that some interfering chit took her off somewhere, fetched her mother too, before Jake could get up her skirts. Shame.'

'Oh, well, um, I see.'

'Wish I'd been there, joining in the deflowering, but I don't stray much from Cambridge, generally. Can get a bit hot for me in Town, too many men out to settle scores.'

Richard gulped, but was saved from answering by Harmour continuing,

'Still, plenty of fun to be had here. But you'll be thinking me quite uncultured, lad. Look, you can see over there, the Hall coming into view. You'll have to excuse me, I'm going to run over and take a look at that lake and its bridge that I mentioned, before we all get herded round the rooms. Housekeeper's a tartar, I've heard,' and he spurred his horse, and vanished in quick order.

At the house the faster riders joined them from the lake, their horses were taken by grooms, and then once they had changed their boots the housekeeper greeted them. She seemed quite a capable woman, as was only to be expected in such a responsible position, but her manner hardly fitted Ebenezer's description. There were about sixteen visitors, but she had a couple of footmen to assist her, which Richard thought was farsighted, as some of the men were quite boisterous.

First they visited the Entrance Hall and then the famous Yellow Drawing Room. Richard was quite overwhelmed with its height, its grandeur and opulence. Indeed he quite lost track of where he was in the house, it was all so magnificent. Somehow, though, he didn't feel it was quite to his taste, especially the chapel with its grandiose views and tromp-l'oeil statuary. There were endless imposing portraits of the Earls and other family members, and Classical allegories of all types, but he thought about his poor little Meer that had been hacked to bits and wondered if the Earl had anything of that nature amid all the sumptuousness.

One painting that took his eye was a very dark picture, with the subject matter illuminated by a light on the table. There was a collection of glassware, and a flame licking over one flask; the audience seemed to be recoiling from what might be a noxious gas emanating from the apparatus. There was a label: Joseph Wright of Derby was the artist, and the title 'Some Chemical Experiments'. He wondered if Professor Wollaston's laboratory looked anything like this, but he probably did his work in daylight hours, he imagined.

He was most wary of Burgess, especially after the man leaned over as he was admiring a classical scene with dancing nudes, and murmured in his ear that he too was a fine-looking bantling, and deuced pretty; before sloping off without pressing his point, whatever that might have been.

It didn't seem sensible to try and question anyone while they were looking around, but he did manage to identify Jake Mackenzie, and made a comment to him about the handsomeness of one of the portraits, to which he replied sensibly that the portraitist had surely omitted that Earl's blemishes in order to earn his fee. John Smart tended to circulate with Jake, and Richard made sure he would recognise both men again if he saw them in different circumstances, hoping that he had not at the same time made himself conspicuous.

He noticed the two footmen were fully occupied in keeping the group together, and preventing the men handling priceless objects, and changed his view about the character of the housekeeper when he saw how she dealt with an errant undergraduate who had tried to penetrate into the private quarters, whether in error or by design he could not tell. However, when he approached her while in the gallery, to enquire if there were other pictures, ones that might be described as more domestic scenes, she was affability itself, and showed him to a small cabinet where there were some paintings that, being out of the fashion, were no longer displayed in the main receiving rooms.

'These are my favourites, sir. Nobody takes notice of them, and I hear the Earl may be selling them to make more space, but they're more comfortable-like, to my way of thinking, than those big pictures.'

She pointed to a small darkish sea scene. 'That's the coast of Holland; I wouldn't like to have been in one of those boats in that storm, I can tell you. But I think you can see the water moving, even though it's just paint. And this one, it's by Van Eyck, it's just a portrait of some man, but look at how he's caught his expression. And here's a street scene, I don't know who painted this one, it's not signed, but there's so much going on, I keep coming back to look when I have a spare moment.'

Richard took a long, hard look at the scene. There were some narrow gabled houses, and a canal or river in front; the brickwork was curiously ornate and the sky full of scudding clouds. It had a jewel-like quality, the wet tiles and cobbles gleamed brightly, it was so detailed, it was truly lovely. He carefully scanned the surface, and then he saw it. Faintly, on a wall, was the word "Meer" with an arrowhead on the left foot of the M. Surely it was the same painter as his destroyed treasure?

'Do you truly not know the painter?' he asked, voice trembling.

'No, sir, I'm sorry, I don't. Master might, of course, but he's away.'

Richard was so excited, he found himself imagining buying the painting, of having it for himself, hanging it on his wall. But then reality hit, it would be far out of his reach, his purse. He could never aspire to own anything in this place. But then, maybe, just maybe, if it was so out of the fashion . . .

'Would you be told if there was to be a sale, madam?' he asked. 'I should be most anxious to attend, if so.'

'Certainly, sir. I should have to make the arrangements for the occasion. And it would be notified in the Cambridge papers, of course.'

Richard dragged himself away from the Meer, hoping he had not neglected his main purpose too much, but resolving to be assiduous in reading the local news from then on. He rejoined the group who were finishing off their tour in the Library, having politely admired the second Earl's manuscripts, and gazed across the park with its vistas and avenues.

And then back to Cambridge, this time mostly in the company of Charlie, Louis and Christian. Richard spoke little, preferring to listen to Charlie discussing the war with the others, and discovered that they had little sympathy with Napoleon, a great deal of admiration for Vice-Admiral Nelson after Copenhagen, and a wish for peace to return so that they could on graduating, further their business interests. There was just something about how they spoke, Richard felt, that didn't ring true. Their praise was just a little too fulsome, their manner did not quite match their words. Or so he thought. But then, surely he was no judge, he was only a beginner in the intelligence game.

Perhaps he did have one advantage over Charlie, and Peter for that matter. He was a girl, and girls he had found were often far better at seeing what men just looked past blindly. So, if he had the chance, he would ask Charlie what he thought about the two Frenchmen, and then consider. Privately, that is. And then he would have to go back to his lists and rewrite them. Especially, to include Ebenezer Harmour, and his high-living friends Jake and John.

*

The next thing, thought Richard as he sat over his papers that evening, is to see if there is any connection between these fellows he'd just met and the Chemistry people. Because, as Peter had said when he visited to show him Stephens' gown that had reappeared in Caius, it was more likely that French spies would be more interested in explosions than hunting or works of Art or Architecture. And Professor Wollaston had reportedly much gunpowder stored in his laboratory, so who knows what other useful substances he might have? Although how this could relate to the death of Stephens in Emmanuel Chapel was utterly obscure. And he may be, they all may be, looking in the wrong places: not everything untoward had to be a Napoleonic plot.

He inscribed the names of Harmour, Mackenzie and Smart to the list of those involved in all of hunting, chemistry and Art, and then remembered Christian Martin, so he added him as a friend of Price. There were just too many names, he couldn't see where to go next. He hadn't been out with the hunting boys, and he really didn't want to. He'd not fit in with that company at all, and they'd try and get him to drink heavily, and he'd have to refuse, and it would all be dreadful. And he would quite like to visit Professor Wollaston's laboratory, but he didn't see how he could, without seeming most out of character for a new undergraduate. What reason could he give?

But perhaps . . . if he could organise an official visit from one of the discussion groups? Or better, if Peter could, because he had more standing as leader of the Emmanuel society. Then they could at least see what was going on there, get some ideas. And then, maybe, see if there was anything that any Napoleonic sympathisers might want to find out about?

Almost immediately he squashed his own idea. Why did it have to be Frenchmen, anyway? It was probably something else entirely, something Stephens had said or done that had outraged someone, or maybe there was an insulted paramour who had arranged a revenge. He hadn't known the man, and he couldn't speak to his parents, wherever they were, it was all so unsatisfactory. And what was that noise coming from below, while he was trying to think? Was it from Edward's rooms? He got up and went to find out, thinking he had been shamefully neglecting Edward of late, and maybe he had spent too long on this puzzle.

Edward's room seemed to be full of men, with his table covered in bottles of assorted sizes and unknown contents, a few half-empty glasses indicating that at least some of them had contained beer and others port or other wine. Most of the glasses though were in the process of being emptied down gullets, though a few, and also many bottles, lay upon the floor surrounded by little pools of their previous contents. Richard recoiled as he opened the door, it was so like unpleasant scenes he had witnessed at balls when in his feminine form. But, he told himself, you are Richard, this is quite safe for you, nobody is going to impugn your virtue. Or make ribald remarks about your person, or, well, anything else. Nonetheless he hesitated. He almost went back upstairs and locked his oak, but then steeled himself and plunged into the fray.

Edward was certainly there. His voice was upraised in a drinking song made unidentifiable by his lack of musical ear, and the uncoordinated accompaniment of his other companions. Richard thought it might have been something about a sailor, and involving seduction of some sort, but it was hard to tell. He was clearly enjoying himself thoroughly bellowing out the words, and refreshing himself at frequent intervals with ale.

Just as Richard was deciding to make his exit and leave the jolly lads to it, Edward caught sight of him, and breaking off in mid-stanza hailed him heartily.

'Rich, me old shipmate, where've you been all these hours? Catch up a flagon, haul in a chair and make merry!'

'Er, hello Edward. Um, having a good time?'

'The best. Trusty Trouts and assorted others,' he gestured expansively to the room.

Richard cast his gaze around. There were men in all states of inebriation sitting or lying on every surface it seemed, and that one with his eyes closed . . . Oh no, was that not Charles? Brother Charles?

He caught up the nearest bottle and held it to his mouth to cover his face. It was disgusting, even though he only swallowed a small mouthful.

'That's Stingo you've got, that's the best one, top pick me old hearty.'

Richard, flagon still to his mouth, turned his back and made as speedy an exit as he could with the crush, not even pausing to put down his beer. He fled up to his room and locked his oak, leant against it and breathed heavily. What was Charles doing in Edward's room? And, more to the point, how had Edward met him? And, what might he have said about himself, Richard? His brain buzzed with questions. What if Charles had said he was the brother of an old boy of Emmanuel, Sir George Clarke? And then, what if Edward had mentioned he was friends with Sir George's cousin? And then Charles would profess no knowledge of the cousin, and want to meet him. And then of course, disaster. Disaster on all fronts. What to do indeed?

He tried to calm down, put his unwanted beer on the floor by the hearth, sat in his chair, tried to think. He could just hide until the men had dispersed, but then the longer he left the pair of them together, the worse - if he had not already been undone. He could leave college altogether, and then Charles wouldn't see him . . . but where would he go? The only place he knew outside of the University here was Peter's home in Milton. And they knew him as Rose, of course. Help! Quick thinking was called for, and he was so overcome with anxiety he couldn't string one sensible thought to another.

Peter, though. Perhaps he could ask him for help? He was a man of resource, calm, sensible, and he knew his secret. Of course.

Putting on his hat so it partly covered his face he cautiously opened his door and peered out. Nobody around. He descended the stair as quietly as he could, careful of the treads that squeaked, and especially careful outside Edward's room. Then, once safely past, raced down the next two flights and out into the Close. And to Founder's Court, praying that Peter would be in.

He was, praise the Lord! Richard opened the door at Peter's word, threw himself onto Peter's couch, and tried to speak calmly, without it must be said, much success.

'Please, you've got to help me,' he began, 'It's Charles, he's in Edward's room, and I don't know what to do.'

'Charlie? Why the uproar?'

'No, not Charlie French; Charles. Charles Clarke. My brother. My twin brother, Peter. In Edward's room. Drunk and asleep, fortunately, I think. I hope. But he'll have said things to Edward and Edward to him and they'll know about me, I mean Richard, being here, but Charles doesn't know about Richard, of course, and they'll find out about Rose and then I'm finished.'

'Calm down, Richard. Well, sorry, silly thing to say, nobody in the history of calming down has ever calmed down by being told to calm down. But just hold hard, let me think.' He sat down in his chair and toyed with his quill. 'What you're saying is, that Charles will say he's the brother of Sir George Clarke, who was at this college, and then Edward will say, Oh, I know Sir George's cousin Richard, and then Charles will want to see you . . . and will of course recognise you, and then . . .'

'Yes, yes, yes. And then I will be thrown out of college and it'll be all awful.'

Peter stood up, and began to pace. 'You just sit there, lad, I'll think of something.' He consulted his pocket watch, he went over to the window and opened it, put his head out. The sounds of revelry were quite clear across the orchard. Closing it, he asked, 'Do you have your feminine attire with you in college?' and on receiving a negative, continued to pace.

'Are most of the men in his room undergraduates, do you suppose?' he asked as he walked.

'I don't know, but there were a few gowns lying on the window-seat. And Edward said several of them were Trusty Trouts, which are his drinking friends from the Eagle and Child, and other taverns, I think Magdalene and Caius men mostly. And Trinity. Yes, some of the gowns were blue now I come to think of it, not that I was really noticing, you know, what with, well, the shock and everything. But they could be Caius ones, of course, I'm forgetting.'

'I've noticed you notice things, lad, and very useful it is.'

A few minutes later, he halted and wagged a finger. 'I think I have it. It's now, what, just before ten o'clock, and everyone has to be in their colleges before eleven or be in the late book and risk a fine. Yes?'

'Of course.'

'Except, Charles not being an undergraduate, doesn't need to obey those rules, but then he shouldn't be *in* a college after eleven either.' He broke off. 'Do you know where he is staying?'

'Nary an idea.'

'No matter. So, the first thing is to get the other lushes out of college, and then, convey Charles to his lodging, if he can remember where it is, of course. And finally, discover what Edward knows of Charles, and then impress upon him that Charles is not a good person to know, because . . . well, I shall think of something. And threaten him with . . . I don't know what. Tell me, is Edward good at keeping secrets?'

'Not one whit. He means to, but then when he drinks he loses discretion. Remember how James Smith found out about the Pink Houses business last term, and then tricked him away to be taken onto the barge?'

'Of course. Right. It will have to be quite a threat then. So, first, I shall go and engage the assistance of the porters to break up the party, saying that Mr Griffith, being disturbed, insists the noise is curtailed. You stay here. I shall lock my door, you'll be fine. And help yourself to my whisky if you wish.' With that he was gone.

Over half an hour passed, during which Richard first paced, then sat chewing his nails, then gave in and poured a large measure of whisky and sipped it guiltily. Then paced again, looked out of the window, and finally took down a volume from Peter's shelves and stared at it sightlessly.

The sound of a key in the lock brough him to his feet again. 'How did it go?' he asked, before Peter had even got through the door.

'Hold hard, lad, let me get in. It went well, so far as it has gone. Mr Dean, Mr Chapman and I escorted eleven men from college, some of whom required assistance from their friends to stand, and having had a brain-wave on the way to the Porter's Lodge, I asked Mr Dean to establish the name and college of all the miscreants before turning them into the street, on the pretext that their tutors needed to be informed of their misbehaviour.' He brandished a paper. 'And here is the list.'

'And Charles?'

'Ah, yes. Charles. He was quite unrousable, I am afraid to say. Dean and Chapman had to carry him across the court to the small room they have set aside for such overenthusiastic young gentlemen to sober up, and will keep him there until I can visit him tomorrow, early.'

'I never knew there was such a room.'

'Nor I. They call it the Royal Suite, though it resembles nothing so much as a cell in the workhouse.'

'Oh.'

'He will be quite safe, you know. They check on their visitors every hour or so, and there is a pot, and blankets.'

'And Edward?'

'Ah, Edward. Most unhappy about his revels being curtailed, I am afraid. Quite maudlin in fact. He swung at me, so incensed did he become, and of course being foxed, he missed, fell over his table and cracked his head. He will also be sleeping in tomorrow I suspect. I took the precaution of abstracting his keys and locking his door until I can interview him after visiting Charles.'

131

'Oh, Peter, you've been wonderful! I'm so grateful to you.' He went to give him a hug, then thought better of it, then carried on anyway.

'What are friends and allies for? You have done so much for me too, you know. And now we have another list to add to your others, this one being potential confederates who know Charles.'

'You can't think Charles is mixed up in the murder, can you? Surely he isn't that stupid? Or wicked?'

'I don't know. But let's compare the lists, shall we?'

He went to his box, unlocked it and spread the papers on the table.

'Hmmm. We have Mr John Smart of Caius in this new list, I see. And Mr Christian Martin of Trinity too. Most interesting. But I think I need to establish which ones of these are just Edward's usual, Trusty Trouts did you call them? And which are newly added to the party. And those presumably are the men who came across Charles and included him in the group. We'd best leave this till tomorrow. And get to bed, I'll be seeing Charles by six: I think I'll have to cut chapel.'

CHAPTER 10

PETER JOINED RICHARD FOR BREAKFAST after chapel, and settled himself to eat before he'd discuss anything, much to Richard's frustration. He looked satisfied with himself, though, which gave Richard some comfort in his anxiety. Of course he hadn't slept well, and had spent the whole of the chapel service willing it to finish, and now could only pick at his rolls. Eventually, Peter wiped his mouth after finishing his chocolate, and pulled out the lists.

'So, my lad, this morning has been most illuminating. Your brother is quite a mine of information, all unknowing. When I went to see him I passed myself off as a constable from the town, investigating drunken misbehaviour in the taverns. He was most sorry for himself, with as you would imagine a thick head and a queasy stomach. He kept repeating something like, "Bloody Stingo", and vowing never to touch it again.'

'That's right. He got dreadfully drunk on that beer in Bath last year, and there was some in Edward's room last night.'

'Anyway, he moaned and groaned but eventually told me that he had been drinking in the Eagle and Child with Smart and Martin, and then Edward and his crowd joined them and things got a bit lively; and somehow they repaired to Emmanuel carrying a large number of bottles which had appeared from somewhere, he knew not where, and were supplemented he thought from the college's buttery, as he was required to contribute to the expense. And then there was great merriment and banter, until he found himself so drowsy that he fell dead asleep and missed all the rest of the fun. And he said he hadn't done anything wrong, and what was this all about.'

'I see.'

'No, but you haven't heard the best bit. He said, when I pressed him about why they had come here, to Emmanuel I mean, that he had heard some of the men were from this college, so he had said,'

'That would be Edward and I guess Will Peabody.' Richard interrupted.

'Yes, but to continue, he had said, why didn't they go back to Edward's rooms to carry on the party, he fancied visiting the college again. He'd been here before once, for a lark, and he wouldn't mind going there again. So I asked him what was the lark, and he said he'd quite liked the idea of having a fancy gown like the other men he'd been going around with, and someone said he could have one to wear if he'd go to Emmanuel and leave it in the chapel on a hook, and take another blue one he'd find in a box in a little room off the lobby, and come back wearing it, and he had. But then he'd been bawled out by the chap who dared him to do it, he'd got the wrong gown or something, which was all baloney, but it had been sport to swank along the streets as if he was an academic cove, and worth it anyway.'

'Charles! It was he that took the Caius gown?'

'It seems so. And being an outsider, he wouldn't be able to tell it from a Trinity one, would he?'

'Of course not. Well, nor could we until the differences were pointed out to us. So, he took the Caius one to the chap who sent him on the errand, one of the men he'd been going around with, and got called out for it. And then that chap, after a little while, left it on a stair in Caius, so as to dispose of it, but he'd be still short of his own gown.'

'Indeed.'

'So now we know who sent him, the Trinity man, don't we?'

'You may well think so. But unfortunately not. Charles, being unobservant and unfamiliar with the colleges, only knew that he was in Trinity, because it had such a big court. He did not know which room he was in when he was assigned his task, not even the staircase. Nor, unsurprisingly, the man's name. Except that he was quite short and had a beard.'

'Louis Price!'

'Well, maybe. There may be many other short bearded men at Trinity.'

'Not on our lists, surely?'

'We shall see. Now, I also interrogated Edward, who was most put out at being confined to his room.'

'Did not Mr Fenn release him when he came to wake him?'

'I had the foresight to arrange for his gyp to forget to rouse him this morning. A small expense, to be sure.'

'And?'

'He was most contrite when he learned that he had been entertaining an enemy of the state.'

'Who?'

'Why, Charles of course.'

'But . . .'

'I know, but Edward does not know, and that is what matters. He of course is familiar with my role as an agent of His Majesty, because of last term's arrests. So if I say Charles is an enemy agent, then he will believe me.' He grinned at Richard. 'You know, he really is an accessory, even if unknowingly?'

'I suppose so.'

'Anyway, Edward says that he only met Charles last night in the Eagle for the first time; that he had hardly spoken a word to him, in fact he didn't know his name even. He only knew John Smart, from previous encounters in taverns, and that is how the two groups came together. All the other men were what he calls Trouts, only Charles, Smart and Martin were recent additions.'

'So, Charles is mixed up with the conspirators?'

'It seems so. I gave Edward a stern injunction not to associate with Charles if he came across him again, as being likely to prejudice his standing in the university. I think that hit home. I hope it did. So, you are undiscovered, Richard. Edward does not know who Charles is, and Charles, as far as I can see, does not know anything about Edward, except where he lives, or about anyone else on this staircase.'

'But my name is on the door post.'

'Not your real name, remember. Just, Cox, R.'

Richard let out a breath that he hadn't known he was holding in. 'What a relief! Thankyou, thankyou so much, Peter. I just didn't know what to do when I saw him in Edward's room. I was in such a state.'

'Understandably. But you did know what to do, you came to me. You obviously couldn't have done any of this yourself without exposing your identity, so you sought help. One of the first rules of intelligence work is to know your limits. Call for help. Don't run unnecessary risks.'

Something struck Richard. 'What has happened to Charles?'

'I let him off with a stern warning about his behaviour, and he scuttled off to his lodgings, which are in St John's Lane, with someone who he has been traveling around with for a while, I didn't ask his name.'

'That sounds about right, he has a wide circle of acquaintances he sponges on, though it pains me to say so.'

'Very well then, what is our next move?'

Richard was taken aback. He hadn't considered doing anything more, this whole business had upset him too much. But Peter was right, they knew more, and could look more sensibly at what to do next. Except he hoped he wouldn't have to do it just yet, he was quite overset.

'If our identification is correct,' Peter continued, 'Price is clearly in the plot, if I may call it that, and involved Charles to retrieve his gown. And from what you told me when you came back from Wimpole, his friend, what was his name?'

'Martin.'

'Martin, yes, he might be in it too, since he was consorting with Charles last night. And if Martin is in with Smart, presumably Smart is one of them also. And perhaps Jake Mackenzie, because those two were together at that ball at Somerset House? Then there is Noakes, but I can't see what he might have been doing.'

'Don't forget James Eldridge, he was at the ball too, with the others.'

'Yes, but he is in Oxford, as far as we know.'

'We still don't know why Stephens was murdered, you know.'

'No, and who did it is equally obscure, though I wager it was one of the men we've just been talking about.'

'If he was taken to see the painting, it must have been someone he knew from the Art group?'

'Which is all of the men on our latest, rather long, list, of course.'

'Oh yes.' Richard's face fell.

'I think, you know, we should leave the murder for the moment, and see if we can find out if there is anything going on which might be attractive to French intelligencers.'

'Sorry?'

'Well, we know someone is trying to do something, I have to believe, with all this complicated business with the murder. It's not just a stabbing in the street, it was planned. Whoever it was took extreme pains to cover his tracks. So, something else must be behind it. I can't quite believe Stephens just happened to offend someone in the normal way, and they organised this whole farrago. There must be more to it.'

'What about looking into the hunting crowd?'

'I'll ask Charlie to nose around there, that's his line of country. But as for us, we need to get a way in to Professor Wollaston's laboratory, to whatever he might be doing there.'

'Oh yes. I had thought about this myself, but all this other business had put it out of my head. And as the men at Caius said, he's very secretive about it.'

'Indeed. But today being Sunday I think we shall have to wait before acting.'

Richard sighed in relief. Perhaps he could have a normal kind of day, listening to Mr Simeon, dining in Hall, reading his Principia. It would be so much more peaceful than the last few hours. But Peter continued,

'You aren't quite safe yet from Charles, you know. He is still in town, and he could turn up anywhere.'

'Oh.'

'So what I think is, you ought to keep to college in the hours of daylight, perhaps even to your room unless you are in Hall or chapel, and only go out after dark, when you will be less recognisable. And always go out with someone else even then. Except perhaps for your walks to Grantchester for tutorials, I suppose, if you leave directly across the Leys.'

'I can't imagine Charles doing that sort of exercise for fun. Though I suppose he might be shooting on the Leys, perhaps. But surely I can go to church? Charles is even less likely to darken the doors of Holy Trinity. And what about the fencing club?'

'But you would be vulnerable on the way there and back, would you not?'

'I suppose I would. But how long would this last? I need to be able to live my life, you know. Lectures, and rowing, and fencing, and socialising.'

'I don't know. I shall make enquiries at his lodgings: I took the address saying I might need to question him again.'

'You think of everything, Peter.'

'No, not at all. But you are getting to be very important to us, in the intelligence service, you know. We wouldn't want to waste your, er, special talents.'

Richard felt a warm glow in the bottom of his chest. He was a good old chap, Peter, really he was.

'Before you go, could I have a little more instruction with the pick-locks, please? Then I can practise while you are away.'

*

Just before lunchtime, a man knocked on his door. He said he had missed him at Holy Trinity that day, and hoped he was well. Also, he wanted to know how the investigation into his friend Philip's death was going, and he hoped it was in order to enquire.

Richard was rather taken aback, though touched by the man's concern. He invited him in and offered him a glass of wine or whisky while trying to both remember exactly who he was, and decide how much he could say, but the man declined refreshment. Richard had met so many new people in the last few weeks he had lost track of who many of them were, and without his lists he was floundering. Except this chap must of course be a Simeonite, he realised.

'How was the sermon today?' he temporised.

'Splendid, as always. He expounded Paul's letter to the Romans, chapter five. Concerning justification through faith, not through works. A powerful word.'

'I'm sorry I missed it.'

'Indeed. Now, I have been speaking to some of my friends at Caius, and we have heard of your continuing efforts to find who might have killed Philip. It is quite a sensation.'

Of course, this was one of the men who had pointed him to Hugh Sterne as Stephens' closest friend. Now he had it: he was Mr Danns. 'It is slow work, I'm afraid, Mr Danns. And we have so many names – if you recall, I was collecting names of Stephens' associates in your college and beyond – that to mention any would be rather unfair on the innocent, you see.' He paused, wondering if he ought to tell Danns about the solution of the problem of the gowns, and how the murderer had inveigled Stephens into Emmanuel chapel. 'I think,' he said slowly, 'that the fewer people who know about what I am doing the better. I don't want to be awkward, but I'm not any kind of official, obviously, and I don't want to upset people.'

'I see. But, do you feel you are closer to a solution than you were when we first realised who had been killed?'

139

'A little, maybe. But we still don't know why he was murdered, and whether there is more to it than a personal matter.'

'Philip was amiability itself,' Danns declared. 'Nobody could take offence at anything he said or did.'

'Really?'

'Well, yes. I mean, he might disagree with a chap over a point of theology, or knock into one as he walked past by accident, or spill a man's drink in Hall, but he was always most conciliatory and apologetic. He was such a good example of the Christian faith.'

'You know, I'd love to tell you more, and I think you have a right to know, once we have a solution, but I don't think I ought just now. I'm really sorry, you know. But I am pursuing the matter. As best I can, which I am afraid is not well enough to solve it.'

'I see. Well, if you could let us know anything, it might be that some of us at Caius could help you.'

'I know, you're absolutely right. But, equally, it might be someone at Caius who is guilty, and that would be most difficult for me if . . . well, if he knew about my actions.'

'I see. It could put you in danger, you mean. Well, I shall hope for more news in due time, sir. Good day.'

After he had left, Richard stood stock still for a while and worried. He lit a cigar and paced, then locking his oak behind him, went out and smoked the rest in the garden before, finding it far too cold for loitering, he threw the stub into the pond and made his way to Hall for some lunch. He needed to consult with Peter again.

He hadn't realised, though he ought to have, he really ought, that by going around and investigating this business, he would become a target of the gang, or person, that had arranged the murder. It wasn't just meeting Charles that was a danger if he went out of college, but meeting someone who wished him ill. And he didn't like that thought at all.

Peter wasn't in lunch, but Edward was, and he wasn't happy.

'Your merry-begotten friend Winton was giving me jaw this

morning, cub, and I'm not best pleased about him breaking up my party, you know. I'm thinking of complaining about it.'

'Er, who to?'

'Well, I don't know, someone. And he locked me in my room last night, made me miss chapel.'

'And you are much distraught about missing Divine Service? I understand completely.'

'Not one buck, noddy, but I will be in trouble with the college if I cut many more.'

'So what is it you are talking about? What happened to cause all this distress? I am quite in the dark.'

'Nothing at all. I just had a few friends round for a couple of drinks, and I don't say we were silent as the grave, but that was no call for old Griffith to send up the boys from the lodge to throw all my friends out. You were there, at least at one point, I think.' He shook his head, as if to clear his memory. 'Anyway, when the porters came a-spoiling for a fight, what was Winton doing there with them?'

Peter tapped him on the shoulder, having just come in. 'I was passing the Lodge, as I told you, and the porters requested my assistance to deal with the complaint from Mr Griffith as they were but two in number and you had quite a party of jolly lads.'

'Well, it's not fair. My Trouts will think I'm a Cock Robin, letting that happen to them.'

'Nice mixing of watery and avian metaphors, Edward,' said Richard mock-appreciatively. 'Meaning?'

'Gone soft, of course, cully. Don't you know anything?'

'Clearly not.' Richard paused to attend to his meal. 'Never mind,' he said with his mouth full, 'you'll get over it, I'm sure you'll still be welcome in the taverns by tomorrow.'

'But it's an outrage,' Edward grumbled. 'Can't a man have fun it he wants?'

'Seems not,' put in Abel Johnson. 'Well, not if it involves upsetting the tutors. Why don't you get your fun from Euclid, or Herodotus. Much less risky. And cheaper.'

'Those hicks? Huh.' He stared into his soup.

Richard followed Peter out of Hall once he had finished eating, and asked to go to his rooms. With the door safely shut, he put the question to him about his safety from the supposed conspirators. 'I hadn't thought of this before, you know. They're not going to like someone going around asking questions like I've been doing.'

'No, I didn't realise you hadn't worked that out, I'm sorry, I should have checked. But you were so capable in what you were doing, it didn't occur to me that you hadn't.'

'What does it mean, then, Peter? Do I have to give up looking for the answer? Mr Danns came to see me just now asking about the investigation, I'd met him at Holy Trinity; and I didn't really tell him anything, because I didn't know who would get to hear. But then if we don't share what we know, there might be someone who could tell us something we haven't thought of asking about. Or, contrariwise, the murderer might hear of it and want to silence us. Perhaps for good.'

Peter rubbed his chin. 'You know, Richard, you might have something there. Is it . . . is it possible that Stephens heard something about the conspirators, and said he had to tell the authorities, and that was why he was killed? To silence him?'

'Oh. Yes, I see, it might be. But,' with a shudder, 'I don't want to be silenced like him.' He felt his neck, and gulped.

'The thing is, we don't know there is any conspiracy in the first place, you know. Or if there is, what is its target. Let alone who is organising it, even if we have a few names of people who might well be involved.'

'Like Price and Martin and Mackenzie, you mean.' Richard ran over in his mind his trip to Wimpole. 'You know, I don't think I said anything about the murder to Price or Martin while we rode out, and the only words I spoke to Mackenzie were about a portrait.'

'Maybe, but they will have heard about your list-making. From gossip at their colleges, you see.'

'I suppose so. And I did talk about the murder to that chap Ebenezer Harmour, who was so interested in the details: he's a friend of theirs so he might have told them.'

'And those who gave you the names for your lists will have probably told the men they told you about. I expect everyone in Caius and Trinity will know about those lists.'

Richard shoulders dropped and he looked most woebegone. 'So I can't do any more, is that it?'

'By no means. There are plenty of things we can do. But, I think, we ought to do them all as a pair. Much safer with two. Unless there are things to be done after dark.'

'After dark?'

'Indeed. I have been thinking, that as Professor Wollaston is most clammed-up about his laboratory, it might be easier to gain entry in the evening, and take a look around.'

'Really? Burglary?' Richard started to tremble. 'I'm not sure I'd be happy about that. It sounds most dangerous. What if we are caught?'

'Ah, well, the idea is not to be caught. We shall proceed on a reconnaissance first. We shall, as I'm sure your young friend Edward would inform you, "look at the place". In daylight, naturally, to start with. How do you feel about a little before-dinner visit to the Botanical Gardens to inspect the early shoots and see the glass houses?'

Richard still didn't feel quite sure. 'I thought you said I oughtn't to leave college?'

'I did. And you should keep to that advice, mostly. But I shall be with you, and it is only a short step along Bird-Bolt-lane, is it not?'

'It is.' He screwed up his courage. 'Very well, I will come. But I shall wear my scarf over much of my face and my hat pulled down.'

The feeble late February sun was doing its level best to shine through thin cloud as they left college and crossed St Andrew's-street. A chill wind from the East had got up. Peter called it a lazy wind: he said it didn't bother to go around you, it blew right through you. Richard wished he was back by his fire, and also that he'd worn his gown for extra protection, and thought how dreadful it would be if he had been out wearing a muslin dress even with a pelisse; he would surely perish in short order.

Past the empty Beast market and Slaughterhouse-lane; and they were at their goal. Trying his best to look as if he was out for a stroll, and perhaps a little education in the matter of botany, Richard couldn't help but shiver and sink his neck further into his scarf. They passed through the gates and began to wander.

'Deuced cold, lad, I think we might make this a quick visit? But we need to give a semblance of inspecting the plantings. Come on, we'll look at the pond: it is a branch from Hobson's Conduit via the King's Ditch, you know. As are our ponds, by a different route.'

Richard was in no mood to take in such exciting matters of hydro-dynamics and town planning, and merely grunted. Eventually they had circled the waters and pretended to admire the aquatic plants, before heading towards the buildings that backed onto Slaughterhouse-lane.

'I believe that several of the Professors have their University rooms here,' Peter said, 'though most of them bemoan the inadequate provision of space.'

They proceeded along the frontage, Peter inspecting each high-set window and shutter while giving the impression of lecturing his younger friend on matters of botany. At least, that was what Richard thought his odd gesticulations and sudden pauses were supposed to imply. He himself just tried to stay warm, and only briefly put out a hand from inside his coat to try the main door's handle, firmly locked.

'Richard, come here a moment. Let me give you a step up, can you see inside this window?'

He gave a rapid look around, but the garden was deserted. Standing on Peter's clasped hands he was lifted up and could see inside merely a pile of papers on tables.

'Nothing here,' he reported.

The procedure was repeated at several more windows with negative results. Then, they circled behind the building and at length saw several vials of coloured liquids on a window-ledge through the dirty glass.

'This must be the one,' Richard said, quietly. 'That chap at the Caius discussion group, John Eames I think he was, said the laboratory had that kind of thing on show.'

'Could you lift me up this time, please? I want to check how the window is fastened.'

Soon however Peter jumped down. 'It has been screwed shut from the inside. Someone is most zealous to keep the contents secure.'

The only other window to the laboratory was fastened in like fashion. Also, the back door, though fitted with only an ordinary lock, was, according to Peter who tested it, securely bolted top and bottom.

'I think we have seen enough plants for one day,' he said, 'let us return to college, I want to warm my rear on a blazing hot fire.'

To which Richard could only concur, 'Amen'. Though he was to be sure, rather troubled by a mental image of Peter's bottom being thrust towards the flames, and the emotions that were engendered deep within his belly.

CHAPTER 11

NOTHING HAPPENED THE REST OF that day, Peter having declared himself greatly behind with his reading for his tutorial on the next afternoon, so Richard was able to sit with his Principia in front of his fire, and luxuriate in the acquisition of a different type of knowledge, one that was unlikely to lead to his untimely death. On the Monday, however, he returned from chapel in a more positive mood, and decided that some action was needed. While he ate his breakfast he gathered together a few things that might be needful: a paper on which to record any observations he might make, a pencil to write them with, pen and ink being out of the question, and his picklocks, just in case. He put on an extra shirt underneath as the wind had by no means softened since the day before, and chapel had been deucedly cold.

As a last thought before leaving, he went to his trunk and took out the Trinity gown. He looked at it, and thought a while. If he was to wear this over his Emmanuel gown, then he would be both disguised from a casual inspection, and also a lot warmer. He added action to thought, and descended the stair with his cap on his head and his chin set determinedly.

'Where are you off to?' asked Edward as he passed his open door. 'And what are you doing in that blue rag?'

Richard stood with his mouth hanging open for a moment, then rallied. 'None of your business, cully,' he shot back.

'Don't give me that ballocks, oaf. Look, I'm sorry about all that business over the party, I think I might have gone a bit too far with the old ale that night, and I had the most terrific hang-over all Sunday. Was I a bit tetchy in Hall?'

'Just bit, just a bit.'

'Anyway, I've turned all studious now. I'm forswearing drinking for the delights of Greek prose.'

'I don't believe you.'

'Honest, swear on my . . . well, my empty flagons, perhaps?'

'We shall see. Does this mean you have calculated how many lates you have in the book and how many chapels you have cut and decided you have been sailing a little close to the wind? And tutorials you may have missed, to boot?'

'Might have.' He shifted from one foot to the other. 'Still, doesn't explain your blue dishcloth.'

Richard plucked at his extra gown. 'It's Arctic out there, and I found this thing, so I thought I'd give it a try for extra warmth.'

'So why not have it under your own gown, so you don't look like a Bulldog?'

Richard was a bit stuck for a reason. He resorted to abuse, as being generally effective with Edward. 'Hulver-head! What's it to you what I wear, lob-cock?'

Edward retaliated with a punch to the ribs which Richard parried with a chop of his hand, and amity was restored.

'Can I come with you, then, whatever you're doing. Haven't seen you much for ages.'

'You've been looking for me in the bottom of a tankard, I'd say.'

'All right, all right, leave it, cully. But can I?'

Richard thought, decided he would be safer out of college if he was accompanied. 'I suppose so. But we're only going to the Botanical Gardens, to see a man in the chemistry laboratory.'

'Why?'

'Ah. For me to know and you to remain ignorant of, don't you see?'

They set off through college, with Edward nagging at Richard to tell him and Richard ignoring his pestering. It was much warmer in the extra shirt and gown, to be sure. Also, he cut a more sturdy figure. He did get an odd look from the porter on duty, but didn't break his stride.

'So, my inquisitive friend, what we are going to do is ask if we may see into Professor Wollaston's laboratory, and observe what researches he is pursuing.'

'What for?'

'I'm not going to tell you, so you can shut up about it. However, you can see what you may notice, and keep an eye out for anyone you recognise, and warn me if you do.'

'Not likely in that sort of nunnery.'

'Well, do so anyway. And don't interrupt me when I'm talking to the people there.'

'Very well, but it sounds dull as a dunghill.'

'That's a good thing, in this case. We don't want any excitement today; I've had quite enough recently.'

Arriving at the door of the building, they found it unlocked, and entered a short corridor. Enquiring of the occupant of the first room, they were directed to the left at the back of the building. 'But don't expect to be let in,' they were advised. 'Nobody is allowed these days.'

Wondering about this intelligence, the lads followed directions and soon Richard was knocking on a plain door. After a considerable wait, a small shutter opened, and an unkempt man addressed them.

'What d'ye want? No visitors. And I'm busy.'

'Good morning, sir. We are two undergraduates who wondered if it might be possible to view the Professor's laboratory. We are both greatly interested in Chemistry.' Richard had to elbow Edward who was beginning to dispute this description of his enthusiasm.

'No visitors I said. Now be off with you, I'm expecting a delivery and I need to get all ready.' And he slammed the shutter closed, and that was that.

148

'Charming,' was Edward's comment. 'Now what, is the show over?'

Richard thought. They stepped back a little from the door. 'Not quite yet,' he said quietly. 'First, what did you detect from that brief interview?'

'Nothing, except I wanted to baste him, but the hole was too small.'

'Did you not see his appearance?'

'Only that he was a filthy blackguard.'

'You did not see the black stickiness of his hands, nor the stains on his clothes? And the charring of his front hair?'

'Oh. Well, no.'

'And did your delicate nose detect aromas beyond those of the unwashed?'

'Er . . .'

'There was a distinct scent like of coal-tar. Or pitch, or bitumen, maybe. I could not quite place it. And also, a roaring sound, as of a flame playing on a vessel.'

Edward made a mock-bow. 'I am your servant, sire. I did not perceive any of this. Actually, I'm impressed, cully. Most impressed.'

Richard felt himself blushing and tried to pull his scarf higher.

'How on earth do you know about these things?'

'By attending lectures, you know, those things that are the purpose of our sojourn at this great University? Have you heard of them?'

'All right, you make your point.'

'Professor Hailstone has been most informative concerning such deposits of unusual substances in his discourses.'

'It's all very well, but that sort of thing isn't in the examinations, so why bother?'

'Do you have no spirit of enquiry?'

'Well, not if it involves extra work.'

Richard sighed.

'Anyway, like I said, what now? Is the show over?'

'Not at all. Did you not hear what our hospitable friend said? He is expecting a delivery. Now of what? And from where? And from whom?'

'So what?'

'So, we await its arrival. But first, let me have a look at this door lock.'

Once he had examined the pattern of lock, Richard signalled Edward to hush, and they retraced their steps. They walked around behind the north wing, and leant against the wall.

'I propose to wait and see what is delivered. Well, wait until I freeze too solid to bear it any longer, at any rate.'

'Which will be about five minutes, I'll be bound.'

'Unless we could find a sheltered spot, or maybe even somewhere in the building?'

'Worth a try.'

Edward shot off immediately, and soon returned with news that there was an empty boxroom just inside the door, with only a few brooms and dust and spiders for company. They decamped there and waited.

'Dashed dull, this,' Edward observed after about three minutes.

'You don't have to stay. Perhaps you ought to be at a lecture? Or in the library?'

'Fair enough, cully.'

Fortunately for the patience of Edward, and the patience of Richard at Edward's fidgeting, there was soon a sound of horses' hooves and creaking of a cart, and they pressed against the window to see better. A man entered the building and went down to the Chemistry laboratory, where they could hear him receive more of a welcome than the boys had. Meanwhile, Richard had dodged out of the front door and was looking at the goods on the cart. There were several crates, stamped with strange lettering, as well as labels announcing their destination as being 'Wollaston, Botanic Gardens'.

Hearing the man returning he slipped behind the corner of the building and listened intently.

'All these crates are to go into that room,' said the denizen of the laboratory.

'Right-oh, mate. But you'll need to give us a hand, they're well heavy.'

'Fair enough, Tom. We need to be careful, mind, they're breakable.'

And the two of them disappeared, panting, with the first crate. Richard took out his paper and pencil and tried to copy the strange printing. It seemed to be in quite a different alphabet. Perhaps it was a code?

Before he had finished, the men returned, and once they had gone again he completed his transcription. He tried to see what might be in the crates but they were tightly fastened. Then it was just a matter of waiting until all the five crates had been unloaded, and the cart departed, while hoping Edward had the sense to stay in his hiding place.

After retrieving him from the boxroom with the glad news that the show was indeed now over, they set off back to college. As they passed the Beast Market, raucous and smelly, and reached Bird-Bolt-lane, Edward, as usual turning this way and that to see what there was to see in his fidgety manner, made an exclamation. Richard hushed him quickly.

'What have you just seen?' he asked, quietly.

'That cove from the Eagle and Child, that we met on Saturday. He's just turned into the garden. What's he down this end of town for? He's a Trinity man, I think. Don't know his name, but he's a friend of John Smart, who knows a lot of the Caius Trouts.'

'Very interesting. Most interesting. Hmm.'

'Hmm what? Just what is going on that I don't know about?'

Richard considered. 'Wait until we get to my room, and then I'll tell you. I think.'

In his room and in front of the fire he stripped off both gowns and his cap, and threw himself on the sofa. 'See here,' he said, 'this is what was written on the crates.'

He showed Edward the copy he had made, which looked almost like English, but altogether not like. It read: 'Ухта́ коми *Россия*'.

'What's that nonsense? Is it mirror writing?'

'Er, no, of course not. Some of the letters are the right way round and some not. And what is that big bent Y?'

'No idea. So, what now?'

'Well, we try and work out what it means, of course.'

'And how do you propose to do it? Not to mention, you said you'd tell me what all this is about, didn't you? Is it more of that stuff like from last term? Coded messages?'

Richard thought quickly. He did need someone to help him with the problem, as well as Peter, and Edward had been in with him on the previous adventure. 'Might well be. It certainly might be to do with a French plot, I guess, but hopefully you'll keep your mouth shut this time and not end up tied and gagged in a barge bound for Lynn and need rescuing. I haven't got any more spare boots and the river will be even colder in February.'

'Point taken, cully. So give, won't you?'

'Well, we think,'

'We?' interrupted Edward.

'Peter and I,' he answered, annoyed at the diversion. 'We,'

'I'm not keen on him being involved,' Edward grimaced, 'not after Saturday night.'

'Tough. So you want to hear me out? Or not?'

'Alright, then.'

'We think there might be something going on with the Chemistry laboratory, that some Frenchmen want to discover, and that the killing of Stephens in our chapel was something to do with it.'

'Big stuff! Aren't you getting in a bit over your head, lad, with this sort of game? I don't want to be a stiff just yet.'

'Nor I, obviously, bacon brain. Hence, a little caution, and a lot of discretion, for which you are not exactly famous.'

'Hold back! I can keep a secret.'

'Can you? James Smith, remember?'

'I'm a changed man, remember?'

'We shall see. Meanwhile, the obvious thing to do is to get the stencilling on those crates deciphered, yes?'

'Well, yes, I guess. What do you think it will tell you?'

'I don't know, we haven't deciphered it yet, have we?'

'No. Well, I don't know, but it looks like some of those papers in Mr Watkinson's rooms, you know. The ones I put aside because I couldn't read them to know how to organise them. He'll know all about it.'

'Excellent. So, do we go and ask Watkinson for a translation? The fewer people who know about this the better. So, perhaps not yet, I think. I will ask Peter first, he knows all sorts of out-of-the-way things.'

Peter was most intrigued. He said he was sure it was Cyrillic script, in other words Eastern European, possibly Russian; and that he knew a man who he was sure could translate it. In London, unfortunately. And he agreed with Richard that they shouldn't bother Mr Watkinson unless they had to, because he didn't want to spread the information around. He set to to write a letter, copying out the writing as accurately as he could, and asking for any information about what it might imply.

He had a tutorial in a couple of minutes, so he gave the letter to Richard to post, and the transcription to keep safe. Richard, remembering the injunction not to leave college unnecessarily or alone, tasked Edward with the job of taking the letter to the receiving office to make sure it caught the first mail. Too late, he realised he had given him the transcription too, but thought, well, I need to trust him, he will bring it back.

An hour later Edward banged into his room cock-a-hoop. 'I've found out what it means,' he carolled, 'it's a place in Russia.' He consulted the paper. 'It says "Ukhta", that's a river, and the area around it; "Komi", that's the region; and "Russia". And I found out what comes from there too. Old Watkinson came up trumps. It's rock oil, whatever that is.'

'Edward! I thought we said not to go to your tutor? Now what have you done?'

'I thought you'd be pleased.' Edward looked decidedly grumpy. 'Initiative, that's what I have. No point waiting for days for an answer from London. Hever solves the riddle in one swoop.'

'Yes, but . . .'

'But nothing. Go on, hop off to your precious Winton and tell him Hever has done it. And don't take all the credit for yourself, mind.'

Peter sought out Richard the following evening, and reported that he had been to visit Professor Wollaston after hearing about the likely contents of the crates, to confront him about the matter directly, much as he did not want to reveal his double identity. He described the visit in some detail, hoping Richard might get some ideas from it. After trying several leads, he said he had run him to earth in Trinity Hall at dinner time, where he was deep in conversation with the Master over a large haunch of venison. Biding his time, he begged for a private word once they had finished eating, and sat down in a corner of the Fellows' Room to talk.

First, he gave him evidence of his credentials as an officer of the Intelligence Service, which considerably surprised the Professor, and led to his wondering what he was doing in the garb and gown of an undergraduate. When this was all settled to the Professor's satisfaction, he began to probe, treading very delicately at first.

'Sir, I know your lectures and demonstrations are very popular, and have attended several myself. I also arrange a Chemistry discussion group in Emmanuel, and have attended a similar one in Caius.'

'Flattery, boy. Get to the point.'

'Ah, yes. Well, you may have heard of the murder of a Caius man in Emmanuel chapel earlier this term?'

'I had not, but go on. Presumably not some sort of brawl, then, as it exercises you in your official capacity?'

'Indeed. We have reason to suppose that he inadvertently came upon evidence that someone, probably a French sympathiser, was trying to gain access to the experiments which we surmise you may be carrying out in your laboratory. I say this because it is well known that you have recently barred all visitors, and have, er, refused to discuss the topic of your current research.'

Wollaston made the noise usually written as 'Harumph' and looked wary. 'You have deduced this? You do not know anything of what I am doing?'

'Indeed. Except, that, well, I do know a little more.' He lowered his voice further. 'It seems you had a delivery yesterday of some crates from a place called Ukhta in Russia. Some heavy crates. Sir.'

'How can you know of this? It was most secret.'

'Sir, we are intelligencers. We also understand that the crates are likely to contain quantities of rock oil, for that is the main product of the region that is exported. Am I correct?'

'I am saying nothing, sir.'

'That is understandable. However, we believe the conspirators are very serious about discovering your researches, and will stop at little to achieve their aims. I do not think your own person is at risk at present, because otherwise the researches would not continue, but it may be in the future. And we want to catch the perpetrators of the murder as well as foil the machinations of the spies.'

'I see. So why have you come to me?'

'For several reasons. First, to confirm whether you have researches underway that may interest French agents, which might benefit M Bonaparte?'

'I neither confirm nor deny your suggestion.'

'Secondly, to ask if you might be willing to cooperate in setting some sort of trap to catch the perpetrators if we gain information that they are likely to try and break into your laboratory and steal the secrets, whatever they are.'

'I am not willing, sir. My laboratory is private.'

'Thirdly, to warn you about the likely dangers. To yourself as well as to your research.'

'For that I thank you, sir, but I believe my precautions are adequate.'

'I understand from a member of Caius who was permitted to visit your laboratory before it became necessary to exclude visitors, that you store a quantity of gunpowder there. I should entreat you to be most careful in its storage, as it would be a most tempting target for anyone hoping to destroy your work.'

'I thank you again, sir, but we are fully protected, I believe.'

'Very well, Professor. If you have anything you wish to say to me in the future, you may find me at Emmanuel. I quite understand your reticence, and hope we can resolve this matter without disrupting your studies.'

'So I left him to it and came back here. Mission unsuccessful, I suppose.'

Richard sat back, and laughed. 'I should not have been so tactful, Peter. The awkward old cuss. "I am not willing, sir. My laboratory is private," indeed.'

Peter cocked his head. 'He's not so old, only just above forty,' he mused, 'and he may have his own reasons for silence. I wonder what they might be?'

Richard scratched his head. 'There's something I ought to be able to remember, but I can't quite place it. Something I learned only recently, I think.'

'About what?'

'I can't remember. It's so frustrating. Maybe it'll come back to me later.'

'Well, I put in that letter that I wrote to the Foreign Office about the Russian script, a request to be informed if the government has sponsored the Professor to do any research on their behalf. Anything of military value, that is. We ought to get a reply in a few days. So maybe that will tell us whatever it is you can't remember.'

CHAPTER 12

RICHARD FOUND THAT THE MORE they discovered about this problem, the less he felt he understood it. His head was full of names and ideas and motives and movements of people around the University that might or might not be relevant. It made him feel on edge, and irritable, so he snapped at Abel when he asked him something trivial before divine service. It was time for one of his lists, he decided a few minutes later in chapel, failing to rouse any interest in the service. So, after breakfast he chased Edward out of his room and sat down to write. Again he wrote and rewrote, and rearranged, and eventually had something that might summarise their position concerning the murder side of things:

> About the execution of the murder (how it was done):
> 1: Murderer (M) is one of the Art group (many possibilities).
> 2: He persuaded Stephens (S) to go to look at the Amigoni painting with him.
> 3: M was wearing a Trinity sizar's gown and S a Caius pensioner's one (both blue) and arrived at college around the same time as the Davies party just before dinner so nobody would be around in the chapel.
> 4: After killing S, M hid both blue gowns in the box in Rev Burton's room and left the chapel in an Emmanuel one (black) from the hooks in the antechapel.

5: M also took S's personal possessions except his Simeonite cross. Might we find these at some point?

6: Implication is that M is a Trinity man (but may have merely worn a Trinity sizar's gown, I suppose).

7: He will have wanted to go and show himself as soon as possible to provide an alibi. <u>But where? And can we find out where the main suspects were at around 4 o'clock on the day of the murder?</u>

8: Charles, a day or two later, went to the chapel in the Emmanuel gown and replaced it on the hooks, and took the Caius one in error for the Trinity one from the box, and delivered it to the short, bearded man who had commissioned him in the task. Who may or may not be the same person as the murderer.

9: The Caius gown (with S's initials) was left on a stair in Caius a month later and is now with the Trinity gown discovered four days after the murder, in my box.

Richard rubbed his eyes, and set down his quill. This was hard work, worse than construing Aeschylus. He'd missed out all that part about the alibi the first time he made the list, though, and that was something he really needed to look into. As well as point 5, he hadn't ever thought about what Stephens might have had in his pockets.

Now he ought to do something about the motive, that was even more difficult, because they didn't really know anything for certain.

<u>About the motive for the murder (why it was done):</u>
1: (Supposition) S had heard something about a plot (from whom? And was it one of the people in his three social groups?) and needed to be silenced. He was a most scrupulous man and would feel it his duty to report such matters.

2: The plot is centred on whatever secret work Professor

Wollaston is doing in his laboratory (we have no evidence that it is, though).

3: The work may be to do with rock oil from Ukhta in Russia (if that is indeed what was in the crates, it might be something else entirely). And we do not know anything about rock oil anyway.

4: It may be to do with military matters such as explosives. (Pure speculation).

5: Or it could be anything else in the world, that we haven't thought of.

He didn't like this second list at all, it was all What if? and Maybe? and It ought to be. Most unlike a mathematical problem, where all the starting information was certain: axioms and propositions, after which everything followed tidily and logically. He felt so frustrated with the whole business. Was there anything he could do to clarify any of the suppositions? He thought point number one was quite likely true, though, because as Peter had said, somebody had gone to a lot of trouble to cover up the murder, it wasn't going to be just a killing of passion.

They could try and break into the laboratory and see what was being researched, he supposed. But that would be most dangerous, not to mention difficult, and they were liable to be caught and exposed and sent down, which would be a disaster. What about finding out more about Ukhta, or rock oil? The laboratory smelt like tar or pitch, but what exactly was it? Would it be in a book? He could try the college library. Or would someone else know? Who knew about rocks, or deposits?

Then it came to him. Professor Hailstone might: he was the geology expert. Could he go and see him? He'd have to check this with Peter first though, and then he could . . .

All of a sudden he felt overwhelmed by the enormity of it all. He burst into tears, sobbed and sobbed, it was all too much. He wanted . . . he didn't know what he wanted, really. Somebody to look after him, and tell him it was going to be alright. Somebody, no, not Peter, but perhaps a man, . . . like Mr Blackburn, really. It was such a strain pretending to be a boy, and studying, and doing all this intelligence work, and he just wanted to be cared for and not to have to worry for a little while.

And, he remembered, it was the twenty-ninth today, when ladies were supposed to be allowed to propose marriage. Not that she wanted to propose to Mr Blackburn, or anyone else for that matter, but it would be so nice just to be a woman for a bit, and not have to exercise her brain so much with puzzles, and cope, and everything. It was odd, really, she was so intimate with Peter, but she still thought of Mr Blackburn by his title, not as William. And she did miss him, though she hadn't had much time to think of him. And now she was thinking of herself in the feminine mode, it was all too difficult.

Was it wrong to want to be looked after? Shouldn't she be able to stand on her own two feet? Did she ought not to be crying? She didn't know. But she was. Oh dear . . . Perhaps she ought to just go and have a lie-down; it was another dull day, and she hadn't got a lecture. That was it, that's what she'd do. This investigation would have to wait. She needed some time for herself, to just do nothing.

By lunchtime Richard felt a lot better. The reason for his het-up state was clear: his courses had begun. No pain, this time, though, fortunately. He did a calculation, it was thirty-three days since the last one. Very well, he would leave his lists and work in his room on Newton for the rest of the day, or perhaps try and make headway with the final chapters of Euclid, and then tomorrow plan what to do next. He still thought it would be good to have a man to depend on, though; well, not depend on, exactly, more, be in partnership with. But for the moment he (well, let's be clear about this, Mr Blackburn, William) was miles away, and leagues from knowing about his situation here at Emmanuel.

This good intention lasted until early evening when Edward bounced into his room with news.

'I saw that cove Smart in town,' he began, 'so I thought I'd do a little intelligence work. Can't have you being the only brain-box around the place.'

Richard found his insides clenching up. What had the idiot done now?

'You haven't told him . . . what did you say?'

'Well, I was all subtle and foxy, you know. I got him to come for a drink in the Angel, we go there sometimes, it's quite near Caius; and got him relaxed a bit before I started on the tricky questions.'

'And you were also quite relaxed, I see,' said Richard, noting his slightly flushed appearance and raising an eyebrow.

'Verisimilitude, my boy, verisimilitude. Anyway, let me tell you. So I asked him about his friends that we had at the party, like I said, I knew him, Smart I mean, but not the others. He said one was Christian Martin, he was a Trinity cove, a Bulldog, you know, he was a quiet sort of man, but quite interesting, he'd travelled on the Continent when the war was on hold, and he knew a lot of Frenchmen who could supply brandy and lace and silk and so on. He pronounced his name funny, too, like a Frenchy, sort of, Martain, I suppose.'

'I see.'

'And the other one he didn't know much about, he wasn't an undergraduate, but he had been hanging around with some lads from Trinity on and off for a few weeks, and he wasn't much good at paying his share, but he was good for running errands and things.'

'Things?'

'He didn't say what. But he said this cove, Charles he called him, was a bit of a hobnail, he wasn't in on things.'

'In on things?'

'Right. So that's when I got interested, I asked him, what things? And he clammed up, and said never you mind, and that, but I said, look, I'm a Trusty Trout, you can tell me. But all he said was, that Jake would kill him if he said anything, so he wasn't going to. And I said, surely not actually kill you, and he went all serious and said, yes, quite dispatched into the pit, though he wouldn't do it himself, he'd get his Turk to do it.'

'Turk?'

'You don't know anything, do you? His hard man, chap who likes to do harm to people for fun.'

'You didn't say anything to him about this Charles, did you?'

'Calm yourself, cully, not a word. Your nobby friend Winton made that quite clear: I don't want to be sent back to Keswick just yet, too much fun to be had here. I just said, who was he, but Smart didn't know. Said they'd be giving him the push soon, anyway, he was getting to be a nuisance.'

'And then?'

'Well then this serving wench with the neat apple-dumplings came over and we moved on to other topics, you see. So, that's all I know, but come on, tell me I've done well.'

Richard put his head on one side and considered. He felt relieved, more than anything, that Edward hadn't let any cats out of their sacks. 'Yes, I think you have been quite useful, actually. You say this Martin fellow is quite in with the French, I mean, people who are actually in France?'

'Seems so. I'll wager he's in some kind of smuggling racket, by the sound of it.'

'And the man he called Jake, I think I know who he is, he's a friend of Smart's, Jake Mackenzie, he isn't an undergraduate but he goes around with the Trinity crowd, hunting and so on.'

'How do you know about him?'

'Intelligence work,' temporised Richard. He didn't want to say he'd seen Jake at the Somerset House ball, of course not; nor yet that he'd been on the trip to Wimpole. Edward was a loose cannon at the best of times; he ought only to tell him what he needed to know.

'Well I want to know all about this business,' Edward complained. 'It's no good telling me just little bits.'

'We have a motto in intelligence, you know: "Do they need the information?".". And you don't.' He felt guilty about this invention, but squashed the feeling.

'Huh. Well, don't go sending me on errands like they send that Charles fellow, unless you're going to let me in on things, then,' and he stalked out, offended.

Richard, the diversion making him unwilling to get back to Newton, cast around for what to do. Reluctantly, he looked out his notes and reread them. Number seven bothered him. Did they know of anyone in Trinity who was definitely on their side, who they could ask about the various suspects? Where would the murderer have gone to show himself around four o'clock on the day of the murder? Somewhere public, obviously. Perhaps, in Hall? Did Trinity dine later than they did? It was possible. He ought to find out.

He could go there and ask the porters about meal times; or he could ask anyone from the college really. Now, was he due over that side of town tomorrow? He checked his lecture-lists. Indeed, he had a geology lecture in Trinity itself, by Professor Hailstone. Capital. Except, he wasn't supposed to leave college, was he, at least not alone? Surely he would be safe at a lecture? And he could go with someone, perhaps Peter? Or even, Edward, maybe? None of his other friends was interested in geology, they all said there was enough to study with the subjects that were actually examined, or else they were more interested in having a good time. Obviously Edward was among those of little curiosity about the makeup of the Earth, but he might be willing to help if it was intelligence work?

Having discovered in morning chapel the following day that Peter had a tutorial he couldn't miss, he persuaded Edward to come with him to Professor Hailstone. First he had to flatter him a little by saying that on reflection, he had realised how useful it had been for him to have found out that information about Christian Martin and Charles, and by extension, the other men. Then he let him in on his plans by explaining a little about the concept of an alibi, and how he wanted to see if any of the men on his lists were dining in Trinity's

Hall on the day of the murder. Paradoxically, he explained, those who were there might be seen as more likely to be guilty, not less so, but he wanted the information and he didn't know how to obtain it yet. Hence the expedition. Not to mention, he wanted to know more about geology.

Edward said he didn't mind, as long as they could go to that coffee house opposite Caius on the way back and see if that comely wench from last term was serving that day. He'd try not to fall asleep in the lecture, but not to worry if he did. So they were agreed.

Richard had a stint to do in the library before they left, and so he walked along by the Brick building, and into the chapel arcade. No sooner than he had reached the passageway, than he heard a voice in the court calling, 'Winton!'. A most familiar voice. Who was greeting Peter? Surely not? . . . But yes, that was Mr Blackburn's tones! In college! Torn between a desire to flee and an urge to listen to what they were saying, he pressed himself against a column and strained to hear.

'What are you doing here, Blackburn?'

'Thought I'd drop in and see you, I've been staying with my old friend Oliver James in Caius, I'm on my way back from the Midlands.'

'Good to see you. How goes it?'

'Slowly. I'm still on that theft of the Bakers, you know. So much information, so little makes any sense.'

'Always the way. Same here, everything muddy.'

'Anyway, what I really wanted to know is, do you know where that girl Rose Clarke is? I've been trying to find her, I'd love to see her again, but she seems to have disappeared.'

'Rose? She was at my place in Milton at Christmas when I came back from Scotland.'

'I know. I was fortunate enough to escort her to the fireworks in London on Twelfth Night, but then she seems to have vanished.'

'Am I to suppose you have developed a *tendresse* for the young lady?'

'You know I have, Peter, you flat. And I've written, but I've not had a reply.'

Richard tried to make himself even smaller. How he wished he'd run away when he first heard Blackburn's voice.

'Where did you write to?'

'To Milton. She told me her plans were undecided, but she had heard the roads to Gloucestershire were in very bad condition. She had thought of visiting her cousin in Cheshire, but the roads there were if anything worse. And Sir George said she would be visiting your sister Julia again later in January, so I addressed my letter there, but I called by yesterday, and although she had been there until recently, she had lately departed again to London. And from there, they did not know. By the way, your mother sends her greetings.'

There was a pause. Richard wondered if they had moved on, but there was no sound of footsteps on the cobbles.

'Could the post have gone astray? It can be most unreliable from the Northern towns, I hear.'

'It might, I suppose. Your mother said she had not seen the letter, but that Rose is likely to have intercepted the servant when he had collected letters from the office, before she saw it herself. But what I really want is to see her in person. I have a book of hers to return, and I know she will want to catechise me on its contents, and my opinions of the same.'

'What is this volume?'

'"A vindication of the rights of woman" by Mrs Wollstonecraft.'

'I see. A most contentious subject, to be sure.'

'It is most forceful in its ideas, though the arguments are somewhat convoluted. I am not sure I wholly agree with them, but I can sympathise to a certain extent. But I want to talk with her about it, even if it leads to a contretemps, as well as about many other things. She is a most invigorating person.'

'Well, the best of luck, Miss Clarke is certainly a force to be reckoned with in herself, you know.'

'I do, and I admire her the more for it. Why, she was telling me at the Somerset House ball all about the Oxfordshire poundstone, and fossils, and the like. I was most enamoured with her learning.'

'What of her person?'

Mr Blackburn's voice dropped in volume, but he was still clearly audible to Richard.

'She is perhaps not so fine of figure as some, but she has a sweet countenance, enlivened by a lively though at times a stern eye. Nonetheless I find myself dreaming of, er, burying my face in her bosoms, and dealing with her . . .well, her rump, in a manner thoroughly satisfactory to both of us, shall I just say.'

'Well said, sir. I wouldn't mind a bit of that nuzzling myself, but I fear she would be too arch a partner for me. Yet, she is a worthy prize, I am sure. Though not possessed of much dowry, I believe.'

'No indeed. And so it may be a goodly while before I am able to proceed with the increased intimacy I have indicated. Marriage must be postponed for some time. If she will have me, I mean. For sometimes she seems quite the flirt, and even forward in her manner, othertimes she is most reticent and distant.'

'Women, eh?' and they both laughed.

Their voices receded, and Richard heard the opening of a door as presumably Peter invited Blackburn up to his keeping-room for refreshment. He leaned against the pillar and sighed. It felt most peculiar to be discussed in this manner, to have his – her – body lusted over. Pleasing? Or weird? Or offensive? Or all three?

Gathering himself, he made for the library, after poking his head cautiously around the pillar to make sure they had really gone. Mrs Winton was a real trouper, she was. To have invented all that story on the spur of the moment was a marvel. And so necessary, really so crucial.

While performing his slight duties in the library he had ample opportunity to look through the volumes to see if any had information on this mysterious rock oil. There were a few books on geology, but on oil they were all silent. And was this oil made from rocks, or found in rocks, or what? Oil usually came, he thought, from animal fat, or possibly from some plants like olives, if his Roman history was correct.

By the time he collected Edward to go to the lecture he had calmed down considerably. Life though seemed to be a jagged line of emotions lately, and so very, very complicated. They strode through the streets, Richard keeping slightly behind on the inside so as to shield his face from recognition, but they saw no acquaintances for once, not even when crossing the Great Court at Trinity. The lecture room was quite sparsely attended, the only person Richard recognised was Mr Sterne of Caius, to whom he tipped his cap as they settled themselves at the back.

Mr Hailstone held forth on the coal deposits of Britain, and to a lesser extent, the world. He described the work of William Smith on the Somerset Coal Canal, and other such excavations, and what it meant for the history of the formation of the rocks under our feet. It was most fascinating, if difficult to comprehend. For example, how could the solid rocks be moved through thousands of feet? And where had the coal come from in such orderly layers? There were theories, to be sure, but it was all such a confusing mystery.

Nonetheless, hearing all this spurred Richard on to wait behind when the lecture ended and importune Mr Hailstone with his questions. He was wary of doing this, having spoken to the man at the both the Pemberton and Somerset House balls as Rose, and indeed made one figure with him, but he dragged Edward along and tried to lounge in as unfeminine manner as he could and lower the pitch of his voice a little. He took comfort from the fact that he was of course in cap and gown, and must cut a very different figure from a young girl in muslin.

'Sir, may I ask a few questions about your lecture?'

'Indeed, lad, I'm flattered to rouse any interest in my subject. You see how crowded the room was? However, I believe the great Newton often lectured to a completely empty room, so I am not too downcast.'

'No, sir, I am greatly interested. You talked of coal deposits, and how they may have formed, and the uses of coal, not just for fuel.'

'Indeed.'

'I have heard of a substance called rock oil, and I wondered if you were familiar with it? Is it related to coal?'

'Yeah,' put in Edward, 'my tutor says it comes from this place in Russia, but he didn't know what it was.'

'Rock oil? Well, well. It is not widely known, or indeed widely found. And yes, Russia, and a few other places. It is a dark, sticky liquid which oozes out of the ground in the Ukhta river basin there, it is thought there must be great deposits of it in underground caverns but as yet little use has been found for it. I am by no means an expert concerning it, but it may be in some way related to coal, in that it will also burn in part, like coal, or pitch; but it is a strange kind of burning, I hear, and not at all satisfactory. Else, no doubt, the Russians would be extracting it and making their fortunes from it, as men do when they find a new mineral resource.'

'Thankyou, sir.'

Edward chimed in. 'Do you know if it might be useful in warfare?'

'Why do you ask, lad?'

'Well, I heard someone say that they're trying to make better munitions from it.'

Richard curled up inside at this disclosure. And who had said that about munitions: he certainly hadn't?

'I don't know anything about that, lad. It's too new a substance in Britain, though I believe the Russians have known about it for many years.'

Richard took charge again. He had to trust someone in Trinity, and this Professor seemed as likely to be safe as anyone.

'There is another thing, sir. You may know about the murder of a Caius man in the chapel at Emmanuel last month – no, it was in January – which remains unsolved?'

'I heard of something of the sort.'

'We are trying to find out who might have done it, I mean, committed the murder, and we are searching for a way to establish alibis.'

'Alibis, eh? "He was elsewhere". I am intrigued.'

'Yes, sir. Well, we wanted to ask somebody who was in Hall here in Trinity on the, er, twenty-fourth of January, if they saw other people there, that we could then exclude from our enquiries.'

'That's a long time ago, lad. I couldn't say where I ate only last week, and I dare say nobody else could give you an account either.'

Richard's face fell. 'I should have thought about this ages ago, sir. But I didn't, and . . .'

'What you want, lad, is the college steward. They keep records of who has dined, so as to bill them correctly for the food.'

Of course! Richard cursed himself inwardly. He had had such a bill last term, and he had never thought about how it was calculated.

'I am a bumpkin! It never occurred to me to ask. I shall go straightways to the man and enquire.'

The Professor gave him directions, and the two of them left. Richard wished he had brought his lists with him, but he thought it worth asking at least about the men whose names were most familiar to him: Burgess, Price, Martin, Noakes, and of course any guests they may have had.

The steward was unforthcoming. He said, with a sniff, that members' financial affairs were private, and he could not undertake to release information to anyone, let alone undergraduates from another college, without instructions from the Master. He was quite obdurate about this, and so they left with their tails between their legs.

'A pudding-head if ever I saw one,' was Edward's opinion. 'What do we do now, break in and steal his ledger?'

'Not a good move, noddy. We go back to college and think.'

'You do that, cully, I'm going for a nice warm cup of chocolate and hopefully a nice warm eyeful of apple dumplings. Coming?'

CHAPTER 13

Peter looked at Richard's newest version of his lists and whistled. 'Good work, lad. So first, we need to find a way to get Dr Mansel to open up.'

'Dr Mansel?'

'Indeed. He is the Master of Trinity.'

'How do you know this?'

Peter gave him a sideways look. 'I am, I believe you may have guessed, an intelligencer. Many things are useful to us.' Breaking into a grin, he added, 'Besides, we've been interested in Mr Burgess for a long time, and so I've made it my business to know about the college. Plus, one of our agents is an undergraduate there, like myself and Charlie.'

'Very well. So how can this be arranged?'

'Hmm. I don't know just yet. But, could you write me a list of the men we are particularly interested in? Then I know who to ask about once we gain access to the accounts.'

Richard nodded. 'And what do you think about the rock oil business?'

'I don't know what to think. As you very cogently put it, all our ideas about this are pure speculation. Stephens may have been killed for a wholly different kind of reason. Nonetheless, the secrecy of Professor Wollaston is important, and more, the reason as to why he has taken such precautions. Has he become aware himself of some threat to his researches? I could not say from my interview with him, he kept an impassive expression. I should not like to face him over the card table, for sure.'

'Would rock oil be a useful substance in the manufacture of munitions?'

'I do not know. And did Edward say where he heard the suggestion it might?'

'Huh! He just said he made it up on the spot. But somehow I don't think I believe him. He isn't that kind of thinker. Not that he's stupid, mind, but his interests lie elsewhere.'

'In the tavern and Barnwell?'

'I don't think he frequents the knocking houses, no. Too careful of his skin. But certainly, the Trusty Trouts are his main source of education in this great University. So, is it possible he heard it from one of them or their drinking friends?'

'It is possible, but . . . well, I don't know.' He shook his head, sighed. 'Now, moving on, I must tell you I had a visitor today.'

Richard coloured. 'I know. I was there: well, I was behind the pillar, in the chapel arcade.'

It was Peter's turn to look uncomfortable. 'You were? What did you hear?'

'Enough. I shall take what you both said as a kind compliment. But I must thank your mother for dissembling for me, and all without warning, on Mr Blackburn's unexpected visit.'

'Good old mater. Never thrown by anything.'

'Also, I imagine she has intercepted Mr Blackburn's letter to Rose, and been uncertain as to what she ought to do with it.'

'I imagine so.'

'Could you please retrieve it, and deliver it without fanfare to me?'

'I can.'

'And you will?'

'Indubitably.'

'Good.' Richard pulled a face. 'Nuzzling, indeed. Huh!'

Meanwhile, Edward had disappeared. He wasn't in Hall; or in evening chapel, not that that was a surprise; and he didn't appear in his room all evening. Nor was he there in the morning when Mrs Fenn banged around with the coal scuttle and reported that his bed had not been slept in.

By breakfast time, Richard had the same horrid sinking feeling he had felt last term, when Edward got himself taken by the bargees, and he had had to rescue him. This time, though, it seemed more serious: these conspirators had shown they were more deadly. And, he didn't know where to look for his friend this time. Well, unless they might be holding him in a room in Trinity, which seemed unlikely. Or Caius, for that matter. And either way, far too many places to search.

Peter had been unmoved when he had told him about it in chapel. Well, more accurately, he thought they should leave a little more time before acting. But Richard decided he ought to report the matter to somebody more urgently, except that he didn't know whom to approach. The Master? His, or Edward's, tutor? Nobody seemed to be the right kind of person, or reporting would only make things worse.

Half way through the morning, though, while trying to concentrate on a passage of Ovid, he thought he heard noises below. Trying not to get his hopes up, he clattered down the stairs and poked his head in at Edward's door.

'Where've you been, you hulver-head? I've been so worried about you. And I thought you said you were a new man, no more breaking college rules and staying out late? *Sterculinum publicum!*'

'What's that one? That's new to me.'

'Latin, *stultissime*. It means, you public dung-heap, as you ought to know if you ever did any work.'

Edward was unrepentant. He said that he thought he would have another go at finding out some more useful information from Smart about his friends, so he had set out on a tour of the inns, but ran him to earth in the Caius coffee house, which was a bonus as his favourite serving girl was on duty, and she was quite cooperative with his admiring her decolletage, which was a word he learnt from Smart just then, and it sounded quite fine and elegant, he said, so he was in handsome sorts, and he had the brain-wave of asking Smart about his rooms in Caius, and how they compared to his own in Emmanuel, since he had visited them, and that he expected they could not be as commodious, especially now he was the sole occupant of his set.

So of course Smart had to keep his end up, and gave a lot of jaw about his magnificent abode, being a pensioner and not a lowly sizar, and in spite of his bluffing about how spacious his keeping-room was, Edward had demanded to see it, or he wouldn't believe a word. So he had been taken there, and of course they were a mean hovel and a pathetic hole compared to his, so he chaffed Smart some more, and Smart told him that the best rooms around were in Trinity, where he spent a lot of time with his friends.

Of course Edward jumped on this, and said he didn't believe him, and in the end they fetched up in rooms belonging to a man called Burgess, which were enormous, and so he tugged his forelock, and admitted he had been bested. But Burgess had some fine wine open, and he seemed very hospitable, so they had a small libation, and one thing led to another, what with a whole crowd of chaps turning up, and they all made off to Hall for dinner, and very fine it was, much larger than at Emmanuel, with an old-fashioned beamed ceiling like a church or a castle, and the food much better too, so afterwards they went back to Burgess' rooms and had a lot more wine, and it all got very lively and great sport, and then a couple of wenches appeared, but they were spoken for, sadly, disappearing into the bedroom with one of the blades, with only squeals for entertainment for the rest of them.

'And a terrible swell called Venables turned up to see Burgess about some hunting, and Smart told me that if we were comparing rooms, this Venables chap lived in the very residence previously occupied by Mr Newton, so match that to your grubby little set, scaly; but anyway we rubbed along famously after that, what with the wine and everything. And after that, someone started playing a fortepiano, which Burgess had in his keeping-room, which was most singular I thought. And they sang all sorts of songs, some in French, I think it was, at least Smart said so; and then somebody said, why don't we go out and look for a few snobs and have a mill, it's a fine night for it?'

'I tagged along, to watch the fun, not to partake, because I'm not that keen on having my brains beaten out and trodden on, and they went up to the Great Bridge, knocking up a few other lads along the way, and set off a little way along the towpath. But Smart and I and a couple of others stayed on the bridge, which was a capital plan, because a whole crowd of bargees hopped out of an inn there almost at once, and set on the men, and it was fine sport to watch. Though a bit hard to see exactly what was going on, being quite dark.'

'But the fight spilled over back onto Bridge street, so we thought it time to make a move. And after that we fetched up in a different room, belonging to this cove called Price, who'd been one of those who'd watched the fun with me from the bridge, he was a bit short and weedy-looking, so I don't blame him. So there was more wine, and brandy, which I thought was as vicious and evil as your whisky, and we all got most illuminated and foxed, and before I knew it it was morning, and there we were, waking up on Price's floor, stiff as a board and freezing cold.'

'How is your head, Edward?'

'Remarkably fine, must be from not mixing drinks, I should say. All from the grape, y'see. Anyway, what was that other thing you called me? After the dung-heap one?'

'Can't remember.'

'Stult-something, it was.'

'Oh yeah, *stultissime*. Complete idiot. Which you are, often.'

Richard envied him his capacity for drinking, but not his fool-hardiness. 'And in the midst of all this revelry, did you discover anything about your new friends that might help our search for our murderer?'

174

'Well, um, not exactly, but I did get to see their lairs, and all that. And I have a lot of new friends, don't you know. You're interested in people in Caius an' Trinity, aren't you?'

Richard considered. What might Edward have discovered apart from new sources of alcohol?

'Can you tell me about anything these coves had in their rooms? You said Burgess had a fortepiano. Anything else?'

'Not to notice. Lots of wine bottles, like I said.'

'You mentioned Burgess had a visitor, Venables I think: they hunted together. Were there any hunting things lying around?'

'Of course. Well, he had prints of hunts on his walls, naturally, and a pile of muddy boots and clothes and so on waiting for the gyp to clean, and spurs and whips and that. But nothing unusual.'

'How about Price? What did he look like, apart from being short and weedy? And was there anything odd in his rooms?'

Edward thought for a moment. 'Well, he had a beard, rather a scrappy thing, though. Nothing in the rooms, well, I wasn't noticing too much by that time, to be fair.'

'Hunting things? Paintings? Chemical equipment?'

'None of that bosh. Prints, I didn't notice particularly. P'raps he's tidier than Burgess. No, hang on a minute, he did have a gun propped against the wall by a bookcase in his bedroom. Saw it when he went in there to put his greatcoat away in his closet. Thought I'd have a look-see at his inner sanctum, being a nosy sort of cove.'

Richard sat up at this intelligence. 'Gun? What sort of gun?'

'I don't know, I'm a grocer's son, we don't go for that sort of thing back in Keswick.'

'Well, can you tell a pistol from a musket? Did it have a long barrel?'

'Long barrel, of course. And a sort of shiny silver rod under the barrel.'

'Was it a musket or a rifle?'

'How'd I know? It was a gun. Brass bits, polished wood, sort of mechanism over the trigger. Like any other gun.'

175

Richard left it. He didn't know what a Baker rifle looked like in any case, and he only imagined this gun might be one because of trying to make sense of all the information he had accumulated over the last few weeks. It was probably just a fowling piece or something like that. People who hunted usually shot as well. He oughtn't to try and add twos to make five, he really oughtn't.

'Now come on, Rich, let me in on all this. What are we really looking for with these boys? Are they all a gang of Frenchies? Or are they going to set a bomb, like last time? Give, won't you?'

Richard set his teeth. He would have to tell him more, or he might well do something that would really get him into trouble. But then if he told him, he'd likely tell someone something he shouldn't, and put him and Peter at risk too. It was so difficult.

'Well, alright, I will, but remember the Black Prince, and James Smith, and keep your lip buttoned up, right?'

Edward mimed silence, gestured him to get on with it.

'We think, mind, only think, that Stephens was killed because he overheard someone plotting to do something, and he was going to tell the authorities. We know, or at least we are fairly sure, that he was invited to our chapel to look at the Amigoni,'

'The what?'

'That big painting behind the communion table, ignoramus; anyway, the man who did it probably knew him from the group that visits places to view the Art and the architecture, I have a list of its members, they're mostly Caius and Trinity men, but there's far too many of them to know who. So, then there was a lot of business with swapping the gowns, and your Charles bloke got sent to retrieve the Trinity one but took the Caius one by mistake, and that's why I wanted to know if any of the Trinity coves had missed their gown, because I've got the original one in my box.'

Edward broke in. 'Yeah, we went to check on that Noakes fellow, I remember, I went to see if it was his, he had a new one. But hold hard, he's a second year, and a poor sizar, you told me.'

'Yes, I know.'

'So why has he got a new gown? Had he lost his original one?'

Richard clapped him on the shoulder. 'You do have a brain, after all, and I'm a, what do you call it, a nocky boy? Of course. So he must be the chap who did the deed, and then he had to get a new gown, because his was lost.'

'Or, someone borrowed his gown to do it, maybe?'

Richard's shoulders slumped. 'Of course, yes, I forgot. And I can't remember if Noakes is on the list of Art lovers either, I need to check my papers, just a minute . . . Hang on, though, he isn't, he didn't come with us to Wimpole, did he? Oh, no, I remember, Harmour said he'd fallen out with Burgess and had sensibly stayed behind that day, so he is in that group.'

'So, then, Mr Intelligencer, what had Stephens discovered, that meant he had to wear the old elm overcoat?'

'The old elm . . . oh, I see. We don't know. It might be something to do with Wollaston's secret laboratory research, but we can't find out anything about that, except what you discovered about rock oil. And what Hailstone told us at that lecture, remember?'

'Sure. But, come on, Stephens was killed weeks and weeks ago. Why has nothing happened yet, no bomb, no plot, no burglary of the secret laboratory?'

'I hadn't thought of that; I really am a nocky boy at the moment. Maybe Wollaston hasn't made any progress yet with whatever it is?'

'They could still break in and look around and find out what he's trying to do, though.'

'I suppose.'

'And what happened about trying to find these coves' whatsit-called, you know, where they were at the time?'

'Alibis? I don't know, Peter's looking after that part.'

'So what now?'

'I don't know. It'd be good to get a squint at that gun you saw in Price's room, to see if it was a Baker rifle, the latest Army issue, because a load of them were stolen, and we think someone took a shot at Peter at Christmas with one. They're much more accurate at distance than a musket, you see.'

'So Price is going to shoot someone, is he? Sounds a bit far-fetched to me. He seemed to be a timid kind of blighter.'

Edward went in search of some late breakfast, and Richard returned to his Ovid, feeling he was missing something, some big thing. More questions, he thought, more information, and even fewer answers. It was all so very very confusing.

Richard caught Peter at dinner, and went back to his room with him. He outlined what Edward had been doing, and relayed some of his ideas. Peter said that it was most enlightening to have a fresh point of view, but he still didn't see how it got them any further.

'Do you think that gun Edward saw is important?'

'I shouldn't think so. Lots of chaps have guns for fowling like you said, and all sorts of reasons.'

'Would you recognise a Baker if you saw one?'

'No, I've never set eyes on one. Blackburn knows about them, but he's gone off to London. I do know they have a brass plate inset in the stock on the right, to hold tools, he was telling me about that yesterday, something about how well-designed they were.'

'How could I find out how to identify one?'

'I don't know, sorry. You could have asked him if we'd known.' He thought a moment. 'Well, no, you couldn't, of course, not as Richard. But I could have asked for you.'

'So then, what about his idea that there ought to have been some-thing happen by now, some treasonable action?'

'I see what he means, but what? Probably it's just taking time for their plans to get worked through. They might be waiting for Wollaston to discover something.'

'And have you discovered any way of unlocking the steward's records at Trinity? Any progress with contacting Dr Mansel?'

'Sorry, no, I've been so busy with my studies.'

Richard felt most let down by Peter's lack of enthusiasm. He decided to set to and find out how to discover more. But how? Where could he find a Baker to see how to identify one? Or could he find an engraving or something?

Understandably, the college library was no help, though he looked through all the cataloguing to make sure. It was while trying to study in his room the next day, being Saturday, that he heard a booming noise from the direction of Parker's Piece, and remembered what Sir George had told him about the militia camping there and training. Surely that would be cannon fire? And where there were cannon there would be rifles?

He set down his Principia and found his scarf and gloves immediately. Then it was off posthaste to the camp. Unfortunately there was a sentry on guard at the entrance who refused him admission: No civilians, he said, obdurately. But Richard would not be baulked. In a flash of inspiration, he said that he was thinking of joining the militia, and could he talk to the recruiting officer? This got him taken to a tent within the compound, where he had a most complicated conversation with a somewhat corpulent sergeant who started on an encomium about the benefits of joining up, before he could get a word in.

Eventually, and after apologising for his duplicity, he asked about the Baker, explaining that he thought he might have seen one in the hands of an undergraduate, which he believed might be most irregular. The sergeant explained that they had no rifles of any sort there, just the standard Brown Bess musket, and he rather thought only special rifle regiments had been issued with the new rifle, and sharpshooter detachments. He had never seen one, and could not describe it, though he had heard of the weapon.

So, failure. Richard thanked the sergeant profusely and extracted himself from further pressing persuasion to join up in the undergraduate company, with some great difficulty.

Back in his room, he felt most Hum Drum, as Edward would have said. Newton seemed dull; Ovid irrelevant. His investigations seemed irretrievably foundered. He poured himself a small whisky and sat there in a brown study, wondering what next.

Edward bounced in, threw a letter at him, told him he ought to check more often at the lodge, and bounced out saying he had an invitation to dine in Caius, he'd see him later, and not to look so peppered, which Richard could not interpret at all, but it sounded rude, as usual.

The letter was thicker than normal, he opened it curiously, and found an enclosure, addressed to 'Miss Rose Clarke'. His heart did a bump, and he quickly thrust it into his inner pocket, jumped up and locked both his doors, and tried not to panic. Well, why was he so flustered by this letter? He couldn't tell, but he reached for the whisky and poured himself another slug before daring to sit down and open it. He broke the seal, began to unfold the page, and then set it down on his lap and put his hands to his face. Then, taking a determined breath, he opened it and read.

January 23rd, 7, Panton street, London

My dear Miss Clarke,

It seems such a long time since I was honoured to escort you to the firework display at Vauxhall, and I daily recall our time together there, and wish that I could again spend time with you. I have been in the Midlands for some days and have only just returned to my lodgings. I was so hoping you would still be in Town, but Sir George your brother informs me you have returned to visit your friend Miss Julia Winton at Milton. If only I had known, I could have visited you there as I returned from Grantham.

Richard gulped, and tried to think whether Mrs Winton and her family would have returned from Ely by this point: if not, the ruse

180

would have been uncovered. And why hadn't George told him of this dissimulation? He might just have forgotten, of course. Something was bound to crack in his careful plans, if Mr Blackburn was as persistent as he thought he might well be. He couldn't take anyone else into his secret, could he? And even so, if he were to, he couldn't cope with relating to Mr Blackburn, to William, as being a boy, when he, that is, Richard, or rather, Rose, felt as he (or she) did towards him. And overhearing the conversation William had had with Peter made it worse, much worse, incalculably worse. Nuzzling, and ravishment, and more, to be sure!

Nonetheless I harbour aspirations which I hope you might reciprocate; to see you in ~~the flesh~~ person and not simply rely on letters. I have inscribed my London address above: might you furnish me with intelligence of your current whereabouts as I would travel some considerable distance if you would receive me, duties permitting? I have read Mrs Wollstonecraft's book that you lent to me, and would be glad to return it and discuss its contents with you. I must say I found her arguments difficult to follow, being couched in more words than are quite necessary, but I understand that this is the style of philosophical discussion. Unfortunately I have not read M Rousseau, to whom she alludes so frequently, but it seems he is the cause of the current demeaning intellectual attitude towards women that Mrs Wollstonecraft rails against.

Notwithstanding, that is not the principal aspiration of my request. I do earnestly wish to see you, to spend time with you, I find your image quite intrudes upon my activities on a daily basis. In short, I consider I hold a great admiration for your person, and wish to become far better acquainted. It has been too long between each of our meetings, and they have been much too brief for me to truly know you fully, but I hope that this situation might be remedied in the nearest future.

In 'other news', as the fashion has it, I have spent the last days in
chasing up and down the country in pursuit of the stolen Baker rifles.
Not so much as to retrieve them, but in order to ascertain where they
might have been distributed amongst persons inimical to His Majesty
King George. I may say with shame I have met with no success in this
endeavour, and will be no doubt asked to switch my efforts in other
directions in short order.

Richard set the letter down, and took a number of deep breaths. How
on earth or in heaven could he meet with this gentleman without
doing violence to his emotions or damage to his subterfuge and disguise? And equally, how could he not accede to his fervent requests
when they chimed so perfectly with his own?

I know that in a few weeks the roads may have improved enough
for you to return to Gloucestershire, and I ardently wish to see you
before this time as my duties do not extend to the West Country.
Are you presently intending to stay long in Milton or will you be
travelling back to London?

I shall be soon setting off for a tour of the northern militia, as far
as York, where I hope to visit my father, and appraise him of the
developments in the war effort, though without revealing my role in
the conflict, and I trust you would wish me well in this endeavour. I
do not know when I shall be back in London but I implore you with
all my heart to respond to this letter to the address superscribed, and
to grant me the pleasure of your company at the earliest instant.

I am, with apologies if I presume too much, yours very sincerely,
William Blackburn

Richard gulped again, and set the letter down, and shut his eyes, and
swallowed several times. He felt all manner of things: exhilarated, per-
plexed, fearful, and embarrassed were only a few of his emotions, all

tumbling over each other to be the most evident. William Blackburn surely was enamoured of him! Well, of Rose, to be sure. And how in heaven's name could he respond to his quite evident overtures? And how must poor William have felt having had no reply to this message for so many weeks? It was now March 2nd, and so, well, his mind wouldn't for the moment function with the simple subtraction, but it must be over a month since he ought to have replied to the letter, had he but received it. What should he do? What indeed?

He stood up, looked around, decided the first thing to do was to hide the letter and its cover in his box and lock it securely away in case Edward might come upon it. Then, well, he ought to, he definitely ought to, do . . . what? Something . . .

In the absence of any rational answer to his self-questioning, he took himself off to the college gardens and walked around smoking a cigar, and paced about and back again until he grew too cold, and then he set his steps towards the chapel and sank into an attitude of prayer.

Receiving no clear answer from above, he was roused by the bell for dinner, and trudged disconsolately to Hall.

CHAPTER 14

'Y OU LOOK OUT OF SORTS,' said Will Peabody as Richard sat down. 'What's happened?'

Richard grunted, and reached for the bread as grace was declaimed from the High Table. 'Well, not much, I'm just feeling off.' What excuse could he give? If he said he'd had a letter, he'd have to explain what it was about, and his powers of invention were on strike at the moment.

'Come on, you're usually such a cheerful body.'

'Well, um, I don't know myself. Just a lot going on, lots to cope with.'

'Like? I know it can't be your Greek, you're pages ahead of me; and as for mathematics, aren't you starting to look at Leibnitz?'

Richard roused himself a little. 'Not up to Leibnitz yet, still only just started on Newton, and I haven't quite done with Euclid either.'

'So what is it?'

'I don't want to say.'

Will gave up and turned his back, started quizzing Abel Johnson about his new low shoes, which he had claimed were in the very latest fashion, sent by his father from Northampton, with small iron inserts at the back of the heels to protect them from wear. Richard sat and picked at some mutton, drank some water, felt as if he might cry if he wasn't careful.

He left the table early, as soon as he saw Peter Winton rolling in late, not wanting to speak to him. He slipped out with his shoulders hunched, and shambled back to his rooms, locking the door behind him. Now come on, Richard, he told himself, Pull yourself together. Bad advice, he said back to himself. Can't be done. So what to do?

Make a list, he told himself. That's what you always do when you're stuck, make a list. So he fetched quill and ink and sat down over a clean sheet of paper and stared at it. No inspiration. Then he thought, what if this were a mathematical problem? What would he do first? Well, write down the known values, perhaps. So he began:

<u>Where have I supposedly been since Twelfth Night?</u>
London until about 10th Jan.
At Milton from about Jan 10th (George told WB) till Feb 23rd
    (Mrs Winton told WB I was gone before 28th by at least a
    few days).
Why didn't WB visit Milton on his way north on about Jan
    26th? Another lucky escape.
London 24th Feb till now, Sat 3rd March (?).
Then where might I be going? Where WB can't easily find me
    out?

Need to write to Mrs Winton and ask her and Julia to pretend I was there if WB visits again. Or should I ask Peter to negotiate?

<u>What does WB say about me? He says he wants:</u>
to see you in ~~the flesh~~ person
to spend time with you, I find your image quite intrudes upon
    my activities on a daily basis.
and wish to become far better acquainted
to truly know you fully,
the pleasure of your company
    . . . Which is all to say that WB is most attracted, and wishes to
    pursue his suit.

185

<u>WB is only slightly circumspect:</u>
apologies if I presume too much

He then sat back and realised that the worst part of the problem is that he didn't really know how he felt about Mr Blackburn, or WB as he had begun to call him, as if he were a mathematical variable. Stirred up, certainly. Flattered, undoubtably. Frightened, probably. Attracted, definitely. And if only circumstances were different, the obvious thing would have been to write a most encouraging letter and arrange for him to call, and then he might have become clearer about his (Rose's) own feelings.

That felt at least a little better, having the problem on paper. There were some conclusions to be drawn. First, he had to work out where Rose was supposed to be for the next few weeks, at least until the end of term on 22nd March. Goodness, less than three weeks to go! And that needed to be where WB couldn't find her out.

Secondly, he had to write to Mr Bl. . . WB, explaining how the delay in reply had happened, and expressing enthusiasm for a meeting, and regret that it could not be for another three weeks. So, perhaps he would say they could meet in London once he had returned. Unless there was any way they could meet in Cambridge, because he didn't know if he could wait three weeks, he felt such a draw towards this man, it penetrated every fibre of his being. But no, it could not be, his feminine attire was in London, and it would be totally impossible. Or could he meet as Richard? Perhaps together with Peter? No, no, several times no, and not just because of enlarging the compass of those who knew of his masquerade. He simply couldn't imagine having a manageable conversation with a man he was attracted to, while in his role as a boy from Nova Scotia. Or from anywhere, actually.

Thirdly, he needed to discuss this with Peter, however embarrassing it might be. Yes, definitely. And he could enlist Peter's help in letting his mother and sister know what they should say if questioned about his visits, and current whereabouts.

186

From the first point, he decided Rose would be visiting friends in Kent, in the opposite direction from WB's trips for his regiment, perhaps in Rye, or some other coastal town. Yes, Rye, because Rose had been there, and could describe some of the sights when Richard wrote. And she would be due back in London on about 24th March, to allow Richard to return from college and change into Rose without risk of discovery. Good.

So the letter would be most encouraging, and full of regret of not being able to meet until then, and written as from Rye. It was as well that the longer-distance post did not give away the sender's location by a frank mark as did the post within a city, was it not? And Cambridge was about the same distance from London as Rye, perhaps, so the cost of receipt would be similar? He was not at all sure about this, though he thought the journeys had taken about the same length of time, albeit at different seasons.

So, to Peter's room, and a most awkward discussion. Better get it over. Come on, Richard, you can do it.

Peter was sympathetic to his dilemma, and said he had wondered when this problem would come to a head. He promised to catechise his family about Rose's supposed movements, and asked Richard to provide a time-table of where Rose had been, or was supposed to have been, during which periods, so there should be no mistake. He was paying a visit home the next day, being Sunday, so that would be easy of execution.

He agreed that Mr Blackburn could not be included with himself and Sir George in the exclusive coterie who knew about the masquer-ade, and hoped that Richard could bear the wait, now he knew about the strength of Mr Blackburn's feelings for Rose. He said that some time ago he had known a young lady whom he found extremely entic-ing, and suffered considerable heartache when they were unable to meet. And, he added, somewhat wryly, more heartache when she told him she was about to become engaged to another man, for reasons of financial benefit and pressure from her mother.

Hence two letters were rapidly composed back in Richard's room: one brief one from Rose to Peter's mother thanking her for her help, and saying that Peter would explain everything. This was to be carried by Peter the next day. Then, a second one to Sir George, from Richard, asking if he had decided on when Richard should return to London, and whether Rose could spend some time at the hotel as before so that she could meet up with Mr Blackburn if he was in town. He also outlined Rose's supposed movements, couching the intelligence in such a way as to appear to be a description of what his 'friend' was doing in case the letter went astray.

That out of the way, he then sat down to compose the letter from Rose to Mr Blackburn. Much more difficult, the more so because as soon as he started, he realised that William would know all about the appearance of the Baker rifle, and could describe it in detail. So he could ask him. Except he could not, because why would Rose want to know these details? And where would he put as the address from which he was writing? Oh dear.

Long-belated greetings from the South Coast, Mr Blackburn!

I am most apologetic that I have not replied to your letter far earlier – or should I say, sooner? I was so glad to receive it, and intended to write straightway, but for some reason I put the paper in a safe place until I was at leisure, and then could not discover where I had hidden it for love nor money. I searched and searched, and turned out my box and my reticule and my pockets, but it was nowhere to be found. Also, I could not by any effort recall your present address, and so I could not reply. And now it has reappeared! It was caught up in the folds of the sleeves of a dress I almost never wear, would you believe? And now, having found it, I realise I could have applied to Sir George for your lodgings, or sent a letter to him to be taken round to the place! I am a fool, am I not? I castigate myself hourly since finding it, as I am as impatient to meet you as you me, if such a statement is proper.

I am at present visiting friends in the Rye area, it is an ancient town by the sea in Kent - or maybe it is in Sussex, I am not sure – though it may be thought a little too close to the French coast for prudence by some. I find that the French have visited the place on numerous occasions and burnt it down each time, and the locals are most derogatory about that race in consequence. The inn where I am at present is near a house called the Mermaid, which was previously an important inn which was razed to the cellars in the fourteenth century, and also hosted the notorious Hawkhurst gang of smugglers in the last century! The town has great thick old walls, but I do not think they would repel invaders in the present day. However, and this is most exciting, there are plans afoot to dig a canal from Rye to Hythe to protect the whole of the coast from a French landing on the shingle and marshland to the southeast of here. It is said work will start very soon.

Which reminds me, have you made any progress with the Baker rifle search? It must be very difficult to find such a consignment over the whole breadth of the country. Perhaps you could describe one to me, just on the chance I might come across one in an odd place: I know this is unlikely but I would feel I was involved in your work at least to a small extent if I knew something of the object of your search. Please give me a description of the main features of the gun: I should be most interested in any case for myself, to broaden my education as much as anything.

I have not put an address on the top of the letter because I shall be moving in a few days, and then again, as I am staying after this with different friends. I shall be back in London, I hope, by the 24th inst., and would welcome your visiting me at the hotel where I stayed previously, as soon as you might manage it. Perhaps you could speak to Sir George about my likely date of return, and in case he arranges for me to lodge at a different hotel?

We have made some trips into the countryside which is very beautiful though muddy. We saw an altar stone dedicated to the Roman god

Mithras in a place called Stone; we visited a church in Winchelsea whose construction stopped when the nave was but half completed, and many more sights that I shall be most glad to describe to you when we meet. Not that there will be a dearth of more personal things to discuss, because I see from your letter that your feelings are tending in the same direction as mine, and I welcome their encouragement.

Yours most warmly, Rose Clarke.

Richard sanded the letter, wishing he could have fitted more on the sheet, but not wishing to use cross-writing. He had several second and third thoughts: was he too forthcoming about his feelings? Certainly the letter-writing mistress at Miss Snape's school would have insisted he strike out many phrases and whole sentences had she seen it. Had he been definite enough about asking for a description of a Baker rifle? Would William respond quickly? And where could he tell William to send his letter of reply?

He just had space in the margin to add a post-scriptum. 'Please could you address any reply to Sir George, and he will ensure I receive it at the first opportunity.'

Unsealing George's letter and quickly adding an explanation of his plan, emphasising how he needed the description of the Baker as soon as possible, he refolded and resealed it, and took the two sheets to the receiving office, pausing only to drop off the other letter and Rose's itinerary at Peter's room. It was done.

At supper on Sunday, Peter told him that he had explained just enough about their mutual friend Rose's movements to his mother and sisters, and no more; and that he had had a reply from his colleague who knew Dr Mansel, and had gained access to the steward and his ledger. It seemed that Louis Price and Christian Martin had both dined on January 24th together with two guests, John Smart of Caius, and Ebenezer Harmour, of no college. Dinner was at 4pm at

Trinity, and he recalled the circumstance, as they ordered a special claret from the cellars, and drank three bottles between them. He also recalled that they had made a disturbance while grace was being said, which earned them a critical glare from the Master, though they laughed it off. John Burgess and Matthew Noakes had not dined that day.

He had also heard from the colleague that Trinity was in a fever of excitement because they were shortly to be favoured by a visit from His Majesty King George, who was to be shown around Mr Newton's old rooms and some of the new building projects, and dine in Hall. He would of course be staying in the Master's Lodge for the one night, before moving on to an engagement in Ely. It seemed his Majesty had recovered from a debilitating illness earlier in the year, which resembled his episode in 1788 when there was a political crisis over the question of the appointment of a Regent. Which Richard may not have known about, being in Nova Scotia at the time, he said with a sideways grin. And only a babe in arms at the time, of course, he added.

'We pay very close attention to the English news, in the colonies,' Richard retorted. 'And we are not at all happy about the antics of Prince George over there either: we are a most conservative set of people who lament his excesses.'

'Well said,' Peter acknowledged with a dip of his head. 'Anyway, it seems that four of our main suspects were lodged out of harm's way at the time of the murder.'

'I'm not so sure. How long would it take to get from our chapel to their Hall? With the right gowns, remember all that business with them being changed?'

'I have a copy of the whole ledger page for that day, lad: there are lots of others we have on our lists who don't appear at all.'

'Yes, I'll go through them, but I still think we ought to look more carefully at Price and Martin.'

'You do that, then. I've got a pile of Greek and Latin to get through, it's a tough job being an agent and an undergraduate who gives at least a fair imitation of being a reading man.'

'I had noticed,' said Richard dryly, and took the list back to his room to consider.

The next day found him meandering around after chapel, looking puzzled. He wandered out into the court and looked up at the clock, and then at the porters' lodge, and up at the clock again. Edward, who was more interested in going to see what Mrs Fenn had brought for breakfast, noticed him staring up into space.

'What'ye doing, spoony?'

'What? Well, I'm thinking.'

'A new experience for you, I'll be bound.'

Richard gave him a Look, and carried on looking at the clock. 'The thing is, you see, all the clocks in Cambridge keep different times, don't they? The bells ring the hour over at least ten minutes, or even more.'

'Yes, of course, that's why we have to keep to our clock for meal-times and so on, which reminds me, do you think Mrs Fenn will have got any more of those sweet rolls, they were extra good yesterday?'

'No, listen. When was Stephens killed? What time, I mean?'

'How should I know? We found him about a quarter after four, I should say. Well, you found him, I suppose.'

'And he had been dead since . . . ?'

'Don't know.'

'Well, we think the two of them came into college after three. I made some notes: Chapman says that they came in, the blue gowns that is, with Mr Davies' party a little after three, maybe a quarter after; and you and I got back a little after them. You remember, I'd been to Mr Laughton and you'd been, somewhere else, I can't remember where.'

'Shopping for a new set of wine glasses, no luck; yes, that day isn't one I'll forget for a long time, nocky.'

'So, when did we get here?'

'Chapel clock said three twenty, I think, because we had to go to our rooms and find our gowns, and change our boots, and I couldn't locate the old academic regalia, so we slunk in almost ten minutes late, remember?'

'That's right. I was fed up waiting for you, now I think of it.'

'But worth the wait for the scintillating company, no?'

'Moving on. So the Davies crowd would have come in about a quarter past, with our men sloping in with them. And then the murderer and Stephens would have had to wander over to chapel, and go in, and look around, remembering it was quite dark already that day, and then go up to the painting, and admire it, and so on.'

'So what are you saying?'

Richard stopped to think a little. 'Well, how long would that all take? And then he'd have to kill him, and go through all his pockets, and get his gown off him, and put both gowns in the box in Burton's room, and fetch the Emmanuel gown, and . . .'

'I see. Would have taken him quite a while.'

'Yes. And then he had to get to, well, I'm saying to Trinity, and appear in Hall. Could it be done?'

'*Nescio.*'

'What?'

'*Nescio.* Remember? It means I don't know, have you forgotten? I thought you knew Latin. *Furfur!*'

'Oh yes. Well anyway. So how do we check it out?'

'We could do a re-enactment. Not actually killing anyone, of course. Unless you have some enemies you want to dispatch?'

'But how would we know how long it takes? We can't see the chapel clock while we are doing it.'

'Have you heard of that new-fangled invention, the pocket watch? Only been around for a few hundred years, perhaps you don't have them in the colonies?'

'Very funny. Yes, but do you have one?'

'No, you know I don't, but lots of men do. Nobs, anyway.'

'Can we borrow one?'

'Surely. I'll try Watkinson, he has one. After breakfast, cully, come on. He's always in his rooms but we can't interrupt him at the trough.'

'And I'll fetch two gowns.'

'Breakfast I said. Come on.'

So in moderately short order, and after spirited arguments about who would have the last roll, and then who was going to be the corpse, the lads set to, to time the murder. Starting at the lodge, and going through all the actions they had attributed to the crime, up to leaving college again, took just about twelve minutes. Well, Edward said it would take longer in reality, because he'd cooperated in the matter of gown removal and pocket emptying, not wanting Richard ferreting around in his trousers, which he thought was reasonable, and he considered he had died rather quickly too, but he rather recoiled at that part of the proceedings, and added that he absolutely refused to soil himself like poor old Stephens, even for verisimilitude.

'Hmm,' said Richard. 'Didn't take long at all. I didn't think it would be that quick.'

'What, haven't you ever strangled anyone before? Even in the wilds of Nova Scotia? Bet you could get away with anything out there.'

'It is a most civilised community, I'll have you know. Much more civilised than Cambridge is, if you want to know. Murders are not two-a-penny; very little drinking and whoring and fighting.'

'All right, all right, I was only bamming.'

'Now, we need to see how long it takes to get from here to Trinity Hall.'

'Trinity Hall? Isn't that a different college?'

'No, bacon brain, Hall in Trinity. As you very well knew,' he added, seeing Edward screwing up his nose at him.

'So, nocky boy, give me that timepiece, I'd better check it's set to chapel time, and then we'll go for a stroll.'

'Fair enough.'

Keeping a steady but not unusual pace, they made their way through town, weaving through the crowds, and taking what they thought would be the shortest route. They arrived in Great Court after no more than ten minutes, and took stock.

'So that means twenty-two minutes from getting to Emmanuel before arriving in Hall here,' said Richard. 'Lots and lots of time.'

'You forget, they had to change their boots and swap the Emmanuel gown for a Trinity one before going to the trough.'

'Oh yes. Well, allowing for them being organised, and depending on where their room is, that couldn't take more than, what, three minutes?'

'So, twenty-five altogether.'

'I thought you had forsworn mathematical study? Which takes us to . . . twenty minutes to four. So, plenty of time, still.'

Edward was examining the watch, and looking up at the clock, and frowning. 'What time did we leave college?'

'Just before eight, maybe a minute or two before.'

'That's what I thought. And we got here at eight and . . . nine minutes past, but their clock says eighteen minutes past eight.'

Richard frowned. So that means . . . Trinity's clock is running about ten minutes ahead of ours?'

'Something like that. I remember, I had a lecture here once,'

'I didn't know you darkened the doors of such events?'

'. . . and I got here in plenty of time, but I was still late for it starting. Not as much as ten minutes though.'

Richard, for the first time, began to get excited. 'That's it! I'd forgotten what colleges all having their own times would mean for an alibi. So, if there was anything to hold him up, he'd have only just made dinner, and it could be that he was one of the men who arrived . . . shall we say, during grace, which would account for them having made a disturbance and got a glare from the Master.'

'Doesn't prove anything, does it, though? I bet these clocks keep on varying how fast they go, that lecture I was late for had only been going five minutes or so.'

'No, it doesn't prove it, but, it all starts to hang together. On the other hand, when was this unique event of you going to a lecture here?'

'Sometime in February, it was the first one after the division of term.'

'Hmm. So, not very close to the murder date, then. The clocks could have been more, or less, different in January. It's so confusing with all these different times. Somebody should sort them all out, make everyone stick to the same times, it's only sensible.'

Edward put his head on one side and considered their timings. 'Look, you said they'd start at three fifteen, coming in with the Davies crowd past our lodge.'

'Yes, we established that.'

'But, come on, if you were going to do a murder, in public nearly, wouldn't you want to be sure nobody would walk in on you?'

'I wouldn't be doing a murder, no way.'

'Yes, but if. You see, if I'd been the garotte merchant, I'd have waited until the chapel bell went for dinner, and then I'd be pretty sure I'd be undisturbed.'

Richard considered this. 'You know, I think you're right. They couldn't have left college until after about another ten minutes, could they, I mean ten minutes later than we said, because of waiting for the coast to be clear. Which means, even if the Trinity clock wasn't as fast as it is today, I mean compared to our clock, they'd still be pushed for time.' He rubbed his nose, shook his head slowly. 'Well done, I'm thinking you're the brains of the outfit, not me.'

'Hidden depths, that's me. Now, look, while we're here, do you want me to go and have a squint at that gun in Price's room? I know you have a wasp in your hat about it.'

Richard's face fell. 'I don't know what to look for, I've never seen a Baker.'

'But I bet you're finding out, some devious way or other. Doesn't Winton know?'

196

'No, he just said it had a brass box in the stock.' Richard bit his lip.
'The stock? Like a cravat?'

'The bit that goes against your shoulder, you sap.'

'Well, look, I could have a nosy, and see if there are any special marks on it, engraving, that sort of thing.'

'It's a rifle, so it will have grooves inside the barrel, I suppose.'

'Great. I'll go and dig out Price, and you never know, he might have some breakfast left. You get back to your old books, I'll see you later.'

CHAPTER 15

'T<small>ELL ME</small> I'<small>M A BRIGHT</small> old cove then. Regular sleuthhound, Hever is. I even remembered to come up with a reason why I was in Trinity so early: I said I'd lost my penknife and I thought it might have fallen out on his floor after the jollification, I'd looked everywhere else, and I didn't have another one, so I thought I'd try and catch him at breakfast before he went out.'

'And we had a good old hunt, and asked his bedder, who is a right dragon, and I said, what about the bedroom, and just barged in, but he was fine about it, and I saw the gun, and admired it, and he said it was just an old fowling musket, but I had a squint, and like you said, the barrel had grooves inside, and there was some engraving on the firing thing, it said "GR" under a crown, and "Tower". And there was a brass sort of lid on the back end, where it goes on your shoulder. I told him it looked a mighty fine gun, and did he get many snipe and such, and said they were supposed to be plentiful on the Leys; and he said he wasn't much of a shot, but he liked the gun, it had been his uncle's, and he was very fond of it.'

'So I didn't find my knife, but I cadged a couple of cakes, and took myself off, and here we are.'

On Tuesday the post brought a letter from Sir George. Richard opened it with his door locked, just in case of interruption, and jigged up and down on his settle with glee when he saw the contents.

George gave him a full description of the Baker rifle: of course, the Foreign Office would know all about these things, wouldn't they? He was a nocky not to have thought of that, a real bacon-brain. It fitted in all particulars with Edward's report! Patch box, engravings, seven square rifling grooves, and in addition it said it had an S-shaped trigger guard and a thirty inch barrel. Real progress. Why would Price have a military rifle, under three years old, in his rooms? Why indeed. And that eyewash about it having been his uncle's. Well.

Also, George said he had seen Mr Blackburn, he had visited him at his lodgings that day, Sunday, and it was a good job he had just received Richard's letter because he could tell him the correct pack of lies, and he hoped he'd done it right, but this sort of situation was only going to get worse, and was Richard really going to carry on with his plan for ever, and how might it all end, and all sorts of elder-brother nonsense, which made Richard both irritated but also quite touched at his concern.

And Blackburn had told him, George that is, that he'd write immediately, and give him the letter to send on, because he'd told him Rose was going to be moving to a new address, and when she confirmed she'd arrived he could enclose it with his reply. Naturally, he would in fact simply readdress it to Richard at Emmanuel, making sure the other name was erased completely, so as not to cause any embarrassment.

Richard imagined the porters puzzling over a letter arriving at the lodge addressed to Miss Rose Clarke: it would be quite a sensation, would it not? He felt himself grinning at the idea, but couldn't decide if it was in amusement or nervousness.

On Wednesday Richard had a bright idea while thinking about the delay in publication of Mr Newton's theory of fluxions, which had allowed Herr Leibnitz to claim priority. If His Majesty had recently recovered from illness, then was this visit rearranged from an earlier date? And might that date have been in January, when the murder had taken place? And what would that mean?

*

On Thursday Richard and Peter attended Professor Wollaston's lecture on the discovery of the elements. He finally understood what an element was, and was surprised to discover that upwards of forty different ones were known. They seemed to fall into groups, with similar properties, and noone knew why. They had widely varying masses, in the sense of how much of one element combined with the same amount of, say, oxygen. There ought to be a pattern, it was thought, but if so it was completely obscure.

He heard about Dr Dalton's recent ideas about the smallest particle in nature which he called atoms, after the nomenclature of the ancient Greek Democritus; about the controversy that this had caused, and the difficulties in reconciling the ratios with which these supposed atoms might combine, in gaseous form and in solid form.

He talked about recent discoveries: Tantalum (or Columbium), Cerium, Osmium; and then described with apparent pride, how his brother William had recently isolated two new elements and was about to publish his findings on one which he had named Palladium after the recently discovered small planet. Richard, attending more closely than some of the others, thought he detected more than a tinge of narrow-eyed jealousy in the Professor's expression while his words were entirely laudatory.

Sudden illumination dawned from his memory. Had not someone told him that William Wollaston, the brother, had become rich as a result of purifying platinum ores? And so perhaps Francis wished to emulate him? Were his researches on rock oil for the purpose of discovering a process which would make his fortune? Perhaps still concerning munitions, though; but his secrecy would be for fear of competitors stealing his process, not of French spies? Had they been hunting the wrong rabbit?

Once the lecture was over he put his ideas to Peter, who was only moderately enthusiastic, which dampened his spirits considerably. He did manage to persuade Peter to come with him to Trinity to

200

interrogate the porters, but he came only reluctantly. They looked up dates in their appointment ledger, and said that the royal visit had been due to come off on January 27th, but due to indisposition it was now scheduled for the twelfth of March, and the college will be full of important people, from the Chancellor down. This was only next Monday! It was a great coup for the college, and was sure to put the Hogs' noses out of joint.

'Now do you believe me?' he said as they walked back to college. 'Now we've been told that date, I remember they were all flustered about a visitor when I came here with that Trinity gown, you remember, when I found it in the chaplain's trunk. Before you came up, you know. I don't think this whole business is anything to do with the rock oil; I think it's something around the King's visit. What, I don't know.'

'You might have a point, lad. But I still think it's more likely to be around the development of a new kind of gunpowder, much more military value in that.'

'But what about the Baker rifle in Price's room? I forgot to tell you, Edward took a look at it and it fits Sir George's description perfectly.'

'Well, if there was a whole consignment missing, and your friend Mr Blackburn has had no joy in tracing them, I expect many French agents have acquired one, for general reasons. Like that fly gentleman who took a shot at me at Christmas, and hit poor Marian.'

Richard's lower lip protruded. 'I think you're wrong. But what do we do next?'

'I think I shall have another try to chat with our tight-lipped Professor. I might take Warburton along, he is older, he is more official than me, and he knows a lot more about artillery, which if we are right about the explosive, is a more likely use to my mind than small arms powder. Perhaps the offer of a ready buyer for his invention, if it indeed exists, might loosen his reticence. It might take a few days until I can reach Warburton, though, I heard he was off to Woolwich.'

'What shall I do then?'

Peter considered. 'I should press on with your Newton, I think. Let's see what Warburton can prise out of our man. And you have plenty of other things to be getting on with: there's a four-oar outing today, and don't you go fencing on Fridays?'

On Friday Richard received the letter from Mr Blackburn. He had hoped it would come sooner and wished it wouldn't arrive at all, in equal measures. He inspected the address carefully: there was no evidence of his former name visible. Well, not his former name, really, his real name. Except Richard Cox seemed to be now so real to him; not that Rose was not real, but Richard had so many opportunities that Rose never could.

William, well, was it proper to think of him as William, at least in private, since he had declared his affection so strongly in the last missive, seemed rather reticent on this occasion. The letter began simply, "Miss Clarke," and sounded more stiff than formerly. The reason became clear in the second paragraph: William had arrived in London on 29th February and knew that Rose had been there since about the 25th, but he had not had any message from her, although Sir George could have taken one and left it for him at his lodgings. Also, he thought Rose's story about the lost address quite unlike her, who had always shown a remarkable intelligence about finding ways around difficulties. She might well have sent her letter care of Sir George, even while she was at Milton, might she not?

He did not know what to make of this. He did not wish to think ill of her, but he could not think of an explanation for the silence. Nonetheless he sent all good wishes for her stay in Rye, and hoped she might help him out by chancing upon a stray Baker in that country, where there were known to be many French agents. Description followed.

He then wrote in a rather convoluted way for two paragraphs in which Richard, or more realistically, Rose, reading between the lines, realised he felt quite hurt by her, and wondered if he had offended her by being too forward, and suspected, though he at the same time thought the idea unworthy, that she might be concealing something of import from him. What that might be he could not imagine, and he hoped it was not anything that he might have done or said that had caused the subterfuge, if indeed there was one.

He signed himself simply, W. Blackburn, and Rose sighed as she folded the sheets and sat back and stared at the letter. Trying to settle his mind by straightening his shoulders and returning to his role as Richard, he put the sheet away in his box and decided that he was going to have to reveal his disguise to William sooner rather than later. He could see no way around it, not at present, but the alternative was perhaps worse, to break off relations with him? And this had to be decided on in the Easter holiday, after Rose supposedly returned from Rye. It could not realistically be earlier, as he needed to stay in character for the rest of the term. And there was the matter of the murder still to solve, and the plot of these traitorous Trinity men to foil, was there not?

Meanwhile he could go and clear his poor brain at the fencing club. Uncomplicated; well, quite complex in how to execute the moves, but not so in regard to relationships with people, who were hidden behind their masks. He took himself off down St Andrew's-street, got to the salle, put on the jacket, glove and mask, and felt his frustration build into a fierce urge to win.

He fenced with his first opponent in quite a controlled manner, as he had been taught, but as the bout progressed his lunges became more aggressive, and his ripostes more forceful. He felt the blood surging, and came out victor by several hits. The next bout was more wild, he suffered several quite painful blows to the shoulder, but still was victorious. The fencing master, seeing this exhibition, came over and urged him to slow down, to parry with more style, to wait for the opening and then strike, but Richard could not heed him. A third match went against him as his opponent was more wily and skilful, but he revelled in the battle.

By the end of the session he was quite worn down, tired but much more self-possessed. He walked home, resolved to do whatever it took to solve this mystery. Coming out of Petty Cury though, he started to feel he was being followed. He glanced around, but couldn't identify anyone, though he thought he caught a glimpse of someone slipping behind a pillar. Probably nothing, he thought. Nonetheless he quickened his pace, and fairly scurried through the college gateway, only calming once he saw Abel Johnson in the court, and fell in with him on his way into dinner.

Thinking back, he had a nagging feeling he had not been quite alone on his trip back from the four-oar outing with Peter yesterday. Just a sense of someone a distance behind, monitoring his habits, becoming familiar with his haunts. As he sat down by Abel he found himself rubbing his neck, and thinking of poor Stephens, and wondering. Peter had said he'd better not leave college alone, but it had proved impractical, what with all the activities that filled his week, and he just felt, well, rather scared.

'Abel, you know about leatherwork, don't you?'

'I should do, the house is full of it.'

'Well, I don't want to seem all lily-livered or anything, but I've been having a feeling I'm being followed, around town, and you know I've been trying to find out who killed Mr Stephens, the man that was killed in our chapel, you know, and I don't . . . well, I don't want to become another victim of the garotte.'

'Me neither. Have you got anywhere with your conundrum?'

'Nothing definite, that's the trouble. Nor has Peter Winton. But we've found out a lot of possibles, and in doing so we think we may have let the real murderers know we are on their trail. And if they will kill once, they'll do it again, and I don't want it to be me.'

'Seems reasonable. So what are you thinking of?'

'Well, how would you protect yourself against a garotte? I know about foils and so on, we have protection when we're learning to fence, but what about strangling?'

'You'd want something to stop the cord biting into your neck, I'd say. Well, like a wide stiff collar, or something?'

'Can one be bought?'

'Anything can be bought, if you know where. Why don't you come with me, I'll take you to a man I know, shoemaker, he is, I'll explain what you need, he'll make it for you, to measure.'

'Really? And can we go straight after dinner?'

'Surely. He's a good sort, I got to know him because he has some interesting new styles in his window, and I went in to see how the trade is down here compared to Northampton. For my father, you know.'

On the way, Richard found himself making excuses for his anxieties, but Abel didn't seem to think he was being silly. He noticed that Abel's new shoes were making a tapping noise on the street, and asked him about it.

'Invention of my father, to reduce the wearing down of the heel. He puts little flat hobnails in, they aren't known outside one or two of his customers who ask for them.'

'I like the idea. Maybe I ought to get some.' Richard felt an urge to be like his friend, who had been so helpful.

'Don't think they know about it here in Cambridge. But we can ask Mr Alsop about it. He might be able to oblige.'

Mr Alsop was indeed very accommodating. He heard Richard's request without seeming to think badly of his fears – well, Abel made the request on his behalf, Richard had asked him to, he was quite embarrassed about it. He thought a while, and then went into the back of his shop and found out a piece of leather that he thought might do.

'A bit like a wide collar for a large dog, do you think, sir?' he asked, holding it up to Richard's neck. 'Yes, I think I can see my way to making one like that. To wear under your cravat, I think. Mmm. Let me see.'

He measured Richard at all sorts of points, noting down as he went, muttering to himself about buckles and lacing and flaring out and other such terms.

'I think we can do very nicely, sir. It will be somewhat uncomfortable, though, however I make it, but, er, may I ask, have you had threats, or attempts on your life?'

'Not actual threats, as such. But I have been dealing with men who have murdered, and I feel they may act again. Perhaps I am being over-fearful?'

'No, I believe you are just being prudent. Now, is that all? I can have this for you tomorrow, after eleven, if that is satisfactory?'

'Very much so, Mr Alsop. There is one other thing, though. Abel, will you explain?'

Abel showed Mr Alsop his shoe heels, and said that Richard was hoping he might try something similar on his boots. The shoemaker examined the heels, and tutted a bit, and then said that he thought he might be able to file down a couple of his normal hobnails to a flatter shape, and they might do.

'But they may not hold, mind. Not on the edge of the heel.'

'We could try, though, sir, could we not?' said Richard. 'I'll come in my boots tomorrow and we can see?'

They left the shop, Richard feeling a deal better. He still kept looking around, behind him and into side turnings, but saw nothing worrying. Nonetheless he kept to his room for the rest of the day and tried to study his Newton, even forgoing supper, and making sure to lock his oak securely.

He took Abel with him again the following morning, for company (well, protection) and for expert advice on matters of leather. Abel seemed pleased to be asked: although he'd had Greek supervisions with him for the last two terms and they'd become more friendly as a result, he didn't feel particularly close to him. He knew he was interested in bowls, and was going to play when summer came, and he was moderately keen on study, but not much else.

'Thanks for coming, Abel. I feel a bit silly doing this, you know.'

'I don't think so. Anyway, when you do a sport, you wear protection; or soldiers, they wear cuirasses and such, don't they?'

'Are you a sportsman, then? I mean apart from bowls?'

Abel tried to look modest. 'Well, a little. I play cricket at home. I'm thought to be quite good. More of a bowler than a batsman, though, but I wear padding on my shins when I bat. And I usually field on the boundary, because I have a good arm. Not found anyone who plays here yet, though.'

'I hope you might. Cricket is played in the summer, though, is it not?'

'Yes. But it needs a large field, and Parker's Piece is full of soldiers, or I might have tried to raise a team to play there. I try and keep my eye in by playing quoits at the Marquess of Granby, you know the pub?'

Mr Alsop had their goods ready for them. Richard untied his cravat and settled the collar around his neck under his collar. It was a good fit, but awkward and quite uncomfortable. Abel tied the cloth for him so as to cover it almost completely, and he moved his head around experimentally.

'Not bad, I suppose. I mean, Mr Alsop, what you have made is very good, but it is bound to feel very odd to start with, is it not?'

'I didn't want to make it too soft or it wouldn't do the job, sir. And I tried to bevel the edges and shape it a bit so's it would sit better. I don't think you could have it any more cut-away, or it wouldn't serve.'

'No, I quite see that. Thankyou.'

The shoemaker produced the modified hobnails and Richard took off his boots. They were quickly hammered into place and he stood up, took a few steps, and pronounced himself most satisfied. He paid, and the lads left, Richard hearing the tapping of the metal with each step as he went.

'Very fashionable, you,' said Abel. 'Latest, in fact ahead of the fashion if truth be told.

'Boot-nails, maybe; but I hope the collar won't catch on,' Richard muttered, wriggling his neck and trying to get more comfortable. 'At least I won't have to keep it on at night.'

'Look,' he added as they reached their staircase, 'I'm going to Trinity on Monday, they're having a very important visitor. Between twelve and one, I'm told. I want to be there, to see that nothing untoward happens. Edward's coming, at least, I haven't told him yet, but he is, and I think it would be better with more of us.'

'Twelve o'clock, Monday? I think I can do that. Who's the visitor?'

'The King. He's not often out of London, so this is quite special. All the nobs are turning out, I think. There'll be a crowd.'

'What about Peter Winton, Richard? You're pretty thick with him, I thought.'

'He doesn't think this is the target of our men. He's focussed on something else. But I'm . . . I don't know. I want to be sure.'

'Fine, then. I'd like to see royalty. I haven't done before.'

'Not sure how much you'll see. He'll be surrounded by nobs on all sides.'

'What do you think might happen?'

'I'm worried about someone taking a shot at him. With a rifle. One of the newest types, they're much more accurate than a musket. At greater distances too.'

'Sounds a lark. Well, serious too, I guess. I'll come and help, wouldn't miss it.'

Richard was on thorns all the rest of the day, and throughout Sunday. He kept to his room on Saturday, mostly with his oak locked, except for dining in Hall; but he did attend Mr Simeon, with collar in place, and found that nobody took notice, or commented on it, though he thought it exceedingly visible however he tied his cravat.

He tried to find out from the Trinity men in church if anyone knew about the timing of events on Monday, but it seemed it was all in the air, because of the uncertain speed of the roads. Messengers would be sent ahead when the King reached Trumpington village, and all would be readied. He would first be taken to the Master's lodgings to have refreshment, and then go on a tour of the college, starting with Mr Newton's rooms which he had especially requested to see. Then to his statue in the ante-chapel, where prayers would be said, and the library and Nevile's court, and then dinner in Hall. Or so the word had it. His informants explained that they might be completely deceived, as mere pensioners were not privy to the plans of the great and good.

Also, the Chancellor was to be in attendance, the Duke of Grafton; and of course the Vice-Chancellor, the Master of Clare Hall, Dr Torkington, and everyone who was anyone in the whole area. The place will be thick with gold tufts and braid and velvet, they said. 'You'll not stand a chance of getting within fifty yards of him,' he was told, 'let alone speaking to the man.'

This reassured Richard somewhat, because if nobody could get near him, nobody could harm him, could they? But he wanted to be there, on guard, he felt responsible somehow. Surely, there would be the courtiers who normally protected the King's person, but, somehow, he wasn't happy. He did approach Peter about the matter, but he said everything was in hand, and not to worry, and to leave it to him and his colleagues; yet he didn't believe him.

He made sure on Monday that he had extra breakfast left by Mrs Fenn, so he could eat late in the morning, as he wanted to be in place well before the hour, and he advised Edward, who was predictably keen on the escapade, and Abel who was more sanguine, to do the same. Setting off at eleven they made their way across town, and through the crowded Market place to St Mary's Church and so onto Trumpington-street opposite the Senate House. Every so often he felt his neck in its collar, and shivered.

The town was far busier than usual. Pushing through the crowds the lads approached the corner of Caius, when Richard halted abruptly. There was Peter Winton up ahead, walking up Trumpington-street, with someone who he thought was Mr Warburton, yes, his broken nose identified him, and also – surely not? – Mr Blackburn again? That was just too much. He couldn't cope with even thinking about him now. Well, they had every right to be here, he supposed, they were in the service of the King, so, well, it just made things a lot more difficult for him.

'Hold hard,' he hissed to his friends. 'I've just seen someone I don't want to meet. Let's go down Senate House Passage and go to Trinity the back way.'

Edward and Abel looked puzzled, but did as he asked. 'Who's the dodgy cove?' asked Edward. 'Is it one of our murderers?'

'No, but I can't tell you who it is, just leave it.'

The other two just shrugged their shoulders at each other, and followed. It was less busy down this route, though still they had to weave in and out of people. They turned right into Caius-lane and passed Trinity Hall, and made halting progress towards Trinity's Queen's Gate. They passed into the Great Court, and took stock.

'Nothing happening yet,' stated Edward. 'Time for a snack, I think.' He pulled out a roll and started munching. Richard's stomach was rumbling, but he had no appetite, though he had some biscuits in his pocket. He didn't even have the will to congratulate Edward on his miraculous powers of observation.

'I think we ought to wait over there, in the corner,' said Abel. 'If you want to keep out of the way, that is.'

'Good plan,' agreed Richard. 'But just a minute, I want to remind myself of where the men we are interested in live.' He addressed himself to the names on the door jamb.

Edward, mouth full, said, 'Noakes is at the top, second floor, on the left of the stair, facing the court; Price is the floor below him on the right, so is Hope, whoever he is, but Price's room faces the street.'

'Good man. I was thinking we'd have to go up the stair to check which was where exactly, now we don't need to.'

'Told you I was foxy, lad, foxy and subtle. By the way, do you have any more food on you?'

Richard passed him a biscuit, and said nothing. He shifted his weight from foot to foot, and wondered how long they'd be standing here. He thought he'd soon want to urinate, and that could be tricky, not that he hadn't gone before they left, but he was so tense.

Abel on the other hand was looking around with interest. 'Never been in here before,' he commented. 'Bit bigger than our place, what?'

'Just a trifle,' said Edward, showering crumbs.

'So, what is there where? You've both been before.'

'That thing with the little steeple is their Hall,' said Richard, pointing to their left, 'and then the Master lives in the range beyond it; then there's the Old Library, the antechapel, the chapel, Newton's rooms are in that bit just round the corner, then there's the Great Gate where I expect His Majesty will come in.'

'Thanks. So, what are we looking for?'

'That's just it, I don't know. I believe our men, that's Noakes and Price and his friend Martin, I don't know where his room is; and possibly John Burgess, though he's not been very much prominent so far; and there's a chap from Caius called John Smart, who Edward here knows, and then some men from outside the University, um, well, there's lots of them we are unsure of, when I say we, I suppose I mean, me. And there might be others. That's why it's so difficult.'

'Price has a rifle, which he claimed was his old uncle's duck-hunting musket,' put in Edward, who had finished his biscuit and was searching his pockets for stray edibles, 'so he'd be my number one suspect.'

'What about you, though, Richard, you've done more on this thing, haven't you?'

'Yes, I have, but I really don't know. I mean, Price could be meaning to shoot the King, I suppose, but, well, I just don't know. Or there could be a bomb, did you hear of that business out at Trumpington where somebody nearly blew up all the top officers of the militia last December?'

'I did. I heard some girl stopped them and got blown up herself with two of her friends, or something.'

'Something like that, I'm not sure. Anyway, Peter says that they

211

haven't traced the rest of the powder, there was barrels and barrels of it, so they could be trying again.'

'They might try and poison him in Hall,' put in Edward, 'that'd be a fine trick. Might not even need much poison, from what I've heard of their kitchens.'

'Doesn't he have food tasters?' asked Abel.

'No idea.' Richard found he was getting even more tense. 'Anyway, you've eaten here, haven't you? You didn't die, I don't think?'

'No, but you can't say anything good about Bulldogs, can you. I mean, it isn't done.'

Richard had to explain about Bulldogs to Abel, which led on to Edward running through all the colleges and their nicknames for his benefit, feeling that his great education should not be wasted. As it passed the time, Richard didn't say anything, but scanned the people passing, and bit his nails.

What could they do if anyone tried anything? How could they stop them? Maybe Peter was right, and he should have left it to him and the official protection men. It wasn't crowded this side of the court, they were a long way from the action; well, he hoped there wouldn't be any action, obviously, but if there was. And what was that over there by the gate? A little disturbance?

'Looks like the messenger has arrived,' said Abel. 'They're all getting themselves readied, in lines, and everything.'

Richard looked around, up at the rooms above him, where he supposed Noakes and Price and who knows who else were quietly going about their business. He stepped a few paces from the wall to see better. All was serene, windows closed and no sign of what might be going on inside.

Just then, a man walked out of the stair, heading in the general direction of the Hall. He was short, and bearded, well, he had a scrubby sort of growth of hair on his chin. Was this Mr Price?

He hurried over to Edward, trying to be inconspicuous, but hearing his boots make a clicking noise on the cobbles. 'Is that man Price?' he whispered, pointing surreptitiously.

Edward glanced over, nodded. 'The same. Where's he going then? Shall I follow him?'

'I don't think so. Well, I don't know. What do you think?'

'He'd spot me in a place like this. Anyway, look, he's gone into that staircase over there. I'll go an' have a nose to see which names are at the bottom.'

In a very few minutes he returned, and gabbled off a list of names before they left his memory. Only one registered with Richard: Martin. Price's friend, and possible co-conspirator.

'And I saw that ridiculously tall cully too, he was going in after Price. What's his name?'

'Burgess?'

'That's the badger. Is he on your little black list?'

'I think so. Look, would you mind, could you go and stand at the foot of that stair, and if any of them come out, try and think what best to do?'

'Right you are. Hever to the sentry-go,' and he took himself off, whistling tunelessly.

CHAPTER 16

THE COLLEGE CLOCK STRUCK TWELVE, well, twenty-four really, plus the quarter chimes, as was its wont, what with there being two bells. It must be running slow today, thought Richard, it seems ages since we left Emmanuel. But then one after another, every few minutes, the bells sounded from the other towers of the town: tinny, resonant, dull, cracked, out-of-tune. And there seemed to be an increase in the noise coming from the street, Trumpington-street, but maybe he was imagining it. More a swelling of a background sound, over noises from the scenes across the court, where people were fussing around, and academic hoods were being shrugged up onto shoulders and caps arranged more neatly, small signs of busyness and preparation.

No, there definitely was more noise from the street. Behind the high ranges of the college rooms it was hard to tell exactly where it was coming from, but there was a definite swelling of sound. Richard wanted to dash to the gate to look up Trinity-lane to see if the procession was passing yet. But he stayed at his post, and just looked out for anything that was wrong, anything unusual, anything different. Edward stood fidgeting around the bottom of the stair two sets away, whereas Abel was still, cracking his knuckles occasionally, and looking across to the crowd by the Great Gate.

What was he looking for? He didn't know. He thought it ought to be to do with Noakes or Price or Burgess or Martin or one of the men on his lists, but which? He looked up again at Noakes' window, which stared sightlessly across the court. Hope's window below was similarly blank. And the other three men were over there up the staircase from Edward, no movement there either.

Now there was a clear sound of cheering, and some catcalling, individual voices occasionally heard above the general clamour. A movement at the Gate, a parting, and a series of men on horseback trotted into the court, plumes blowing, horses snorting. Then the carriage horses, and the gilded coach itself, drove under the arch. It was almost impossible to see, there were so many people in the way, so many worthies and dons and courtiers and . . . well, a huge mass of humanity. A band started up, martial music, it might have been a military band, it was so difficult to tell.

The King presumably got out of the far side of his coach, Richard couldn't be sure, but there was a movement of the crowd to the left, towards the Master's lodgings. He craned his neck up at the windows once more. Surely that was Noakes' window, now open? And what was that poking out? A gun barrel?

He grabbed Abel's shoulder. 'Look up there! Isn't that a rifle?'

'You're right. What do we do?'

'I'm going to race up there, see if I can tackle him before he can shoot,' and he hared off to the foot of the stair, and clattered up it as fast as his legs would take him, leaving Abel looking up and wondering.

Richard hadn't got time to be frightened, he just acted. Bursting into the room he threw himself at the man at the window, trying to wrestle him away. Something clattered through the opening, and fell on the floor. As the man turned, he saw it was Jake Mackenzie. He was far bigger and stronger than him, and he had the rifle. Richard crouched down to spring again, but Jake swung the rifle at him and caught him on the head, sending him reeling into a corner. Lying there, dazed, and unsure if he could get up, he watched Jake take up his position again, settle himself, and take aim.

Another object crashed against the window jamb, and Jake cursed fluently. He again settled, and Richard recognised the stillness that came over a man about to fire. Then, a third missile struck the barrel of his gun, his finger jerked on the trigger, and it went off with a crash, deafening in the enclosed space. More cursing from Jake. He started to attempt to reload, tearing off a cartridge with his teeth, but before he'd got past priming the lock, there was more noise on the stair. Richard began to struggle to his feet; Jake cast the rifle aside, and took off. He more or less fell down the stairs, and there was another crash, followed by his footsteps getting quieter as he fled.

Richard forced himself up on his hands and knees, and moved his head experimentally. It still felt swimmy, but he was alright. He thought. Well, mostly alright. Then, someone else came into the room, surely not Jake coming back to finish him off? No, such a relief, it was Abel.

'What happened? Did I get him? I heard his gun go off, did he hit the King?'

Richard levered himself upright, staggered over to the window, looked across at the crowd. They were still moving towards the Master's Lodge, nothing seemed out of the ordinary, no sign of everyone crowding round a still figure or anything.

'I think you made him miss, at least, it looks like it. Did you throw something at him?'

'Cobbles. I managed to prise some out. I couldn't think what else to do.'

Richard turned. 'Brilliant. My attempts were pretty pathetic. But he's gone. So, well, it's all over isn't it? I hope it is, anyway, I don't want another lam on the sconce like that.' Then his head jerked back. 'What?!' He winced in pain with the movement, but pointed, his hand trembling.

There across the room was a body, blood pooled below a great wound in the side of his head. Richard swallowed several times, took a deep breath. He advanced a little closer.

'Who is it?' asked Abel.

216

Richard leant over, turned him slightly, recognised him. 'It's Noakes,' he said, surprised. 'Matthew Noakes. I met him once. But I thought he was one of the conspirators.'

'He isn't any more,' said Abel. 'But what do we do with him?'

Richard was looking more closely at the wound, squinting to try and focus properly. He fetched the discarded rifle, and fitted the stock to the dent in Noakes' skull. 'I think he probably lammed him on the head like he did me,' he said, 'and then finished him off with a more accurate blow just there on his temple, see, he's cracked the skull open.'

He rubbed his own head tentatively. 'Good job he had an assassination to carry out, or he might have done the same to me.'

'Are you alright, though?'

'I think so. Well, all right enough, for now. But look, this is Noakes' room, yes?'

Abel nodded.

'And the gang picked it because . . . ?'

Abel went over to the window, and looked across at the crowd. 'Maybe because it's high up and they could get a clear shot over everyone else's heads? I know the King's a tall man, at least I've heard so, but all those people . . .'

'So, why is Noakes dead?'

'Search me.'

Richard paused, his forehead furrowing. 'Hang on, that reminds me. We ought to search Price's room while he's safely out of the way. His room's just below.' He thought for a short while. 'Look, will you go and make sure Edward is still on guard, and that they haven't left that staircase, and tell him to talk to Price if he comes out, divert him, hold him up, anything, to give me a bit of time. And then hurry back and help me search.'

'Will do,' and Abel was gone.

Richard took the rifle, and descended the stairs most carefully, one at a time. His head was still not right, and he didn't want to plummet to his death, having survived Mackenzie's attentions. He reached the door: it was locked, as he expected. Taking his picklocks from his waist-coat he set to work. The college locks were simple to prise open, they were even more basic here than in Emmanuel, and he was soon inside.

The room was commodious, and fairly well furnished. He propped the rifle out of direct view and started to look for anything that might incriminate the plotters. Papers, equipment, anything. It was all quite untidy, but no more than anyone else's rooms. He slipped into the bedroom, and found in the closet a sword bayonet in its scabbard – at least, that's what he thought it must be, it looked like the description of the one supplied with the Baker rifle he'd read about in George's and Mr Blackburn's letters. He put it with the rifle and carried on looking.

Now here was something. Letters, filed in a toast rack on the windowsill. As he went to look, there was a noise of the door opening. He spun round, wincing as he did so, but it was only Abel, giving him the thumbs up.

'Can you help look for papers, anything that might be incriminating, please?'

He looked through the papers in the rack. They were of all sorts and ages, but he decided he had better take the lot, he didn't have much time. He kept looking round in case anyone had returned, having eluded Edward. He hesitated, then squatted down to rummage through the clothes in the drawers in the bedroom, trying not to disturb how they were laid. There was a locked wooden box concealed under some unmentionables, a small one inlaid with mother-of-pearl that might have been used to keep jewels, if it were a lady's; he took this too. Any thoughts of his actions being criminal were discarded when he thought of how brutally his own room had been ransacked last term, and his lovely Meer painting destroyed. For good measure he pocketed some loose coins he found in the keeping-room and the two of them left, locking the door behind them and concealing the rifle and sword under their coats as best they could.

Out in the court, all was as before. No sign of pandemonium, just a lot of people standing around waiting on the opposite side, presumably until the King should reappear. Richard beckoned Edward over from his post. He ambled across, shrugged his shoulders, and asked,

'So what now? Nothing doing, eh?'

'Not exactly,' said Abel, 'but come on, we're going back to Emmanuel. Can you carry this box?'

'Surely. Is it too heavy for you?'

'No, ass, but I've got a rifle under my coat, and it's a bit awkward to hide. And Richard's got the bayonet under his. So, we're a bit loaded.'

Edward's mouth dropped open for a moment, and then he grinned. 'You're bamming me, aren't you?'

Abel opened his coat just a little, showed him the lock mechanism. 'Actually, my friend, not this time. Now, come on, before they find the corpse we left up there.'

'Corpse!' exclaimed Edward.

'Hush, we'll explain later. First, we need to get out of here.'

The three of them left the college by the Queen's Gate and tried to walk nonchalantly down Caius-lane. Richard had to ask them to slow down, he found the movement jarred his head so. The crowds had dissipated from this part of town, and when they emerged by the Senate House the street looked almost like a normal day. Picking their route to avoid shoppers, they walked along Trumpington-street all the way to Pembroke before turning for Emmanuel.

Once they had reached the relative tranquillity of Pembroke-lane, Edward demanded an explanation. 'You mean while I was standing over by Martin's stair I missed all the action? Nobody came out, so I was watching the parade, mostly. Nothing happened there either: what did I miss?'

The other two filled him in: how Richard had gone directly for Mackenzie and Abel had put him off his aim with rocks; how Noakes had been killed before they got there; how Mackenzie had run into Abel on the stair and nearly sent him flying down to break bones, but had in fact knocked him into a doorway, fortunately; how Richard was lucky to be alive, and so on. He listened with, for him, almost rapt attention, and even gasped in all the right places.

'I never saw a thing,' he repeated, 'nothing. Didn't even hear the shot.'

'Good; maybe nobody else did either? It must have been the racket from that military band.'

'We haven't reported Noakes being dead, though,' said Richard. 'Shouldn't we have? I feel quite guilty at leaving him.'

Abel thought a moment. 'Best let them find out for themselves. His gyp will see him at the latest tomorrow morning. We weren't involved, so it's best not to get ourselves involved.'

'Do you think Mackenzie did it?' asked Edward.

'Almost certainly.' Richard shook his head, carefully, but not carefully enough. 'The thing is, what do we do now?'

'I need food,' said Edward. 'We missed lunch, you know. It's nearly time for Hall, isn't it?'

But the chapel clock only showed a quarter before two when they entered college. Richard decided: he must find Peter Winton and report. And then, well, Peter would know what to do. And if he was still tied up at Trinity, so be it, but they could eat, he was famished too; and Peter'd be bound to come back soon.

'Look, you two, we need to see if Peter Winton is in, then we'd best leave him a note in his door jamb to come and see us immediately, if he isn't there. And I don't know about you, but I could do with a dram or two. Or three, even.'

'I've got some wine,' volunteered Abel.

Peter was not at home, so Abel volunteered to write a note and take it to his door, and then come up with his wine bottle. They congregated in Richard's room, and he lay back on his settle, and had a little whisky, which felt so good after all the tension; and the other two tried out Abel's wine once he'd got it open, which proved quite difficult, as the cork was crumbly, but they pronounced it fine once they picked out the cork crumbs. Somehow their difficulties made the events in Noakes' room more bearable, they were here back in college, and safe. And then Richard put the rifle in his bedroom, and locked the small box and the letters and coins in his trunk, but he took the bayonet out to examine it.

It had probably never been out of its scabbard, he decided, being still greased from the makers. He made a few flourishes with it, and found it balanced quite differently from a fencing foil, as well as being much heavier. Most interesting: it was probably made only for use attached to the rifle, he thought. He replaced the scabbard, and set it aside on his table. Then of course they went over all that had happened once again, and Edward had another moan about being left out, and they tried to pacify him by saying what a good job it was that he'd been on guard, so Price and his friends wouldn't have been able to come to help Mackenzie, and so on, and so forth.

'I bet they were all holed up in that room, Martin's did you say, to give each other alibis for when Mackenzie pulled off his shot, don't you think?' suggested Abel.

'You must be right,' Richard agreed. 'And maybe they invited someone else that was above reproach to join them, to make sure?'

There was a loud booming noise, that rattled the windows, just then. Richard almost jumped out of his skin, he was so on edge, which hurt his head again.

'Those soldiers on Parker's Piece are having a good time,' observed Edward, 'and you're a bit jittery, old scot.'

'Hardly surprising, noddy, after what has happened, don't you think?'

Which set Edward off again, complaining he'd missed all the fun, and why hadn't they called him over, and all such tripe.

Then at last the chapel bell rang for dinner, so they took themselves off there. Still no sign of Peter, but all of them ate ravenously, and felt a lot better for it.

After dinner, Richard went back to their stair, but Abel had a job

221

to do for one of the fellow-commoners, he being a sizar; and Edward decided he needed some chocolate, so he took himself off to the coffee-house, which meant of course, that he wanted to flirt with the serving-girl there. Richard climbed slowly up to his room, looking around warily, but there was nobody around. He felt his neck again, and thought he would soon be able to dispense with the collar now the danger was over, it was very uncomfortable wearing it for prolonged periods. What he wanted right now was a chance to sit down, or maybe lie down, and rest his poor head.

He unlocked his oak, and then his inner door. He had hardly stepped into his room when something whipped over his head, and yanked his neck back as it tightened. Without thinking, he pulled against whatever it was, raised his heel, and raked it down the shin of his attacker, ending with a hard stamp on his foot.

Yowls of pain and a release of the tension showed he had hit the mark. He leapt forward and grabbed the bayonet from his table, unsheathed it, gripped it and whirled around, dropping into a fencing stance, one foot forward, the other back and turned out, as he did so. The garotte dangled from his neck, but he brushed it aside and faced out his attacker. He recognised him: it was none other than Ebenezer Harmour, who had been so interested in the details of the strangled body in the chapel.

Harmour had blood dripping down his leg through his torn stocking, and an expression of pure hatred on his face. He lunged towards Richard, who, too surprised to do anything else, parried the move automatically with his sword, and then with a fierce riposte and a flashing blade attacked Harmour' outstretched hand. Blood spurted from a severed artery as the steel met his fingers, and bits of flesh dropped to the floor.

Harmour then really screamed. Like a girl, one might have said, but like no human girl had ever cried out. The whites of his eyes bulged, he clutched his mutilated hand to his face, but continued to glare at Richard, his hatred metamorphosing into horror. Richard still stood implacable, poised to strike, the point of his sword tracing a small quivering pattern in the air. Harmour then abruptly turned tail and fled, leaving a trail of blood behind him. The sound of his footsteps on the stair was punctuated by his slipping and falling a few steps, and cursing wildly. Richard sank to the floor, still clutching the sword, overwhelmed at what he had done, shaking uncontrollably, and starting to weep.

CHAPTER 17

RICHARD DIDN'T HEAR THE CLATTER of feet on the stair, he never heard the door bang wide open, he was unaware of the man standing over him. He had curled into a ball, and let go of the sword, and just rocked to and fro on the floor, sobbing.

The man reached to touch his shoulder. 'Are you all right? I mean, sorry, I'm a buffoon, obviously you're not alright, but, I mean, are you injured? There's such a lot of blood, um, is any of it yours?'

Richard couldn't reply. He just moaned, shivered, and coughed a few times, then returned to his rocking.

The man stepped back. He cast around the room, picked up a few things off the floor, grimaced, and set them on the table. 'What you need, my lad, is a shot of strong liquor. Have you got any?' He saw Richard's whisky on the dresser, and poured a hefty slug. 'Come on, drink this, it'll do you good.' He pushed it inside the ball of Richard's body and found his mouth. 'Come on, take a sip.'

Richard smelt the vapours, reached out his lips, sipped, coughed, sipped again.

'Now let me get you up off that floor, it must be cold down there.' He lifted Richard all of a piece, and put him on his settle. He fetched a blanket from the bedroom and covered him with it.

'There, that's better. Now, you don't know me, but my name's William Blackburn, and I was just coming into the college with my colleague Peter Winton, when we met a man sprinting through the court, bleeding heavily, so Peter chased after him and detained him with the help of a porter as he passed the lodge, and I didn't know quite what to do, being unfamiliar with the place, so I thought I ought to follow the blood trails, and here we are. What's happened? Did he hurt you?'

Richard shook even more violently. Mr Blackburn! Oh no! It couldn't be. But . . . it was, and all his plans, and everything; and what could he do, and what would William say when he knew, and his head hurt so much, and . . . Oh!

And with all the noise they'd made in the struggle, other people would be coming, and that would be even worse, and how could he explain, and if only Peter had been here, but that would have been terrible too. And he didn't know what to say, or do, and he couldn't ask William to leave, that would be ridiculous, and he didn't want him to go anyway. And he felt so awful, he'd injured that man dreadfully, Harmour, yes, Ebenezer Harmour, he'd met him on the way to Wimpole, though why that mattered he couldn't say, but anyway, he'd been trying to garotte him, hadn't he, so, well, it was alright, wasn't it? But he couldn't bear having any more people to deal with, so . . .

'Please,' he croaked, 'could you shut and lock both my doors? The oak as well as the regular door. The keys are here.' He fumbled in his pocket and held them out. 'Don't ask why, just do it. I beg you.'

Blackburn did as he was asked, then set the keys down on the table next to the things he had picked up. 'For a start, 'he said, 'there seem to be two severed fingers here. I hope they belong to our prisoner, not you?'

Richard poked out first one hand and then the other in answer. They were bloody, but intact. 'I'm uninjured, more or less, I think,' he said. 'Well, apart from the bang on the head I got earlier in Trinity.'

'In Trinity?'

'Yes, in Trinity. It's a college, you know.'

'I was aware of that.'

'Well, this man called Jake Mackenzie smacked me on the sconce

225

with the butt of rifle, a Baker rifle it was, and I can tell you that's no butterfly kiss.' He was feeling more himself, somehow. The whole situation was so ludicrous it was starting to feel funny. He was still trembling, but he felt oddly as if he might burst into laughter. Giggles, even. Perhaps he was hysterical? Not that it would be surprising, after what had happened. There was nothing for it but to make a clean breast of the whole business, as far as he could see. Which would be awful, but, well, what else could he do?

He began to uncurl slightly. 'Also, you see, that man who Peter arrested, Ebenezer Harmour he's called, just tried to garotte me. See?' He held out the cord that still encircled his neck. 'Could you try and undo it at the back, I think it has jammed in my cravat?' He twisted around to show William the nape of his neck.

William fumbled at the cord, and in the end fetched out his pen-knife and simply cut through it, with some considerable effort. 'How come you aren't dead, then?' he demanded. 'If you've been garotted, I mean.'

'I'm not, am I? I don't feel dead, no, I'm not dead. I'm not. But that would be because of my special collar. I had it made, you see, because I was frightened this might happen.' He sat up, back still to William, and undid the knot of his cravat, and unwound it, exposing the leather under his shirt collar. 'See? You might undo it for me now, I think I'll be safe enough if Harmour is in custody. It's a bit awkward to do it oneself, you know.'

William undid the small buckle, and eased it away. Richard rubbed his neck gratefully, and then pointed to his head.

'Here's the bump I got earlier. I don't think the skin is broken, is it?'

William inspected his scalp and expressed the opinion that it was not.

Richard decided it was no good dissembling any longer. Amazingly, Mr Blackburn had not recognised him from behind, by his voice, but he would soon. He turned round. 'Mr Blackburn, you said I didn't know you, earlier, I mean, well, I do know you, actually, and in fact, and, er, I think you probably know me too?' He turned his face to William, and grinned. 'Richard Cox, at your service, sir.'

William's face was a picture. First it was blank, then his eyebrows stretched up, his mouth opened; then his neck stretched forward, and he began to flush. He drew back, looking most embarrassed, then stepped away.

'Richard Cox, you say? Not, . . . Rose Clarke?'

'The same, sir. Both, I might say. And I am so pleased to meet you at last, I really am. I mean, as Richard Cox. Well, as a rather dishevelled and weepy Richard Cox. But I have had quite a day of it, to be fair. Quite a day, indeed. And now you are here, to crown all the unlikely impossibilities.'

'Are you . . . I mean, um, do you, um . . .'

'Yes?'

William stood looking dazed. 'Er, am I to understand that . . . the young lady I have been, er, courting, well, trying to court, it has been most difficult, almost impossible, I should say, and now I see why, er, that she is in fact a young lad? An undergraduate at this college? And I have been grievously hoodwinked? I cannot countenance the . . . well, words fail me!' He buried his face in his hands.

Richard was overcome with laughter. He rocked once more, gasped and wheezed, then started to sob once again. William couldn't think . . . but he did . . . and that was even worse . . . and, no, he had to explain, but he couldn't speak for laughing – or crying – or whatever he was doing.

'Sir, Mr Blackburn, William. You are a bacon-brain. A lovely bacon-brain, to be sure, but . . . You have it all wrong. Have you never seen one of Mr Shakespeare's plays? I am Rose, really, I am a girl, I am disguised as a boy from Nova Scotia, not that that's relevant, but anyway; I wanted to study at this university, and women are not permitted to, well, attend, so I had to dissemble, and here I am, I am truly a girl, you must have no fears on that count, though I must say I probably don't make a very attractive one at this exact moment.'

William opened his fingers and peered at her through the gap. 'Really? I cannot hardly credit it. You look so . . . well, as you say, not at your best, but like a lad who has been through the wars. Are you sure?'

Rose cackled again. 'I am sure, sir. Quite sure.'

'Sorry, that was a stupid thing to say, I . . .'

'. . . Am just as flummoxed as I am myself by this whole situation? You do not wish for evidence of my sex, do you?' She couldn't believe she had just said that, nor that her hand was at her shirt buttons.

'No, no, NO! Please spare me that.'

'Very well. Perhaps you should sit down over there once you have poured yourself a glass of my whisky, and collect yourself. I shall explain. As far as I understand things, that is. And if I can stop laughing. Not at you, you understand, though you do appear most comical in your expression, but at the whole . . . preposterous situation.' He picked up his own glass from the floor and took a sip. 'And while you have the bottle, could you top my glass up?'

William hesitated, and then complied, hesitantly. 'Ladies do not drink whisky,' he ventured.

'But lads at college do, and very pleasant it is once you get used to it,' said Rose. 'Now, well, first tell me why you are in Cambridge?'

William looked at his glass, at her, and back at his glass. 'I came here with John Warburton to meet with Peter Winton,' he managed to say, 'because of concerns about a plot to steal certain chemical secrets from the Professor of Natural Philosophy. Well, that was the main reason, I suppose, but I also wanted to see the King, who was visiting Trinity college today.' He sipped. 'This is very good whisky.'

'Thankyou. Now, as you may or may not know, Peter and I have been investigating a murder in the chapel here, which seemed to be connected with some conspiracy to do something, though exactly what had eluded us. At first we believed it to be about the Professor's researches, but recently I became convinced it was connected with the royal visit. Because . . . well, never mind about that.'

'Peter was unconvinced, and so I went with my two friends Edward and Abel to the college to stand guard near the rooms of our main suspects, to try and foil any actions they might take. Er, it wasn't a very clear plan, in fact hardly a plan at all, but we didn't know what they might be going to do either, so, well, it was the best we could do. Except, we did know they possessed a Baker rifle, so an attempt of the King's life was always possible.'

'A Baker rifle? So that is why Rose wanted to know about it . . . but she is in Rye . . .no, of course, that was part of the subterfuge, I'm going to have to rethink everything . . . sorry, go on.'

'Yes, well; we saw the barrel of the rifle at an upstairs window, I ran up to try and tackle the sharpshooter, and Abel threw cobbles to put him off his aim, and well, he fired and missed, and then he ran away. Not before I got this lump on my head, of course. And then we, er, burgled the room of one Louis Price, and abstracted certain items, including that sword bayonet over there. And returned to college, and ate dinner, and when I came back to my room, that man,' she shuddered, 'tried to kill me as he had killed poor Mr Stephens, that was the man in our chapel; and he only failed because of that collar, and I raked my heel down his shin, and stamped on his foot, that was one of the few useful accomplishments I learnt at Miss Snape's.'

'Miss Snape's?'

'Yes, Miss Snape's School for Ladies, it isn't important, they thought girls ought to be able to repulse unwanted amorous attentions, well, anyway; I'd had some hobnails fitted to my boot heels, it is an invention of Abel's father, well, so it was a particularly effective manoeuvre, with the iron edges, and he was in considerable pain, and let go of the garotte, and I grabbed at the sword bayonet, did I mention I'm a member of the fencing club here? And I was just trying to protect myself, but he came at me and I reacted, and I cut his hand to ribbons, I feel sort-of guilty about it, but then he was trying to kill me, after all.' He paused for breath.

William had started to his feet on hearing this, but subsided. Rose leaned over and picked the weapon up from the floor, and looked at the blade.

'It is extremely sharp, it seems. I think I'd better put in back in its sheath, in case of further injury.' She fetched a cloth from her bedroom to wipe the blood from it, and then slipped it into the scabbard, which she put away tidily in the bedroom with the rifle.

Meanwhile William had got up and was pacing around. 'Who knows about this?'

'My disguise? Or today's events?'

'Well, both. Your disguise first, if you will.'

'Only Sir George, my brother, and Peter Winton. Nobody else. And it must stay that way, for I am resolved to remain at college and complete my degree. As long as no other French sympathisers succeed in killing me, that is.'

'And today's, er, machinations?'

'I really don't feel up to coping with all that, I just don't.' She had started trembling again. 'Do you think you could get Peter involved, to sort it out? I just want to stay here and recover myself. And my head hurts so.'

'I expect he'll be coming back once he's disposed of our murderous friend. He looked as if he needed a doctor, before anything.'

'The thing is, there's another dead body to deal with. In Trinity, by name Matthew Noakes. He was dead when I got to his room, that's where Jake Mackenzie was firing the Baker from. I don't know who killed him, but I'm almost certain it was Mackenzie. And Louis Price is going to be upset I took his letters and his box, not to mention the rifle and sword. And I believe they have other friends who are in the plot, Christian Martin probably, and John Smart, and somebody ought to arrest them before they do anything else dangerous.'

William clapped his hand to his head. 'More mayhem? I must . . . I don't know what to do. And who are all these people you are talking about?'

'Never mind, just find Peter, that's the thing. But don't go just yet. There's something I want to do first.'

'What's that?'

'Kiss you. If I might. It's dreadfully improper, but noone will know. And I might not get another chance for weeks.'

She moved over towards him, face tilted up, smiling. He shrank back, looking terrified.

'Er, I'm not . . . I don't want to be rude, but I can't cope with . . . I mean, kissing a boy. It's unnatural.'

She paused, her shoulders dropped. 'But I'm Rose. I really am, I'm a girl. I may not have much of a figure, especially at the moment, but I am a girl.'

'I just . . . I can't. Not that I don't want to . . . I mean, I do want to kiss, Rose I mean, I've thought about it for . . . well, I'd better not say, but,'

Rose halted, began to laugh again, nervously. Her face fell a little. 'I can see your point, I suppose. Well, well, I'll just have to stay frustrated for a little longer, until I can be reunited with my dresses and my wig, and perhaps a little rouge. Get on with you, you . . . man, you. I'll let you out to find Peter, and then see about changing into a shirt and breeches that are a little less blood-spattered. And clean the place up as best as I can. You know where Peter's room is? Yes, I know you do, I saw you . . . well, let's leave that for now.'

'I'm really sorry. About everything, you know.'

'Yes, I know, and so am I. Peter and I need to talk, about these Frenchies, and I'm going to look through those letters and in that box once I've tidied. So, off with you. And remember, I'm Richard Cox, pensioner of this college, when we next meet, no forgetting and treating me like a lady. Ask Peter about it, what to watch out for, if you're sure you can't be overheard, he knows the form.'

He ushered him to the door, unlocked it, and stood by it as Mr Blackburn hesitated on the small landing.

'Did you see your neighbour's lock is broken?'

'Dillard? No, I didn't. He's hardly ever in, he spends most of his time hunting or visiting friends, and often stays away for days at a time. I don't know how he'll be allowed to take a degree, he won't have kept his terms.'

'Well, someone's smashed it: look.'

Richard looked; pushed the door a little, thought. 'That must be where Harmour hid and waited for me to come back from Hall, then. So he could come upon me when my back was to him. Ughh!' He shuddered again, and felt his neck.

Looking back at Richard several times with an inscrutable expression, Mr Blackburn descended the stair, and Richard returned to his room, locked both doors, and proceeded to follow the plan he had outlined. Once in cleaner clothing, and having bathed his bruise, he fetched the letters and the box and started to read.

The letters were mostly just ordinary ones about orders for wine, and bills, and one from Price's father, but there was a single half-sheet that caused him to sit up. It was a note from Matthew Noakes. It said that he wished to cease his involvement with the company, in that although he was quite resolved on the necessity of injuring the strength of the armed forces, such as had been attempted before Christmas, he could not stomach the death of innocent civilians such as Mr Stephens, and thought the attempt on the King was unseemly and against all ethical principles, even in wartime. He promised his total silence on all such matters for the indefinite future, and to not interfere with any of their actions, and trusted that his oath would be respected. In this regard he could not allow his room to be used for a vantage point for the assassination attempt, and he hoped they would understand.

So, he was killed because he wanted out, and his room was the one they needed as a vantage point. Poor chap, how had he become involved in the first place? thought Richard.

Next, he turned his picks to the small box. Inside was a collection of even more interest. There were records of meetings that had been held, back as far as last term; coins in gold and silver, some with the inscription "Empire France", and bank notes in sterling. There was a delivery note for gunpowder, dated November of the previous year; and records of a payment to Ebenezer Harmour on January 25th last. There were some letters in French which Richard felt he could leave for the moment, he found he was too exhausted to cope with translating them. In fact, he'd leave the whole lot, and go and have a lie-down.

CHAPTER 18

H<small>E EASED OFF HIS BOOTS</small>, and inspected the nails in his heels. There was blood on them too, but it would have to wait. He was going to flop on his bed. Taking the blanket from the settle, he headed for his room, wondering how long it would be before Peter turned up. A long time, he hoped, he was all in.

He lay down and covered himself with the blanket. He shut his eyes, and tried to relax his muscles, realising as he did so how tense he had been. Immediately his vision was filled with images of blood, spattering all around, of Harmour's horrified face, of his own bloody blade, far more graphic than the reality, filling his whole vision. He opened them again in shock, stared at the blank ceiling. The pictures persisted, but were faded against the peeling paint. Then, the bloody carnage changed into faint scenes of Noakes' body, slumped incongruously against his own bookcase, the one in this set, with the pool of blood underneath his battered head. He turned over and buried his face in the pillow. But the images followed him, and he had to get up again, to be doing something, to be able to cope.

There was a hammering on his oak. In relief, he realised it would be, must be, Peter. He walked across the room in stockinged feet, feeling stiff, and then paused.

'Who's there?' he called through the door.

'Alexander Bedford. From two floors down. I've just come in from a ride, and there's blood all up the stairs to your door. Are you alright?'

'Yes, I'm fine,' Richard called, feeling anything but. 'Look, I don't want to open the door just now, but I'm hoping my friend Peter Winton will turn up and then it'll all get sorted out. Honestly, I'm fine, and it's not my blood. Someone attacked me, and he got hurt. But I'm not keen on visitors at the moment, if you don't mind.'

'Are you sure? I mean, there's an awful lot of blood.'

'Positive. Someone's gone to fetch Winton, I hope he won't be long.'

'But how do I know you don't have a corpse in there? We had one in the chapel, and I've heard they found one in Trinity this afternoon, so one of my friends told me.'

Richard was puzzled. How had poor Noakes been found so soon? And how had Bedford heard, if he'd been out riding? Should he admit knowing about it? Probably not.

'Another corpse? Where, and who, and how did you hear?'

'We left our horses in the stable by All Saints church, and everyone was talking about it. What with the King visiting, and everything.'

'Oh. Who was it?'

'They didn't say. I think it was an undergraduate, though. Not one of the royal party. Look, can't you let me in?'

'Please, I'll come down and explain later, but I need to talk to Winton first.'

'You didn't kill him did you?'

'What?! No, why would I do that? I mean, . . .'

'Well, and you might have another body up there, I don't feel all that safe.'

'Lock your door then, sport your oak. Honestly, I'll explain later.'

There were mutterings and scuffing of boots, and then the man went away. Richard had hardly sat down, contemplating his whisky bottle again, when there was a further disturbance at his door.

This time it was Peter, accompanied by William, who were admitted as soon as his shaky hands could work the keys in the locks. He re-locked the doors behind them, and then sat down carefully on the settle and leaned back, exhausted.

'Where is Harmour?' he demanded.

'Who?' said Peter, looking aggrieved.

'That chap with the cut-up hand. You know, the one you arrested just a while ago.'

'Oh, so that's his name. He wouldn't speak a word, apart from cursing, and we didn't know what to make of him, so we put him in the Royal Suite for now, you know, by the Lodge, where Charles spent the night, not so long ago? But he was quite gravely injured, and we had to deal with the bleeding, and fetch him a doctor, and it all took an unconscionable time. I'm sorry.'

'Has Mr Blackburn filled you in at all?' He turned to William, who was examining the severed fingers, and the garotte cord and the collar, which Richard had laid beside them on the table when he tidied. 'Or do I have to go over it again?'

'He has, to some extent, but I'd like to hear it from you directly. You see, Cambridge is buzzing with rumours, and I don't know what to believe.'

'Yes, I understand they've already found Noakes' body,' said Richard.

'Noakes?'

'Yes, he was killed, almost certainly by Jake Mackenzie, he wanted to leave the gang, but they needed his room for their shot at the King.'

'What?'

'They were trying to assassinate His Majesty as he arrived in Trinity.' He turned to William. 'Didn't you tell him?'

William tensed up, looked most uncomfortable. 'Er, not as such, I was more worried about what had happened in this college, I mean, the attempt on your life, and the injuries to Mr Harmour. I did tell him all about that, you know.'

'Very well. You'd better both sit down, and pour yourself a drink, there's some of Abel's wine left if you don't want whisky, but I'm having another shot, my nerves are not what they might be.'

And once they'd settled, he recounted the events of the middle of the day, and explained why they'd not told anyone about Noakes, and so on.

'But what about the explosion at the Chemistry laboratory? How does that fit in?' asked Peter.

'Explosion? What explosion?'

'Just about a quarter after three, the room was wrecked, all the windows blown out, and all the Professor's glassware shattered. Did you not know?' Peter ran his hands through his hair, making it stand up comically. 'Including his supply of rock oil, I hear,' he added, 'so he won't be doing many more experiments for a while.'

'I'd no idea. A quarter after three, you say? That must have been what we heard, then. We thought it was soldiers on Parker's Piece. We were here, waiting for the dinner bell.'

'So, take me through what happened here after Hall, then. To check William has it correctly.'

Richard recounted the attack, and his resistance. He showed Peter his boot heels, and the severed garotte, and took out the bayonet from his bedroom, feeling churned up again as he handled it.

'This is what I grabbed when he tried to . . . when he attacked me,' he said, finding his voice rather uncertain. 'I didn't think, I just reacted. And it was a good job it was there, too.'

'But why did he come at you once you had the sword? Seems fool-hardy to me.'

'I don't know. But he was so enraged about me scraping his shins, and so consumed with hate, and frustration, I think . . . you know, I wonder if . . . yes, it could be. Um, he was very friendly with Jake Mackenzie, and what if . . . after Jake ran off having failed to kill the King, he met up with Harmour and he decided he was going to get rid of that interfering boy Cox once and for all? And he knew the college, he'd scouted it before, for when he killed Stephens, and so all he had to do was find my name on the door jamb, and come up and wait. He'd know my name from meeting me on the Wimpole trip, you see.'

'Could well be,' admitted Peter. But we need to prove these things, if we are going to be able to take them to court.'

'Ah,' said Richard, 'that's where my little collection might come in handy. Wait there, you two.'

He fetched the letter, and the little box, and handed the items to Peter one by one. 'Here's Noakes' letter saying he wants to leave the gang, and Abel can testify that the marks on his head fit exactly the butt of the Baker rifle that Mackenzie was using,' he put a hand to his own bump, 'and probably this bruise here.'

'Here's the payment note for last term's gunpowder delivery, you remember, we saw it go into the Pink Houses?'

'How could I forget?'

'And a record of several meetings, you'll see there is a list of who attended.'

'Excellent.' Peter licked his lips.

'And here are some Bank of England notes, I believe these can be traced to the original purchaser? And some coins, gold ones, as well as silver.'

Peter took them. 'These ones are *Napoléons*,' he said, excitedly. 'Minted only last year. What a find!'

'And, I like this one particularly, a payment to our friend Mr Harmour for unspecified services, dated January 25th. Which, you will recall, is the day after Mr Stephens met his Maker, and this may well not be a coincidence. Taken in conjunction with the garotte cord, helpfully abandoned by Mr Harmour earlier today, I think it proves he was our murderer.'

'We have them! Richard, you are amazing! But, do we know why Stephens needed killing?'

'The king was originally coming to visit Trinity at the end of January, but he was unwell, so it was postponed until today. I think Stephens must have overheard some of the plotting before that date, and was going to tell the authorities.'

'I remember now, that was one of our suggestions before.'

'Yes, yes. And the other things in this box are some letters in French which I have not read, because although I do speak the language, I am not fluent, and my head hurts, and I couldn't face it. There, that is all.'

'So, while Mackenzie was trying to shoot the King, the others, what, Price, and who else? They were blowing up Professor Wollaston's laboratory?'

'I don't think so. Price and Burgess were holed up in Martin's staircase until perhaps half after one, because Edward was keeping an eye on them there; and though I suppose they could've easily got across town by a quarter after three, and broken in, and set off the powder, it doesn't seem very likely, does it?'

'They might have picked that time because of the King's visit, though?'

'It's possible. But I think Price was more of an organiser, he got other people to do his jobs for him. Like he didn't get involved with the mill with the bargees, when his friends did.'

'What mill?'

'Oh, just a fight Edward told me about. He did a little investigating on his own account, you see. He was most selfless: he was forced to consume a vast amount of wine in the process.' Richard chuckled to himself.

'Looks like we have our work cut out for a little while, then. We need to arrest Price, and Mackenzie, and who else? Martin, clearly. Burgess?'

'Martin, yes. I didn't see anything with Burgess' name on in the papers I read, but you'd better check the French correspondence. And I'm sure John Smart is involved too, but I don't know in what way.'

'I'll read most carefully through all this, but maybe not until a bit later.' Peter got up. 'Will you be alright now? I have to go and take Harmour to the town lock-up, and inform the magistrate, and take some constables to arrest the Trinity pair, and then locate

Mr Mackenzie. And have all their rooms searched, and who knows what else.'

'I'll be fine. Well, not fine, exactly, I keep seeing blood when I shut my eyes. It's horrible.' He shivered.

Mr Blackburn, silent for all this time, spoke up. 'I hear from my fellow-officers, that that is quite normal after battle. Men find it help-ful to talk about what happened, often again and again, and to make a joke of it, if they can. The phenomenon usually subsides reasonably quickly, if so. But they say it is most distressing.'

'It is.' He paused. 'Um, . . . could I ask something of you both?'

'Surely.'

'Could Mr Blackburn first ask Mr Archer to come up, from the room two floors below, so I can give him an edited account of the . . . the events of this afternoon? And stay with me while he is here?'

'I can and will.'

'And then, er, could Peter see if Edward Hever or Abel Johnson has returned? I don't like the idea of being here on my own, and, er,' with a sidelong glance at William, 'I don't think it would be appropri-ate to ask you to stay yourself, William. Would it?'

Mr Blackburn coughed, and turned slightly red. 'Er, no, I suppose not. Definitely not.'

Peter raised an eyebrow.

'It's alright, Peter, William here is now aware of my secret: I hope he asked you for advice as to how to behave so as to keep it a secret.'

'He did not.'

Mr Blackburn coughed again. 'I, er, I was too embarrassed,' he said. 'So, I'll fetch Mr Archer now, then?' and left the room, after a hiatus when Richard had to get up and let him out.

'Don't go just yet,' he asked Peter.

'I'd better. Lots to do. But, er, what about William? He, um, must be, . . . well, confused.'

'He is; mightily so. But how do you think I'm feeling?' rejoined Richard.

'Mmm. I see what you mean. Oh well, I hope you can sort yourselves out. I must get off to the . . . I'll put these papers and things in my box first, then I suppose the first stop is the constables. Once, I've looked out Edward or Abel. Ho hum.' And he was off.

'When you search Harmour's rooms, don't forget to look for any possessions he might have taken from Stephens' body,' Richard called after him.

The interview with Mr Archer passed off without too much difficulty once he was reassured by Mr Blackburn that the proper authorities were dealing with matters. Also that the blood on the stairs could wait until Mrs Fenn attended the next day, unless he would like to clean it himself.

Richard was left with Mr Blackburn. Standing awkwardly at the threshold. Not quite looking at each other. 'I'll be going too,' he said. 'I think Abel was in, I heard someone talking to Peter when I showed Mr Archer out; he'll be up in a few moments I expect.'

There was a short silence. William edged inside and closed the door behind him. 'Er, I've been telling myself for weeks that when I finally saw you I'd start by discussing that book you lent me. Mrs Wollstonecraft, you remember?'

'Yes, I do.'

'I think you might have jumped the gun on that discussion, you know. Put her ideas into practice. Shown what is possible for a determined member of the female sex.'

'Yes, I believe I have.'

'And, well, um, I think, I don't know exactly what I think. But you were very brave earlier, you know, with Harmour. I think I admire you for it, yes, I do. But . . .'

'Might take a bit of getting used to, eh?'

'I should say. Um, but I don't want you to think I . . . I mean, I haven't quite adjusted my feelings, I mean, my thoughts, I don't quite know what I mean. I'm quite overset about the whole matter.'

'Well, shall we try again?'

'Try what?'

Richard trying hard to stand and move like Rose, moved a little closer, and tilted her head up.

'Well?'

'Er, yes, no I mean. No: I can't do it, it's very difficult for me.'

There were sounds of feet on the stairs.

'Sorry to have kept you, Richard. What's been going on while I was doing my chores?' Abel banged into the room, all cheeriness and energy. 'I hear you've been in the wars? Tell me all about it.'

And William Blackburn melted away down the stairs, and off to return to his lodgings, or meet up with Warburton, or something, and no doubt to investigate the explosion at the Chemistry laboratory. And Rose, rapidly returning to being Richard again, comforted himself with the thought that it was, after all, only ten days until the end of term.